"Gayle C... to cap...

Lorraine Heath

*Could she be ...*
*posed for the ...*

Lady Elizabeth Cabot is no longer the reckless girl she once was. Now the darling of the *ton*, she is determined to put her past behind her. But who would have imagined that one immodest act could throw her entire world into chaos . . . and force her toward a loveless marriage? In desperation, she approaches her childhood friend, Peter Derby, with a daring plan.

Peter still remembers the wild and spirited girl who had stolen his heart. But could the rumors be true: is *she* the model for the scandalous painting hanging in London's most exclusive gentlemen's club? If Peter agrees to pose as her fiancé, Elizabeth has promised to reveal the whole truth.

But Peter has his own ideas about this sham "engagement" to the exquisite beauty who's always been just out of his reach—and he's willing to incite yet another scandal to make her heart truly his.

*Romances by* **Gayle Callen**

A MOST SCANDALOUS ENGAGEMENT
IN PURSUIT OF A SCANDALOUS LADY
NEVER MARRY A STRANGER
NEVER DARE A DUKE
NEVER TRUST A SCOUNDREL
THE VISCOUNT IN HER BEDROOM
THE DUKE IN DISGUISE
THE LORD NEXT DOOR
A WOMAN'S INNOCENCE
THE BEAUTY AND THE SPY
NO ORDINARY GROOM
HIS BRIDE
HIS SCANDAL
HIS BETROTHED
MY LADY'S GUARDIAN
A KNIGHT'S VOW
THE DARKEST KNIGHT

# A Most
# SCANDALOUS
# ENGAGEMENT

# GAYLE CALLEN

**AVON**

*An Imprint of HarperCollinsPublishers*

AVON BOOKS
*An Imprint of* HarperCollins*Publishers*
10 East 53rd Street
New York, New York 10022-5299

First Avon Books paperback printing: December 2010

Avon Trademark Reg. U.S. Pat. Off. and in Other Countries, Marca Registrada, Hecho en U.S.A.
HarperCollins® is a registered trademark of HarperCollins Publishers.

Printed in the U.S.A.

10 9 8 7 6 5 4 3 2 1

*To my sister-in-law, Mary Anne Fox: The first time I met you, you were two years old, and climbing on my lap for attention. You've had my attention—and admiration—ever since. You've grown into a lovely woman with a heart so big that you humble us all.*

# A Most
# Scandalous
# Engagement

# Chapter 1

*London, 1846*

**P**eter Derby was not the only man calling on the very eligible Lady Elizabeth Cabot that summer afternoon. At least a dozen men meandered in the sumptuous drawing room beneath frescoed ceilings, waiting their turn to speak to the lady herself. She gave each man his few minutes, dumbfounding them with the radiance of her smile, making each of them dream that they could have her in their marriage bed, connecting their family to that of the Duke of Madingley forever. But of every man in this room, only Peter knew her secret—she'd posed for a nude painting, and even now it was hanging in the saloon of his gentlemen's club.

Through the movement of the slowly thinning crowd, he caught glimpses of Elizabeth, and still, he could be so moved by her beauty. She had the midnight hair and eyes of her Spanish mother, contrasting with a peach English complexion. Those eyes could have been mysterious, yet instead showed her cheerfulness. She could have been cool and remote, a lady so high in rank that mere mortals must look up. But Peter knew Elizabeth had never been like that. She was friendly and compassionate, inquiring about one suitor's ill mother and another suitor's recent broken arm, making everyone feel like a friend.

But Peter no longer wanted to be just her friend. He'd known Elizabeth her whole life, had gotten her out of one scrape after another in her youth. And through it all, she'd never treated him as anything other than a friend. He knew his place in the *ton*—so far beneath hers he might as well have been in a shadowy valley to her shining mountaintop.

But the painting changed everything.

Elizabeth's gaze collided with his, before she quickly looked away, flustered, embarrassed. He'd never flustered her before, and it intrigued him. He liked the pink in her cheeks, the way she linked her hands together—which in turn accented the faint hint of cleavage at the neckline of her respectable blue gown.

Now he had another image that changed his every thought of her. The painting was burned into his brain: against a black background lit only with candles, she reclined on her side, body arched, dark, curling hair teasing at the juncture of her closed thighs. A long, diaphanous scarf draped around her, enhancing rather than concealing. Her head, thrown back, was lost in the shadows, but he hadn't needed to see her face to know it was she.

That Elizabeth would risk everything to pose for something so scandalous it could lead to her utter ruin, suggested that she hadn't outgrown her recklessness, regardless of her proper behavior these last few years.

She still had a wild side, one he now hungered to see. They had something in common.

The last suitor left the drawing room, and the little maid, after a nod from Elizabeth, grinned at him and departed, carrying her needlework. Then Elizabeth dismissed the two footmen, who left the door properly open behind them.

Several clusters of plush chairs and sofas grouped around tables stood between them. Elizabeth remained frozen, a new wariness in her eyes as she studied him. He began to move toward her, each step bringing him closer to an unknown future. Lately he'd been taking risks, and she might be the most dangerous one of all.

He stopped before her and waited. The moment drew out, fraught with tension, as embarrassment pinkened her cheeks. Would she run from him, perhaps refuse to speak about this new secret between them?

At last she rolled her eyes. "Well, what do you have to say for yourself, Peter Derby?"

He laughed aloud. She put her hands on her hips, emphasizing her elegant slimness, drawing his gaze to her other curves, so properly tamed by layers of garments.

She gave a little gasp. "Is that how it will be now, that you'll look at me like . . . like . . ."

"Like you're a woman, and I'm admiring your beauty?"

"You've never looked at me that way before."

In a low voice he said, "Then perhaps you should have considered how men would look at you before you posed for that painting."

Her frantic gaze darted to the door once more, but no one had heard him.

"Or before you and your cousins dressed as boys," he added, "and snuck into a gentlemen's club to steal it. Thank God Julian, Leo, and I were there to keep you from making things worse."

That was another image that would never leave his brain—Elizabeth's hips, sensually rounder than he'd imagined, encased in a pair of boy's breeches.

"That painting was supposed to be in a private French collection," she insisted, "not on display before you ogling men!"

"I don't understand how this all happened. Were you tricked into posing?"

But she only pressed her lips together and glared at him. Very curious. Why didn't she want to explain herself?

"So the artist needed money when the deal fell through," Peter continued. "Perhaps he should have come to *you* for help. You would have done anything to protect your indiscretion."

Folding her arms across her chest, she tapped her foot as if he bored her.

"I know how close you and your cousins are," he continued. "You thought you'd divert our questions, protect each other, by each claiming to be the model. It didn't quite work out the way you'd planned it."

"I imagine we should have guessed how *foxed* the three of you were," she said with exasperation. "But a wager, Peter?"

He spread his hands wide. "We have to discover who the real model is—how can you blame us?" And how else could he protect her, by making sure only *he* focused on her? But he couldn't tell her that part of it. He needed to know *why* she was suddenly reverting to her old risk-taking ways.

Elizabeth sank back into an upholstered chair, and her blue skirts flared and settled around her, the silk rustling almost erotically. But then all his thoughts about her were erotic. He sat down in a nearby chair, their knees almost touching. She didn't move away, so she was clearly distracted.

"I hadn't imagined the Earl of Parkhurst would join you and Mr. Wade in such foolishness." She gave him a suspicious look.

"You practically invited us to determine the truth.

And how could I not bet that *you* are the model? Your cousin Rebecca? I had just seen her at a ball wearing the same diamond pendant that was in the painting. She would never have worn it in public if she'd known it could identify her as the scandalous model."

Her gaze stilled on him. "You never mentioned that last night."

"Why should I give Julian and Leo any advantage? At least we've given you the chance to win the painting outright."

"In a month's time," she added between gritted teeth. "But time won't matter. You'll never be able to prove for certain that it was I. My word alone isn't enough in your game."

"And you don't want to help me win for old times' sake?"

She blew out her breath and rose to her feet, leaning over him. He lounged back, head against the chair, and enjoyed the view of her lovely fury. He'd never seen her like this before, and was enjoying it far too much.

"Mr. Derby, I cannot believe you're treating me this way!"

He grinned, eyes half closed as he watched her. "Lady Elizabeth, I cannot believe you think you deserve special treatment, not after what you've done. If your brother hears—"

"Chris is hunting in Scotland, as you well know."

"Ah, but this helps you, doesn't it? No brother wondering why you're suddenly so ill at ease."

"I'm not—"

"No brother catching you sneaking around dressed as a boy."

"No, I have *you* for that."

His smile died a quick death. "I'm not your brother."

"I know that!" Her brow furrowed. "But you've always been there to help me. Last night, when I saw you, I was actually relieved!"

"Liar—you were embarrassed."

"That, too! But I thought—I hoped—"

"That once again I'd ride to the rescue? I thought you didn't need me for that anymore. You'd thoroughly convinced me that you were all grown up, a sedate, proper young lady."

She studied him impassively. "You've changed, Peter. Something happened in this last year."

He didn't flinch, wouldn't give her any reason to think she might be correct. "You're wrong. But you, Elizabeth—you only pretended to change."

Whatever she saw in his face made her suddenly back away, then whirl toward the double doors. "You know the way out."

"I'll see you tonight."

She stopped and looked over her shoulder. "What is tonight?"

"Lady Brumley's ball. You'll save me a dance or two, won't you?"

She only groaned and left him. Peter's smile slowly returned.

Elizabeth couldn't unclench her jaw. She strode through the entrance hall, ignoring the marble columns, the graceful beauty of twin staircases winding up three floors above her, the pastoral paintings on every wall, some as large as the walls themselves. She could only march, and hope her fury—and fear—would somehow abate.

Peter Derby might as well be a stranger to her. To say such a thing was shocking and unexpected, but there it was. He'd been a neighbor she'd relied on when she didn't want her family to know the foolish things she'd done, like accidentally setting loose her father's prize stallion, misplacing her pet frog in the house, or exploring caves. Peter had understood her. When at last she'd realized her escalating stunts might hurt her family or even harm their reputation—and she had her brother's example to follow there—she'd followed maturity and common sense and become the proper lady her family expected. She and Peter had remained friends, as much as possible with the disparity in their backgrounds.

But now . . . but now . . . he'd seen the painting. She

would have closed her eyes in mortification, except it might cause her to trip up the stairs. She could still remember the exact moment last night when she, Susanna, and Rebecca had walked into the shadowy saloon and seen the painting, so large it almost filled one wall. They'd thought to steal it, had even tried to lift it, before being discovered by—them. Those arrogant, amused men. And Peter—her friend Peter!—had been one of them. She could have melted through the floor when he looked at her standing by all that nudity. She hadn't wanted to meet his eyes, but she couldn't be a coward. And in their depths she'd seen a new awareness that had never been there before. Even now she didn't know what to make of it.

This afternoon she'd looked across the drawing room and seen Peter lounging near the door, just waiting to be alone with her. For the first time, she'd observed him as other women might. He was tall with sandy blond hair, and blue eyes that seemed to blaze as he studied her through the milling suitors. She knew those eyes were bracketed by the faintest laugh lines, for regardless of his circumstances, he'd always approached life optimistically. He had a lean, square jaw: a scholarly sort of face, she'd once thought, though his family hadn't been able to afford to send him to Cambridge, so temptingly close to where they'd both grown up.

She'd hoped he had come to apologize, to say he'd talked his friends out of it and somehow would retrieve the painting for her. He could have fixed everything.

But no, that version of Peter had disappeared this last year, and she didn't know why. She'd heard a whisper or two from friends that he'd behaved in quite a roguish fashion, from gambling with his newly earned wealth, to being glimpsed in the company of questionable women. Now that his circumstances were much improved, she would have thought he'd begin to look for a wife, but he seemed to have no interest.

She could no longer be surprised that Peter was going to prove she was the model. He'd crassly wagered *money* over it! A lot of money. Surely he couldn't afford to lose it.

But she was going to make sure he did. And he'd brought it on himself. Save him a dance, indeed.

Peter wasn't going to ruin the Season for her. She was a popular young lady, with the perfect husband all picked out. She'd put aside her girlish mistakes—mostly.

"Lady Elizabeth! Lady Elizabeth!" One of the footmen ran to keep up with her as she began her march up the stairs.

She looked over her shoulder, forcing a smile, for surely the servant didn't deserve to bear her anger. "Yes, Wilfred?"

His large Adam's apple bobbed in his throat as he swallowed. "Miss Gibson is here. I showed her to your bedroom, as usual."

"Thank you, Wilfred. Will you please send for tea and cakes? Miss Gibson loves her cakes."

"Of course, milady."

In her bedroom, she found Lucinda lying across the bed on her stomach, reading a novel. She was fair to Elizabeth's dark, her eyes bright green to Elizabeth's black, short to Elizabeth's tall, thin to Elizabeth's curves. Elizabeth could chatter with anyone, from servant to prince, where Lucinda was more reserved. They seemed like opposites, but matched in all the important ways: temperament, sense of humor—and loyalty.

Elizabeth felt a pang of sadness, because she would have to forget loyalty for the moment. She could never be honest with Lucy about the painting. She'd sworn a new vow to her cousins, protecting all three of them, just as they had when she and Rebecca were sixteen, and Susanna, already a grown woman, insisted on swearing a real oath to protect each other. And now the painting had placed a barrier between Lucy and her, and Lucy didn't even know it.

"Lucy, you didn't lose my place in the novel again, did you?" Elizabeth asked, throwing herself dramatically down beside her friend.

Lucy made a face. "It's only the tenth time you've

read it. I hate to ruin the ending for you, but the girl wins the prince."

Elizabeth gave a weary sigh.

"You'll win the prince, too."

Elizabeth turned her head and stared at her friend, whose expression was just as determined as Elizabeth usually felt. "Really?" she asked wistfully.

"Really. We will be sisters in truth. We will make it so."

Elizabeth sighed. "If only your brother would co-operate."

"He will. William is simply oblivious sometimes."

"I know it has only been a few years since my coming out. William is in the prime of his life. Most men at his age are not ready to settle into marriage and all it entails. But his flirtation and hints that I was just the sort of woman he'd marry—I wasn't wrong to think he was showing an interest in me, was I?"

"No! He's never shown another lady such favoritism."

Elizabeth shivered as she remembered how wonderful William's initial notice of her had felt. She'd been nervous and excited—and so very curious about what happened next between a man and a woman. Too curious. She had not allowed herself to be alone with William, couldn't take the risks she'd once gladly accepted without thought. It had felt dangerous and far too tempting to be alone with a man. Bad things happened in her family when one lost control. The painting was ample proof of that, proof that a dare had gone too far.

"Then I'll continue to be patient," Elizabeth said with a sigh. "But when I see all those men wanting to marry me, I sometimes feel . . . frustrated."

"Surely you are used to such men," Lucy said gently.

"I am. And I'm flattered. Like anyone else, I enjoy the attention. But I spent my girlhood waiting to be grown, so William—sweet handsome William—would notice me at last. And he did—but not enough." She indulged in a rare pout.

Lucy giggled. "Give him time."

"You've been saying that for far too long. I feel like I've been waiting for him forever."

Lucy bumped against her shoulder, laughing. "I hear you had many callers today."

"More than usual, I admit."

As they discussed the merits of her suitors, they ate their cakes and drank their tea, fortifying themselves before the ball that night. Elizabeth settled in to their laughter and gossip, enjoying herself as she briefly put aside her troubles.

At last Lucy rose to her feet and donned her bonnet. "I will see you there tonight. My brother says he's attending . . ." she added in a singsong voice.

Elizabeth laughed. "Then I'll have to be there."

"And I promise to keep telling you his social schedule—he's bound to realize you're perfect for him if he keeps seeing you all the time!"

Elizabeth's spirits lifted. She would dance in William's arms—and leave Peter dangling.

# Chapter 2

**T**hat night, in Lady Brumley's overheated ballroom, Elizabeth found herself watching Peter from where she stood with her mother. The dancing had not begun yet, but already two men had signed her dance card. Almost impatiently, she looked past them. Though trying to pretend she was only studying the guests, she could not delude herself. She wondered what Peter, Lord Parkhurst, and Mr. Wade, would try to pull tonight in their attempt to defeat each other over something so intimate as that painting.

But Peter was not with his two friends—he was with the Clifford sisters, Lady Alice and Lady Athelina. They were simpering and laughing at whatever he said, gazing up at him with worship in their eyes. Elizabeth thought he was standing a bit too close to them than was proper, and wondered why their mother, a dragon if she ever met one, was not paying more attention to them.

Surely he hadn't always pushed the boundaries of Society's rules, she told herself. She would have noticed—

wouldn't she have? Lately she'd begun to hear a mother or two talk about Peter's exploits at the racetrack or in a gaming hell, whispering that they received their information from their husbands. Shaking their heads with fond regret, they believed that a young woman would come along and teach Peter the error of his ways, calling him a regular rascal waiting to be tamed. Before Peter had made himself rich, none of them had even noticed him.

It had been several years ago, Elizabeth recalled, when she had at last decided she had to mature and represent her family, that she'd no longer needed Peter to help extract her from adventures that had gone . . . unexpectedly. They'd socialized in the country as neighbors, but not so much in London. She'd taken his occasional presence for granted.

Now she watched Peter take Lady Athelina's gloved hand between his and lift it to his mouth. He looked up at the young woman with what could only be a hint of sin in his eyes.

What had happened to spark such a change in Peter Derby?

She was saved from gaping like a fool when Lord Dekker approached to lead her into the first waltz. Powerful, stocky, barely taller than herself, but twice her width through the shoulders, he moved them through the other dancers with confidence, if not absolute grace. He grinned down at her, and she smiled back, reminding herself that she wouldn't let the rest of her life be a reaction to that painting. Sometimes, she needed to simply enjoy a dance, enjoy being an eligible young lady.

And then she felt a breeze at her back, and realized that Lord Dekker had waltzed her toward the open terrace doors. Her smile vanished as she caught a glimpse of torchlit darkness. She tried to come to a stop, but he only took her motion in stride, taking an extra turn before he attempted to pull her through the doors, right in front of a group of astonished elderly ladies.

"Lord Dekker," she said through smiling, strained lips, "the dance floor is the other way." She tried to pull back her hand.

He didn't let go, only winked at her and turned her about again.

With her back to the ogling ladies, she replaced her smile with a glare. "Lord Dekker, I do not wish to leave the ballroom."

"But I *know* you do." His voice was a murmur, his smile a leer.

She couldn't have possibly heard him correctly— could she? She was about to come to a complete stop, perhaps force him to make spectacles of them both if he still intended to drag her out the door.

"Excuse me, Lady Elizabeth," she heard a man say. "I believe this was my dance."

Lord Dekker released her immediately, and she caught herself from stumbling. Together, they turned to face her rescuer—and instead of being grateful, her heart sank further.

It was Lord Thomas Wythorne. He was the younger son of a duke—and she'd turned down his proposal of marriage just last year. He hadn't spoken to her since. Even her brother had been disappointed with her refusal, for he'd long considered Lord Thomas the best match possible for her. From the beginning, Lord Thomas's mother had treated her own mother, the dowager duchess, as a friend, and their attachment only deepened through the years. Many thought her engagement to Lord Thomas a sort of destiny. But expectations were not a reason for her to marry.

Lord Thomas was smiling innocently, looking from Lord Dekker to her.

Whatever Lord Dekker saw in his face—and Elizabeth couldn't tell—it made the man bow.

"My mistake," Lord Dekker said, then walked away.

Elizabeth continued to smile at Lord Thomas, even as she surreptitiously wiped her perspiring hands on her skirts. Her heart was still pounding, and she wasn't sure why. She'd been out on a moonlit terrace before, after all. There were certainly couples strolling in the shadows. But it was one thing to agree to a walk with a man one trusted, another to be forced.

"Are you well, Lady Elizabeth?" Lord Thomas asked politely.

She nodded, trying to make her smile more genuine. "Of course, my lord. A misunderstanding, that is all."

He arched a dark brow and said nothing. He had wavy brown hair that framed his narrow face, emphasizing the aristocratic bone structure of generations of dukes. She had always liked him well enough, but she certainly didn't love him. A romantic, she was lucky enough to be able to wait for the right offer of marriage—the only one she wanted.

Lord Thomas cleared his throat. "I believe several of the gentlemen overimbibed earlier this evening."

"That must explain it," she said, telling herself to relax.

"You could dance with me, my lady," he said, cocking his head as he awaited her response.

Accepting his offer would be polite, since he seemed to be attempting to make amends for his angry reaction to her rejection of his proposal. But before she could agree, she saw Peter Derby—standing with her mother. The evening was getting worse. Her mother might be the Dowager Duchess of Madingley, but she had once been a common Spanish girl, swept off her feet by a future duke touring her country. British Society had not taken well to the unusual duchess, although she was never openly snubbed. Consequently, she did not normally care for London, preferring the peace and gentility of Cambridgeshire, the duke's country seat.

"Oh do excuse me, Lord Thomas. I must attend to my mother, who hasn't been feeling well."

He bowed without speaking, and she gave him a hurried curtsy. He would probably take offense, of course, but she couldn't just leave Peter with her mother! Who knew what he might let slip?

As Peter approached the extended Cabot family, conflicting feelings churned inside him. Except for Elizabeth and her cousin Matthew Leland, he had made a point of avoiding certain members of the family the last several months. He could see Emily, Matthew's bride, nod as she noticed his approach. Classically beautiful, she had champagne blond hair and a slender figure. If she seemed ill at ease, he would make his greetings short and depart. He knew too many of her and Matthew's secrets, although they would never pass his lips. His involvement and guilt guaranteed his silence, and surely she knew that.

But although her blue eyes widened a fraction when she saw him, she gave him a faint smile, easing his worries. He'd misjudged her not so long ago, and her forgiveness still struck him as unexpected.

"Your Grace," Peter said, bowing to Elizabeth's mother.

The dowager duchess was still a beautiful woman, silver threads in her regal black hair. With her darker complexion and strong nose, one could never mistake her for an Englishwoman. Elizabeth bore some of her mother's handsome features, but with a fascinating twist of Englishness.

"Mr. Derby, it is good to see you," the duchess said, her voice melodious with a Spanish accent. "My daughter Elizabeth tells me of your recent good fortune."

He noticed that Emily pointedly looked away.

"Yes, madam, I have been very lucky."

"I don't believe in luck, young man," the duchess said. "You've always been a diligent fellow, something I truly appreciate."

"Your Grace!" a woman called.

They all turned as one to see Elizabeth waving as she moved quickly between milling couples and clusters of chatting guests. Peter immediately understood her concerns, for she smiled too pointedly at him. What did she think he would do, reveal her indiscretions to her entire family? He'd always protected her secrets.

He took the brief opportunity to admire the way she shone under the candlelit chandeliers, her pale pink gown glittering with tiny diamonds, her dark hair glowing, her eyes soft with love. He knew that look, had watched her bestow it on every member of her family. A version was granted to her friends, and he had been the recipient a time or two. He had always contented himself with that.

But he wasn't content anymore.

When at last Elizabeth approached, the duchess said, "Is there a reason for such unladylike haste, my child? It has been many months since I've seen Mr. Derby."

Peter simply smiled at Elizabeth. "I visited Madingley House this afternoon, Your Grace. Elizabeth was in the middle of welcoming many young men."

Just like that, the duchess returned to a mother's favorite topic and gave a faint sigh. "I should never have accepted a shopping invitation."

From beneath her skirts, Elizabeth stepped firmly on his foot. He almost wanted to play her childhood game by lifting his foot and watching her lose her balance, but she was no longer a child—for which he was grateful.

She waved a hand negligently. "It was nothing, Mama."

The duchess frowned. "I'm certain many other young ladies would not think it so."

Peter arched a brow as Elizabeth tried to recover.

"I did not mean that I wasn't pleased and flattered," she quickly said.

"Did any man take your fancy?" the duchess probed.

"They were all very nice . . ."

The duchess rounded on Peter. "What did you think, Mr. Derby?"

Many pairs of female eyes focused on him.

He knew the only speculation of interest to them was if he could reveal something about the men courting Elizabeth. They would never assume that he considered himself one of her suitors. She was the only sister of a duke; her marriage could ally them with another great family, increasing their power in land and wealth and in Parliament.

In fact, he was considered a family friend, nothing more. But last night, in a gentlemen's club, things had begun to change. Now, Elizabeth was watching him with a new speculation.

Peter shifted his gaze to the duchess. "Lady Elizabeth's suitors seemed rather . . . young, madam."

"They were testing the waters, Mama," Elizabeth said briskly. "I didn't mind letting them practice their flirtations on me."

If Elizabeth was grateful he'd deflected her mother's interest, she didn't show it. She was still angry with him.

"Lady Elizabeth, would you care to dance?" he asked, taking advantage.

Those black eyes glittered, but she sweetly replied, "Of course I would, Peter. Perhaps you need practice as much as my young suitors today."

The duchess drew in a quick breath.

Peter laughed. "Try not to step on my toes."

Elizabeth winced as he drew her away. The orchestra played another waltz, and for some reason, she glanced at the terrace doors.

"Do you wish me to dance you outside under the moonlight?" he asked.

She frowned. "No, that would be indecent."

"Indecent?" he echoed, studying her. What an interesting thing for her to say. "I seem to recall practicing your dances on the terrace at Madingley Court in the sunshine. In fact, I believe I helped you learn them after your dance instructor had practically collapsed in fear that he'd disappoint the duke because of your disinterest."

He saw her jaw clench, but she still didn't meet his gaze.

Perhaps it was only indecent now because she was thinking about him as a man who'd seen her painting, rather than as her old friend. He didn't mind that, he thought with satisfaction.

He pulled her a little closer through a tight turn, avoiding a couple plodding along like a ship with torn sails.

Her breasts brushed his chest, and he felt the reaction deep in his gut. Elizabeth's gaze flew to his.

"Too indecent?" he asked innocently. "I didn't want you crashing into the next dancers."

"You never dared try such a thing with me before," she said grimly. "It is only that painting."

"I don't think less of you for that painting."

"Only because you don't want people questioning *your* behavior of late."

Ignoring her, he said, "I just want to know why you did it. What made you want to take such a risk? I thought you'd worked hard these last years to rid yourself of such impulses."

"It wasn't about risk," she said at last.

At least she was talking. He held her close, whirling her about until her skirts flew and her toes barely touched the floor.

"Elizabeth—"

"I don't want to talk about it!" she whispered.

The passion in her expression was about anger, but it was a passion he'd never borne the brunt of before. He saw her temper at last, the "wild Spanish blood" of which some used to accuse her mother.

She seemed to realize the same thing, because her eyes went wide with worry and sadness.

"Forgive me," she murmured. "I don't usually behave in such a way—even when provoked."

"I'm looking forward to uncovering what provokes you, my lady."

The dance was done, and her eyes searched his as she curtsied. He began to escort her back to her mother, but she shook him off and went alone.

Before Elizabeth could reach her mother, Lucy appeared in her path, and they almost ran into each other. Both stumbled back, and when Lucy laughed, Elizabeth found herself reluctantly joining in.

"That was quite a dance," her friend said when at last they strolled arm in arm about the fringes of the crowded ballroom.

Elizabeth tensed, thinking of the way Lord Dekker had tried to force her outside. "Which dance?"

"The one you just finished with Mr. Derby." Lucy gave a dramatic sigh. "You dance very well together."

"Oh!" Elizabeth said brightly, then had to admit, "He was often trapped into being my partner when I was learning."

"He didn't look trapped today. He seemed to be enjoying himself, although you didn't." Lucy gave her a pointed look. "Share."

"There's nothing to share. I always dance with Peter. We are friends."

"But it must be difficult for him to be so closely connected to your great family, yet always on the fringes."

Elizabeth opened her mouth, then closed it. Was that true? Surely Peter didn't feel that way. She remembered that he and her cousin Susanna had briefly flirted with each other, although a romantic relationship never developed between them. But the flirtation alone proved that Peter was always confident about himself and his position in their narrow Society.

"So where is William?" Elizabeth asked, changing the subject to something even more important.

Lucy grimaced. "He hasn't arrived yet. He was meeting several of his silly friends at their club first. Hopefully they're not all foxed."

Elizabeth could only pray that William belonged to a different club than Peter. She didn't want to think about William looking at that painting.

Although perhaps it might make him actually notice her, if he knew the truth.

Oh good heavens, what was she thinking? He might not wish to see her again over the scandal of it. She told herself to stay calm. Susanna had a plan, or so she'd told them earlier in the evening. They were going to defeat those three boorish men, win back that painting—and destroy it!

"I see him!" Lucy suddenly squealed.

Elizabeth found herself dragged too close to the dance floor, where more than once she had to dodge a waltzing couple. At last she and Lucy stood before

Baron William Gibson, so handsome that Elizabeth's eyes hurt looking at him. His hair was a tousled blond, streaked by the sun, green eyes like springtime. He loved to race his horses about London, and more than once she'd seen him driving his phaeton when she'd been out walking. It was as if the sun had come out to dazzle her.

William turned from laughing with his friends and saw his sister. He chucked her under the chin. "Hullo, Lucy."

And then he looked at Elizabeth. She waited for the magic, for him to *really* notice her, as he had when she'd first made her debut.

But then he chucked her under the chin, too.

"Hullo, Elizabeth."

"Good evening, William," she said, holding back her disappointment even as she sank into her most perfect curtsy. Why didn't he say how lovely she looked? Why didn't he notice her gown, and the way it showed off her figure, so that she could see the admiration in his eyes, the way Peter—

She broke off, appalled and angry. There was no comparison between William and Peter.

"Remember to save me a dance?" William asked her.

Her heart skipped a beat and she looked at her dance card. "It is rather crowded, but I do believe the next waltz is still available."

He shook his head. "Can't. Card game in the drawing room. I'll come find you later."

And then they were gone. Elizabeth stood beside Lucy, watching the young men laughing and slapping backs as they paired up for their silly card game.

"I'm sorry," Lucy said softly.

"It isn't your fault."

"He'll remember and come back."

"Of course." Though Elizabeth kept her voice calm, she felt unsteady beneath. In every way, this had been a disappointing evening.

Elizabeth paced her bedroom, unable to sit still for her maid to brush out her hair. After allowing Teresa to find her own bed, she brushed it herself, taking out her frustrations. She glared at herself in the mirror and took vigorous strokes.

She didn't like how this painting—this wager!—was changing her. She was becoming overly suspicious of everyone. The more she thought about it, the more convinced she became that Lord Dekker only wanted to flirt with her under the moonlight.

All of it was Peter's fault. She thought about his smug, laughing face as he'd held her so inappropriately during the waltz. What was wrong with him? He should be consoling her, siding with her against his imbecilic friends. And instead, he was treating her like . . . like . . . oh, she didn't know. She wanted the old Peter back, not this stranger, with blue eyes that seemed almost hot.

After a quick knock, Susanna opened the door and leaned in, gesturing with her hand. Elizabeth gladly tossed away her brush and let Susanna take her arm, pulling her along the corridor to Rebecca's bedroom. It amused her that Susanna, usually so reserved and studious, a bluestocking in every sense of the word, had decided to plot their strategy—and that Rebecca, adventurous and daring since her childhood illnesses had abated, was willing to listen to her sister!

Once inside, Elizabeth sank down on the four-poster, getting comfortable among the pillows.

Susanna put her hands on her hips. "You'll both hear my plan now."

"Of course," Rebecca said, brushing her hair. "Tell us everything."

"We cannot stay in London and let those three men pick us apart one by one, looking for weaknesses, combining their information."

Elizabeth frowned. "But they're trying to best each other."

"And us. And I'm beginning to think that defeating us is more appealing than defeating each other."

Rebecca smiled at Elizabeth. "She assumes that because she knows what's beneath a man's skin, she knows how he thinks."

Susanna was an artist, and she boldly helped her anatomist father by sketching his dissections. This debate between sisters had gone on forever, and Elizabeth impatiently waved her hand.

It was Susanna's turn to smile. "I didn't say that. But I think the best way we can protect this secret is to go our separate ways, not make it so easy for them to question us one by one."

Elizabeth tensed with uncertainty.

"Separate ways?" Rebecca frowned.

"Eventually one of us will make a mistake," Susanna continued. "I think we reduce the risk of that if we don't give them access to all of us."

"But it's like . . . leaving the game." Rebecca's shoulders slumped.

Elizabeth saw her cousin's disappointment, and didn't understand it. *Winning* the game was what mattered, the only way to retrieve the painting and protect themselves.

"No, it's like taking the game elsewhere," Susanna said, her smile growing. "If they choose not to follow, then we win, don't you see?"

"I can't leave," Elizabeth said. "My mother has not been feeling well, and I need to be with her." She left out the fact that William was here, too.

Susanna nodded. "That's fine. We mustn't go together anyway. I've been invited to a house party. I'll attend."

"Mother mentioned it." Rebecca sounded uncertain. "She'll insist I attend, too."

"Not if you're going to visit Great Aunt Rianette."

Rebecca froze with her brush still in her hair. "I beg your pardon?"

"She's been asking for one of us to visit," Susanna continued, "and Mama has been feeling guilty that we've been too busy. Now she won't have to feel guilty anymore."

Elizabeth hugged a pillow to her mouth to hide her laughter as the two sisters continued to bicker even as they made plans for Rebecca's train trip.

Satisfied at last, Rebecca looked at her sister and Elizabeth with confidence. "Should I wish us all good luck, even though we won't need it?"

Elizabeth took both their hands, and they shared a smile. But inside, worry curdled her amusement. She didn't want them to see it. They had their strategy, and they were determined to win. Rebecca was ready for an adventure; Susanna was ready to prove her superiority over a simple male. Elizabeth wouldn't bring them down with her petty concerns.

# Chapter 3

**P**eter tried to leave his family town house early the next morning. He had plans to begin tracking down the artist who'd painted Elizabeth. But just as he reached the front door, he heard his mother call his name. Sighing, he looked over his shoulder and saw her leaning over the balustrade from the first floor.

"Peter, may I speak with you for a moment?"

"Of course, Mother," he said, then went back up the stairs.

Though she smiled, worry was evident in the lines on her forehead. She was still a handsome woman, her figure softer, her hair peppered with gray she didn't bother to conceal. He had always wondered why she didn't remarry after the death of his rather tyrannical father, but she always said that her children kept her too busy. That was code for trying to persuade her eldest to marry and provide an heir. James hadn't cooperated yet.

She drew Peter into the drawing room, looked both

ways down the corridor, then shut the door. "I don't want your sister overhearing."

He sighed, wondering what mischief Mary Anne had gotten into now. "Shouldn't James be here?"

"He's too impatient with her," Mrs. Derby replied. "I think she would do best if it came from you."

He sat down on the sofa beside his mother and took her hand. "Tell me everything."

With a sigh, she said, "I thought when Mary Anne came out into Society, things would be better for her."

"She's more mature, as far as I can tell." He felt a twinge of guilt as he said it, knowing he'd seldom been with Mary Anne this past year.

"Oh, yes, she's much more of a conversationalist, and she no longer speaks without thinking."

"There, now, that sounds better." He grinned. "Too often I used to be able to hear her screeching several floors away."

His mother didn't smile back. "She has developed an obsession. It couldn't be with reading or painting or needlework, something appropriate. No, she has become—a sharp."

He stared at her, trying hard not to laugh. "Do you know what that is?"

"She plays billiards for money and misleads men about her expertise!" She twisted a handkerchief in her fingers, distraught.

"Misleads men?"

"Oh, it is too easy to do. Who would expect such skill from a young lady?"

"I know she enjoyed playing a game or two. I thought she caught on quite well."

"Did you encourage her?"

"I don't think so. But we played together when she was younger. I didn't think she cared all that much."

"And now it's all she wants to do."

Peter's smile faded at his mother's obvious distress. He knew she was not the sort of woman to exaggerate. She had accepted his father's airs, his attempts to seem more than a squire in their little village, which was hard to do when one lived next door to the Duke of Madingley. The old duke had never done anything to offend his father—the duke's very existence was enough. And when the duke had taken an interest in Peter's education—since his father could only afford to send the heir to school—it made everything worse. It was his mother who'd convinced Mr. Derby to allow Peter the access to the Cabot tutors, since it would help him find a good wife some day. His father had grudgingly acquiesced.

"Have you asked Mary Anne why she enjoys the game above all others?" Peter asked.

"She's . . . evasive. I would let it go, Peter—I thought, what harm?—but then at a dinner party she and I attended three days ago, I heard a commotion when I was passing by the billiard room. I saw her at the center of a group of men—she was not the only lady present," his mother quickly added. "But she'd asked to play and they'd allowed her, simply assuming . . ." She trailed off with a sigh.

"That they were humoring her," he finished.

"Later, I heard tell that she played simplistically at first, then took their money with her win. Can you imagine, Peter? Thank heavens those men are friends of ours and talk will go no further. But what will happen if she does this again? Am I supposed to keep her locked in the house? She'll be on the shelf in no time. I think it might very well be what she has planned. She shows no interest in securing the attention of a man—unless he'd like to play against her."

He nodded his understanding. Every mother wanted a good marriage for her daughter, and feared she would end up a poor relation otherwise. He would never allow his sister to feel unloved, even if she had to live with him until the end of her days, but that wasn't what his mother wanted to hear. And he couldn't imagine proud Mary Anne beholden to him, either.

"I'll talk to her," he said, rising to his feet.

His mother sank back against a cushion, the strain in her face already easing. "She loves you, Peter. She'll listen."

Mary Anne was also headstrong. He wasn't certain

she'd listen at all, but he could listen to her. He'd certainly learned his lesson about taking time to discover the truth. "Do you know where she is?"

With a heavy sigh, Mrs. Derby answered, "Where do you think?"

As predicted, he found his sister in the billiard room, bent over the slate table, lining up a shot. He said nothing for a moment, not wanting to disturb her concentration.

Leather benches and small tables lined the wall. Overhead, an oil lamp gave illumination, with a tray hung beneath it to keep from ruining the green baize of the billiard table.

He tried to look at her objectively. She was a pretty girl, with hair the same color as his, a light cross between brown and blond. They shared their father's blue eyes, but thankfully not his temperament. She was overly tall for a woman, which she'd once confessed caused her much concern.

For the first time, he noticed the darkness of her gown, a green so deep it could have been gray. Now that he thought of it, she was never one to wear bright colors or frills and ribbons like Elizabeth did. Even her hair was sedately drawn back into a knot at the base of her neck.

After a crack of ivory balls smacking, Mary Anne straightened and grinned with satisfaction. Peter clapped, and with a start she turned to see him leaning in the doorway.

She smiled. "Good, aren't I?"

"So Mother informs me."

With a loud sigh, she slumped one hip against the table, cradling the cue in front of her chest as she lifted her pert nose in the air. "So she complained about me to you."

"Not complained. She is simply worried, and says that billiards has become an obsession with you."

Rolling her eyes, she groaned.

"Quite dramatic," he said mildly.

"Women played through history," she said. "It's only recently that men pushed us away. Mary, Queen of Scots, played."

"And you know how she ended, parted from her head."

Mary Anne made a face. "Mother simply disapproves because she doesn't understand the game."

He watched her, saying nothing.

Her sigh was milder. "Oh, I'm not demeaning her intelligence. It's just that she's never bothered to allow herself to enjoy the challenge of it. She doesn't understand my skills."

"Apparently several gentlemen didn't, either."

She bit her lip, and he knew she was trying to hold back a smile.

"They assumed that because I am a woman," she said, "I was incapable of mastering the game."

"And their ignorance made you play for money."

"It was their suggestion."

"And you innocently went along with it."

At last her triumphant grin emerged. "It was enjoyable to see their dumbfounded expressions."

"I'm sure it was. Only a fool would underestimate you." Before she could preen too much with his compliment, he added, "Would it be enjoyable if they discussed among the *ton* your new penchant to play for money?"

Her smile faded. "I don't care."

"Mother does. She's worried you'll end up alone like Great Aunt Clementine."

"I don't like cats," she said with a sniff.

"Regardless, Mary Anne, playing for money with men is just not done."

"If this were a card game—"

"It's not, and you know the difference."

She leaned over the table and began to roll one of the balls repeatedly against the rubber-padded cushion. She didn't look at him as she softly said, "I know."

"Promise me you won't do that again."

He saw her jaw clench.

"But I can still play?" she asked, looking up at him.

As always, those blue eyes melted him. "Of course. It is a game you're skilled at. I only ask that you play with close friends and family—and not for money. You do not want a reputation."

"Will it bother you on your great wife hunt?" she asked, her lips twisting in a smirk.

"I am in no rush. I'll leave James to that pressure."

Her smile faded. "And me. You're leaving me to it."

"But you're a woman, Mary Anne. It is part of what you are."

"Yes, we're only complete if we're wives," she murmured.

She didn't meet his eyes, and for a moment he thought there was something unsaid. He wanted to dismiss the thought but found he couldn't. She went back to practicing, ignoring him. The balls clicked against each other or thumped along the edge.

For the first time, he wondered if he knew his sister as well as he'd once thought. He needed to find a way to help her.

At a dinner party given by Lady Fogge the next evening, Peter watched as Elizabeth was escorted into the dining room much earlier than he was, due to her rank, and they sat too distant among the twenty guests to speak. On her left was a pale, red-haired young man he'd met once or twice by the name of Mr. Tilden. It was to him she directed most of her conversation, since the man to her right, Lord Radcliffe, seemed to enjoy looking down her bodice rather than at her face.

After dinner, when the men rejoined the ladies, Peter

made a point of escorting a reluctant Elizabeth, walking her about the room slowly, watching the candlelight glow on her smooth skin. Several women smiled at her as they passed, but she didn't stop to speak with them. When they neared a deserted corner, still within view of every guest, he stopped and faced her.

She gave him a cool look and waited.

"You didn't seem pleased with your dinner partner," he said, gesturing subtly toward Lord Radcliffe.

She sighed. "With his curly black hair, he reminds me of a spiteful cupid. But I don't want to talk about him, Peter. You need to know something that will affect how you *attempt* to win the wager. Rebecca and Susanna have left London. You won't be able to use them against me in your quest for the truth."

"Use your cousins against you?" he said quietly, with faint sarcasm. "Why would I do that?"

"You might think one of them will crack beneath the strain of your questions; you might compare our stories." She lifted her chin with defiance. "Now you won't be able to, and neither will your friends."

"You aren't worried that my friends will now join me in questioning *you*?"

She shot him a sly smile. "Have you seen them today? I do believe they were invited this evening, were they not?"

"I see," he said slowly, letting his admiring gaze

roam her face. "Your cousins led them away."

"Like puppies on a leash."

He laughed, and more than one head turned toward them, but his merriment took a while to fade. "Well done, Elizabeth. Whose idea was it?"

"Susanna's, of course."

"Of course. Where did they all go?"

She only shrugged mischievously. And although she was besting him, he enjoyed the sight, for she seemed to be recovering from whatever had caused her tears. But he wouldn't forget them.

He decided it was time to counter her cleverness. "Do you know where I was today, while everyone was fleeing London? I went to the Royal Academy."

"Whatever for?" she asked too innocently.

Her smile hardened, but didn't disappear. The game was still on.

"Several of Roger Eastfield's paintings are on display there. You remember him, don't you?"

"The artist who painted me. Did they tell you where to find him?"

"I imagine I could have asked you, but didn't think you'd answer. And yes, they did tell me where his studio was."

She hesitated briefly, then said, "I hope you said hello for me."

"He wasn't there. A neighbor said he journeyed north, and was uncertain when he'd return."

Her relief was subtle, but it was there.

"What a shame," she said, reaching to pat his forearm.

He put his hand over hers, and her eyes darted to the other guests. But Peter's body blocked their touch from sight.

"It was not a very good section of London, Elizabeth."

"I know. I was careful."

"So he painted you at his studio?"

"Would you rather he painted me in the Madingley drawing room?" she asked, blinking at him.

He watched her intently. "And you were alone with him?"

"My cousins were with me."

His shoulders and neck were so stiff with tension, it was hard to relax them, but her words helped.

"You think I would allow myself to be alone with him, Peter?" she asked in a soft, affronted voice.

He barely controlled his astonishment, then whispered between smiling lips, "You posed *nude*, Elizabeth. Can you blame me for wondering if you did so because you were enthralled with the artist?"

She blinked. "By enthralled, you mean . . . you think I would let him . . ." Then she sputtered, as if she didn't know how to say it.

"Then I'll be blunt." He leaned a bit closer than propriety allowed, and in the same room as their host and her guests, he asked, "Did you lie with him, Elizabeth?"

She inhaled sharply, straightening away from him. She looked about, seeing that they were still being ignored, and hissed, "I would never do such a thing. I think less of you, Peter, for even suggesting it."

There were two hot patches of color in her cheeks, and she seemed to have trouble meeting his gaze—but not because she was lying about her relationship with Eastfield. He knew that with certainty. And he felt relieved.

"I'm not an artist," he said. "I don't know how one resists a beautiful naked woman day in and day out."

"It was professional. It was *art*. We didn't even talk, for it disturbed his concentration."

"How did you—"

"I don't wish to speak of this anymore. It is time for me to converse with our hostess. Oh, Lady Fogge!" she called, raising a hand and smiling as she left Peter alone.

He watched her go, keeping his expression neutral even as his mind turned over and over her reaction to his investigation of the artist—and what it might mean.

# Chapter 4

The next day, Elizabeth desperately wanted to make morning calls with her mother. She didn't wish to be in the house to receive, but her mother, so excited by this new interest in her daughter from so many men, was determined to see for herself.

Elizabeth almost took a nap midday before the men arrived, but restrained herself. She'd had a hard time sleeping the previous night, feeling strangely alone in Madingley House, the great palace where her mother and aunt slept, not to mention dozens and dozens of servants. But her brother, Christopher, and cousins Daniel and Matthew, were gone, and she hadn't imagined how much she would miss the security of their presence, their deep booming laughs, even their protectiveness.

At three o'clock the men began to arrive, by singles, or twos and threes. To her surprise, Lord Thomas made an appearance. She and her mother exchanged looks. He slowly circulated about the room as one by one various men took their turn conversing with her.

Always, her gaze would go back to Lord Thomas. He was one of the highest ranking in attendance, the younger son of a duke. He could have approached her at any time, and all would have made way for him. Instead he admired the intricately carved fireplace that stretched up to the ceiling, then wandered past each painting as if in a museum.

At last the duchess seemed to be wilting under the demands of being hostess, after so recently recovering from a fever.

"Take your ease, Mama," Elizabeth said, bending over her. "There are only a few gentlemen left, and surely you've spoken to them all."

"That nice Lord Thomas is so thoughtful."

"Yes, isn't he," Elizabeth said, glancing at him again, only to find him watching her, a faint smile on his handsome mouth.

"He always brings me word from his mother." She lifted a folded letter from her lap. "I'll retire and read it."

Bows followed the duchess as she left the drawing room. The last three men finally took their leave, and Elizabeth faced Lord Thomas. As he came to her slowly, she found herself more and more curious.

He stopped before her and said nothing, simply studying her face.

Almost nervously—and she was never nervous!—she said, "I still regret that we did not have the chance to dance the other night, Lord Thomas. I hope you have forgiven me."

"I have, my lady. I contented myself to look upon you from afar."

And then he allowed his gaze to travel slowly from her face to her bodice. She kept waiting for him to catch himself, as men usually did, but . . . he did not. Her skin began to burn with humiliation and the first touch of worry.

"Lord Thomas?" she said coolly.

He smiled when at last he met her eyes again. "You are a lovely creature, Elizabeth."

He didn't use her title. "Creature? Not exactly what a lady wishes to hear."

"But are you still being treated as a lady?"

She swallowed, remembering Lord Dekker trying to force her to waltz out on the terrace. Why did Lord Thomas bring that up? Only one man had treated her as less than a lady in his eagerness to spend time with her.

"I think you should leave." Her voice was cool now, full of the noble hauteur that she'd been bred to.

He chuckled softly, glancing over her shoulder at the matching footmen lining the double doors to the entrance hall. He held out his arm. "I think we should stroll about the room. Such lovely artwork."

She wanted to leave, but something terrible would happen if she did. All she could do was control her trembling as she laid her hand lightly on his forearm. He led her toward the far wall, where large French doors opened onto the terrace.

"I believe we can be seen together out in the open," he said. "So much more private out there, too."

It wasn't any more private than inside the servant-filled house, for many gardeners worked in the extensive beds that made one believe one was in the country, rather than in the heart of Mayfair. But on the terrace, though they were in view of servants, they could not be overheard.

He guided her to the balustrade. She removed her hand from his arm, resting her palms on the marble, as if enjoying the view.

"What do you want?" she asked coldly.

He waited until she was forced to look up at him. His smile faded as he said, "I know about the painting."

She inhaled so swiftly it was as if she'd been struck a blow to the stomach. *Oh God,* she thought, and it was a fervent prayer. Clutching the balustrade, she stared with aching eyes out at the gardens, unable to look at him for fear of giving herself away.

"I do not know what you are talking about," she said, wishing she sounded less formal. "My cousin Susanna is an artist, not I."

"No, but you're the model. I admit, I did not deduce it myself. Another gentleman—if you can use that word—whispered it to me. He said he saw Miss Rebecca Leland wearing the same jewel as in the painting—and of course, since she wore it, she can not be the model, nor, of course, her spinster sister."

It was exactly the same reasoning Peter had used.

She tried once more to bluff her way out of the accusation. "Again, I don't know—"

"Stop, Elizabeth. I don't know if you realize where that painting hangs, but many men of my acquaintance have seen it."

This explained Lord Dekker's belief that he could be alone with her on a terrace and she wouldn't protest. If more people found out, she'd be ruined, her family's name disgraced.

"I don't know why you risked yourself in such a way," he continued, "but I know you need protection."

She took a shaky breath, not certain what he was saying.

"I can ensure that the rumors go no further, that Madingley never needs to know the truth of his sister . . . as long as you marry me."

Her shocked gaze flew to his. He was watching her closely, his expression solemn but his eyes glittering faintly. She'd rejected him, and perhaps he felt humiliated enough to find another way to have what he wanted. The painting had played right into his hands.

"Marry you?" she whispered, as if the words didn't want to make sense.

"Yes. You were not so interested before."

There was a hard edge to his words, and now she knew that he had not taken the blow to his pride well.

"But by marrying me," he continued, "all of your problems will go away. My name will protect you. We'll join two ancient families together, and make them even more powerful. No man would dare spread rumors if he knew he'd face my wrath."

She still gaped at him, her mind frantic, her fear growing into fury and desperation.

"I can't marry you," she said, almost breathless. "I'm already engaged."

Where had that lie come from? she thought wildly. What if he became furious over another rejection and told everyone the truth? An engagement would only protect her from marriage to him, not her secrets.

To her surprise, he chuckled. "I don't believe you. There has been no word—and you, my highborn lady, could not hope to keep such news a secret from the gossips."

"But it *is* a secret," she said desperately. "I can't even tell you his name until he's able to speak to my brother."

That, at least, was a realistic barrier to a public announcement.

Thomas shook his head. "Ah, Elizabeth, you're making this so much more challenging. I don't mind a challenge. I'm determined to have you. But my patience will only last so long. If there is an engagement—which I doubt—I suggest you break the poor man's heart."

"I can't do that."

"You can—and you will. After all, you can't go to your brother with this dilemma, for then you'd have to reveal what began all of your problems—posing for that painting."

Her mind was racing—he was right, she had no one to fall back on for help, no one she could risk telling—and no fiancé! What was more, she did not doubt that Lord Thomas's proposal would soon be a matter of public knowledge within the *ton*.

"I assume the duke is returning in time for the Kelthorpe Masked Ball?"

She could only nod helplessly.

"You have three weeks, then, to see this settled. You won't be able to keep the painting and your guilt from your brother. But with my help, together we can solve all your problems. I'll even do my best to control knowledge of the painting—for now. What else would protect your reputation better than marriage to me?" With his finger, he lifted her chin until her mouth closed. "Three weeks, Elizabeth, to make me the happiest man in the world."

With a smile, he turned and walked across the terrace, disappearing into the drawing room. Sinking onto a wrought-iron bench, she put her face in her hands. The rest of her family might enjoy scandal, but she did not. She'd spent her childhood thoughtlessly doing whatever she'd wanted—and saw the toll such a life had taken on her brother, and her mother. With maturity, she had realized she'd be content with a simple life and the man of her dreams. What was she supposed to do now?

Could she spend three weeks pretending she had a fiancé? But . . . another man—maybe even more— knew about the painting, according to Thomas. Though Thomas said he could control them, they might believe they could press their advances, as Lord Dekker had. Somehow she had to protect herself.

That night, at Lady Marlowe's dinner party, Peter looked for Elizabeth. Lady Marlowe could seat fifty people at her dining table, and they'd all crowded into her overheated, overdecorated drawing room, conversing before the meal. He'd had no time to get Elizabeth alone, so now that the meal was over, and the gentlemen were reunited with the ladies in the drawing room, perhaps he would have a chance.

He had tried his best to visit Elizabeth that afternoon, but with his promise to his mother weighing heavily on his mind, he felt obligated to escort his sister on several morning calls. She was as polite as always—to the women. With the occasional man, she seemed to lose her tongue and her good sense. She'd never been hesitant to speak her opinion, to women *or* men. On the way home, he asked her what had changed, but she pretended ignorance. When he pressed her harder, at last she said she didn't intend to marry, that she wanted an independent life, that there was nothing he, or their mother, could do to force her.

She flung herself from the carriage at their town house, and he watched her march away, astonished. What had happened to his even-tempered, friendly little sister?

Since she had refused to attend the dinner this evening, he concentrated on Elizabeth. At last he caught a glimpse of her across the drawing room, where she stood with her friend Miss Gibson and family. The carpets had been rolled back, the small orchestra warmed up and playing the first country dance. Elizabeth stood beside William Gibson, to whom Peter had never been introduced. He perfectly expected her to be led away by Gibson before he reached her.

But that didn't happen. She looked frustrated, and her toe tapped, a sure indication, but Gibson was ignorant. Fool.

Peter stopped before her and bowed. "Good evening, Lady Elizabeth."

Her curtsy was brief and perfunctory—and then her gaze sharpened on his face.

He raised his eyebrows in response.

"Mr. Derby." She drew his name out, as if in consideration.

"Lady Elizabeth," he repeated, grinning. At least she looked more like herself tonight. "May I have this dance?"

Without a single hesitation, she put her hand in his. Surprised, pleased—then wary—he led her out onto the floor. It was a quadrille rather than his favorite waltz, so the steps took them apart and brought them together, circling other couples, before they could link hands again.

When they came together, she murmured, "I need to speak with you in private."

He smiled. "You know I am at your command."

As she rolled her eyes, the dance separated them again. Several minutes later they spun together and she whispered, "I knew you'd have no problem—I heard you've been alone a time or two with questionable women."

He widened his eyes with innocence. "Why, Elizabeth, I have no idea what you're saying. You almost sound jealous."

She ignored his taunt. "Meet me in the family parlor at the end of the main hall."

"The men are playing cards there."

"Drat."

And then they were separated, and he couldn't help

chuckling at her frustration. She seemed desperate to be alone with him—an enjoyable thought.

When they were together again, she said, "The library."

"And if that's occupied," he said, "we could adjourn to the gardens."

Instead of quickly overruling his suggestion, she gave him such a troubled look that his amusement faded.

"Elizabeth—" he began, frowning, but she interrupted before the dance separated them.

"The library," she repeated. "You go first and make sure it's unoccupied. I'll follow five minutes later."

And then she curtsied, he bowed, and they walked off the dance floor in different directions.

He was waiting in the library beside the door when she entered. She gave a start to see him, but he silently held up the key, and she nodded. After locking the door, he leaned back against it and watched her.

Her usual calm grace had deserted her. Her movements were hurried, restless, as she circled the leather wing-back chairs, and looked up at the bookshelves as if about to choose a title. Peter waited and watched, curious but patient.

At last she took a deep breath and turned to face him. Those dark eyes seemed to roil with emotions, uncertainty and determination mixed with anger. He approached her, his unease growing.

He took her hands and she didn't even stop him. Though her skin was soft and supple, her fingers were cold. "Elizabeth, tell me what's wrong. I've known for several days that you've been upset, but I can't believe it's simply because of this wager."

She opened her mouth, hesitated, then the words seemed to tumble from her lips quickly. "I need you to pretend to be my fiancé for the next few weeks."

*That* was certainly nothing he'd ever imagined. Stunned and worried about her, he still felt a jolt of desire as he wondered what it would be like if that were real. But she didn't want it to be real. Something was making her desperate.

She tried to yank her hands away. "Say something, Peter!"

He didn't let her go, saying mildly, "You can hardly propose to me and not tell me why."

"It's not a proposal! Not really," she added, shoulders slumping.

"Elizabeth—"

"I can't talk about this, Peter. I thought, for the sake of our friendship, you would help me."

"Elizabeth—"

She interrupted again. "And if our childhood friendship isn't enough, then I will make a bargain with you. If you agree to a false engagement, and allow me to break it off when I need to, I will tell you the truth about the painting. You'll defeat your friends."

She watched him closely, waiting, not even breathing, Peter thought. Something had driven her to such a desperate act, and he had to understand why. To hell with the wager.

"Elizabeth, you could not possibly have thought that I wouldn't have questions about something so outrageous."

"I won't answer your questions, Peter. That's part of the bargain. In return for your help and your silence, you'll defeat your friends. What more do you want?"

He pulled her hands up to press them flat to his chest. "Elizabeth, this is . . . insane. You're going to tell your mother we're engaged? Your brother? All of your friends? Why would you do something so drastic?"

Stubborn, she seemed determined not to confide in him. But did she not realize that if he agreed to her insane plan, they would be forced to be closer than ever? Certainly then he could find out the truth, help her somehow. He'd always been the one who rescued her, who hid her secrets—and now she was asking for that again.

She stared at her hands where they rested on his chest. He rubbed her fingers gently with his palms, wanting to warm her, to ease her. Again she pulled away, and this time he allowed it.

"Peter, this is not something I've asked lightly." She

didn't quite meet his eyes. "I understand how it will affect me, what I'll have to do. But it's temporary, and it will not affect my family. But you—how will it affect you? Will you mind lying to your family?"

*I once lied to yours*, he thought, then submerged his uneasiness. That was the past.

"Or is there a woman you're courting?" she continued.

Now she searched his eyes, and he was able to say, "There's no one." And it was only partly the truth. There was no one else he'd ever seriously considered. Since Elizabeth had grown up, she was the one always lingering in his thoughts.

"And those women I heard about?"

Though he smiled, her expression didn't ease. "We only amuse each other, games and not commitments."

Nodding, she looked away. Only in mourning had he seen such unhappiness shadow her face. He felt sympathetic, and had to try reasoning with her one last time.

"But Elizabeth, I'm not sure you *have* thought this through. To convince your family, we'll have to appear as if we've suddenly fallen in love."

She bit her lip even as she nodded.

"And your mother will believe that?"

"She has to." Her words were low and tense, fraught with anxiety.

But Elizabeth wouldn't confide in him, ask him for

his help directly. She wanted subterfuge, regardless of who might be hurt.

He'd spent years wondering if they could have more than a friendship, and now she was presenting him with the opportunity. But by risking everything with a false engagement, she would have to live with the results.

He spoke slowly, clearly. "You do understand that in order for our parents to believe this, we won't be playing this safe."

The relief in her eyes was obvious. "Then you'll do it? Be my fiancé?"

"Yes, I'll do it."

A frown grew as she understood his previous words. "Safe? I know this can't be safe. We're lying to the people we love—to everyone."

"And you've had much practice lying lately."

"You'll discover the truth once you've helped me. Isn't that what you want, Peter?"

"I don't do anything halfway. To convince them we're serious about marriage, you'll do everything I say, accept anything I do." At last, openly, he let his gaze drop languidly down her body. He'd hidden his regard and admiration these last few years; it felt brazen and exciting to show her his desire.

Her eyes went wide as a blush stole across her cheeks. "You don't need to look at me that way."

"Then who will believe me?"

He stepped even closer, close enough to feel her breath coming too quickly.

"They'll think you lost your mind to give up a wealthy, expected marriage with a peer, for someone like me," he said in a low voice. "The only reason could be a love match. Had you not thought of that? Are you sure you want this?"

He almost didn't ask that last question, for now he desperately wanted to be close to her, to taste the forbidden before he had to let her go forever.

And he had to discover her secrets.

"I need this," she whispered, looking up at him.

He gently brushed a curl from her forehead, let his palm linger and cup her cheek. She was trembling but didn't back down. His courageous Elizabeth. "I'll touch you often." His voice grew low and husky. He didn't try to hide how she affected him. "I'll look at you as if I never imagined you would grace me with your love."

She swallowed heavily, unable to hide a wince. "Oh Peter—"

His thumb brushed over her lips. "You have to be better at make-believe than this, Elizabeth."

At last the dark fire of determination rose again in her eyes, and he was glad of it. Whatever was wrong, she needed to be strong to combat it.

"If you can do this for me, I won't let you down," she said almost grimly.

But she was still trembling lightly as he stroked the smooth skin of her cheek, then along her bottom lip.

"No one can see us," she whispered. "Why are you doing this?"

"Because I have to think of you in a new way. I have to let it show in my eyes when I profess my love to your family."

She gave another wince, but he didn't let her speak. He put his hands on her upper arms.

"You have to become used to my touch. You're going to have to look like you wish I could be doing more than holding your hand."

"Oh, but I couldn't!" she cried, then looked about the library in guilt, as if someone might have overheard. "Surely that is not done."

"Have you ever watched two people in love?"

He saw her giving it real thought, knew she'd watched her cousins and her brother fall in love. How could a young lady not envy the love and trust and devotion those couples shared when they looked at each other?

She kept staring at him, and he saw the dawning truth in her eyes. Something had caused her to panic, to make her think of this crazy idea, more risky than any scrape from her youth. But she'd tried so hard not to be that girl anymore. She would back down now and tell him the truth, ask for his help.

But instead she slid her arms about his waist and leaned against him, looking up. He'd never had the chance to hold her, to feel her body against him, though the possibility had tormented his dreams. Her breasts were soft and round and so tempting.

"Is this right, Peter?" she asked tremulously. "You'll guide me in how to do this? I can't afford to make any mistakes."

It was all about her desperation, her problems. He knew that. She'd only viewed him as a friend.

But now he had the chance to make her think otherwise, to see him as a man.

He slid his hands over her shoulders and down the smooth, elegant slope of her back, pulling her even closer against him.

"It's a good start, Elizabeth," he said, bending down toward her upturned face.

Her eyes widened the nearer he came, but she didn't pull away.

He stopped just before their lips met. "But you have so much more to learn."

Then he stepped away from her, unlocked the door, and walked out of the library.

# Chapter 5

Elizabeth stood in the center of the library, feeling dazed and overwhelmed and almost shaky. Everything she'd ever thought about Peter had been turned upside down in the last few days. And tonight—tonight had gone beyond anything she'd imagined.

What had she done?

Suddenly, the door opened, and she whirled about, not knowing whom to expect.

Lucy closed the door and leaned against it, staring at her. "I followed you and Peter. You were alone together! What were you thinking?"

Elizabeth opened her mouth, but nothing would come out. Wringing her hands together, she didn't know what to reveal, what to hide from her best friend. She felt like bursting into tears, but if she did, she might never be able to stop. She'd been so desperate to escape Thomas's subtle threats, but already regretted blurting out an engagement. It was too late.

"Oh, Lucy, everything is such a muddle. I've been so

frightened of being forced to marry a man I didn't love."

"Forced to marry?" Lucy cried, rushing forward. "What are you talking about?"

"One of my suitors attempted to . . . be alone with me. And the others look at me too—intently, too disrespectfully. Somehow, I've become the prize of the Season." She was lying about her suitors, but she needed to find a reasonable explanation. And what if there were more men who knew about the painting? What would they feel free to do?

Lucy gaped at her. "That does not sound at all exciting."

"It isn't. It's frightening. And I so want your brother to notice me. I had to come up with some way to make it happen yet still protect myself."

"Tell me," Lucy said, taking her hands.

Cold and trembling, Elizabeth welcomed her friend's warm comfort. Taking a deep breath, she said in a low voice, "I asked Peter to pretend to be my fiancé."

Lucy's mouth dropped open.

"I know, I know. But it will protect me from these men, don't you see? My brother isn't here to do so. And I'm hoping that *your* brother will realize what he's let go, after hinting that he wanted me as his wife not so long ago. When I'm free again, surely he'll propose."

For some insane reason, she had thought she could attract William's notice tonight, somehow convince him in one evening that they belonged together, that he should marry her *now*. That foolish thought had fled her mind almost immediately. She had to leave William out of this, to somehow make him see what he was missing when she became engaged to someone else.

Lucy frowned in confusion. "So you still want me to tell you what events my brother will attend?"

"Of course!"

And meanwhile she would string Thomas along, waiting for her brother's return. Somehow she would make Thomas realize he couldn't go against the whole Cabot family. And that painting would be gone, she'd make certain of that. What proof would Thomas have against her? Then she'd be "free" again, and William would realize he had a second chance.

"But . . . Mr. Derby?" Lucy asked with doubt.

Elizabeth sank onto the sofa and her friend sat beside her. "Tonight, I saw him across the room, and knew he was the one person I could ask for help." She didn't mention that she had something to offer him in return, the solution to that wager.

"And he agreed, just like that? Knowing he would look in the wrong when you broke it off?"

Elizabeth nodded. "To help protect me." The satisfaction and relief had almost overwhelmed her. But how was she going to keep her lies straight? She hadn't told Peter anything about the men harassing her, because that might lead him back to Thomas. No, she could not have them confronting each other.

"Then he knows about your *tendre* for William?"

"No, he doesn't. Perhaps that is a mistake, but . . . he pointed out that in order for us to be convincing, we have to seem like we've suddenly fallen in love."

And then Peter had touched her. Their casual friendship seemed to dissolve in a mad rush of sensation that had only confused and worried her. But even that hadn't made her change her mind.

"Your mother will believe that? Your cousins?"

Elizabeth winced. "My cousins aren't in residence, and my mother—I must protect her from the truth of how I'm being treated. She would believe it's all her fault, because I'm of her Spanish blood. Having never felt respected, if she believes the same has happened to me . . . oh, it might weaken her even further."

"But you've never shown even one bit of romantic feeling for Mr. Derby. What will you do?"

"He's going to . . . guide me."

Lucy covered her mouth on a gasp. "What does *that* mean?"

"He will make it look like he's fallen in love with me, and I will respond." She thought of the way he'd cupped her face, the strange sensation of warmth and pleasure. He'd looked deep into her eyes, and in that moment, she'd known he was capable of displaying emotions he didn't feel—but was she? "I've decided to make the best of my plan."

"What do you mean?"

"I'm going to learn everything Peter does, every romantic touch—and then I'll try them with William."

Lucy closed her eyes on a groan.

"Well, I have to make him notice me, Lucy! He's putting off marriage, but I don't have that luxury." It truly bothered her how William could make her feel inadequate about herself. She wasn't inadequate; she was taking control, making her own future happen, dealing with threats.

Lucy sank back against the sofa. "It is all so . . . dangerous, Elizabeth. So many things can go wrong."

"I know, but I won't allow it. I can control Peter, and with an engagement, I can control those men trying to force me to choose them." *Including Thomas.* "So you will still tell me which parties your brother chooses to attend?"

"Of course. And you'll be able to keep this from Mr. Derby?"

"I'll do my best." She pushed to her feet. "But right now I have to prove to him that I can play my part." She ignored Lucy's worried look, knowing that her friend suspected there was more to the story.

Lucy followed along behind, but they didn't hurry back to William and the rest of the Gibson family. Elizabeth paused in the doorway to the drawing room, hand lingering on the frame, her gaze sweeping across the guests. She let herself pass over William, absorbed the emotions he aroused, and then she settled soft eyes on Peter. He was talking intently to several men, gesturing with his hands. It was a habit that had always amused her, and she used it even more to remind herself of her fondness for him.

But fondness wasn't always trust, though once she would have thought it so. At last he saw her and went still. The two men with him turned to follow his gaze. It was not difficult to blush and lower her eyes, for she remembered too well the way he'd touched her face so intimately. Beneath her lashes, she looked up, saw one of the men elbow Peter good-naturedly and the other shake his head with a wince.

No, it would not be easy to quickly convince any among their circle that they'd suddenly fallen in love with each other. But they had time. Three weeks until the Kelthorpe Masked Ball—and her brother's home-coming. It would have to be enough.

While she hovered in the doorway, trying to decide what to do, the orchestra played the first notes of a waltz. Out of the corner of her eye she saw more than one man bearing down on her, but she kept her focus on Peter. He left his friends and came toward her. Walking through her approaching suitors, she ignored them, as if she had eyes for only one man. She told herself to think about William, but strangely, that didn't work. Peter was grinning at her, and though his demeanor was gentlemanly, in his eyes there was amusement and knowledge and the promise that he would make everything work out.

Because it would benefit *him*, she was certain.

He swept her into his arms, and although the drawing room was on the small side, he expertly maneuvered through the tight quarters, drawing her against him far too provocatively when it looked as if they might collide with another couple.

She gave a little gasp and murmured, "I know we're making a point, but perhaps we don't need to be quite so scandalous."

He didn't bother to hide his laugh. "After everything that's happened the last few days, can you honestly call a waltz scandalous?"

She looked up into his eyes, a blue that seemed darker, more mysterious, as if the real Peter was a man she'd never truly known before. A lock of sandy blond hair fell over his forehead, making him seem . . . rakish. She found herself smiling, then laughing, letting her head dip back just a bit as he spun her through the corner of the room.

To her surprise, she felt the brush of his thigh between hers, and it made her aware of his strength over her, the power in his frame. And then she blushed, for it seemed somehow . . . embarrassing, to think of Peter that way.

"Elizabeth?" he murmured, leaning closer, as if he'd touch his lips to her forehead.

She shook herself, forcing a smile. "Yes?"

"You were . . . gone for a moment there."

"Simply losing myself in the dance."

When the waltz ended, she sank into a deep curtsy, looking up at him with a smile she knew was a bit too sly with the secrets they shared. He bowed, his own smile more mysterious, hinting at things others might wonder about. When he should have released her hand, he placed it on his arm instead, walking her to the edge of the floor, claiming her.

Elizabeth knew they were being watched by the small crowd of guests. She looked up into Peter's amused face. "Before I joined you, your conversation with the other men seemed quite . . . heated."

His smile broadened. "Railway mergers bring out the passion in some men."

"In you?"

"It's an exciting time to be in business, Elizabeth."

She exaggerated her look about to see if they were overheard. "Don't let some of the old lords hear you say that."

"Surely I cannot make myself any less in their eyes. And more than one 'old lord' has tried to pry for my knowledge." He cocked his head as he studied her. "You don't seem surprised."

"Of course not. You're an intelligent man. I remember how you were with my brother's tutor. Competition with you drove Chris to work harder than he might have wanted to. My father appreciated that."

"Compliments already."

She smiled. "For a new fiancé."

"Back then I felt the need to prove that your father's faith in me wasn't misplaced. And I enjoyed every bit of knowledge I could amass, for I never knew when it would cease."

"Oh, my father wouldn't have—"

"Not *your* father."

She studied him, knowing that she had him trapped. "You never spoke much about Mr. Derby, and I didn't know him very well."

"He was not the sort of man the duke was. My father felt the need to constantly prove himself better than others—better than a duke. The fact that he could not afford to educate both his sons embarrassed him so badly that I almost received no education at all. My mother made him realize that I'd never marry well without one. The chance to improve the family fortunes finally changed his mind."

"You never told me this," she said slowly.

"You were younger, and unaware. Why should you know that there could be men in the world like my father?"

"It must have made you want to prove yourself to him." His expression remained impassive.

"And you *have* proven yourself, Peter," she said softly.

"That's not important. Success on my own terms is."

She took a deep breath, looking about at the guests, who tried to watch them without really watching. "And perhaps you will have even more success with this new connection to my family."

"You mean the one I'll lose within a few weeks?" He cocked his head.

Her face flushed. "But until then, you will meet new people—perhaps even the woman who will wish you were available again."

"I have a good deal of success with women on my own, thank you."

"So I heard," she murmured.

"And what did you hear?"

Would this humiliating evening never end? "Nothing specific, of course. People are quite circumspect."

"In our circles?" he asked dryly. "Then we can't know the same people."

She looked away.

"You're attempting to be lighthearted, now that I've agreed to your scandal."

A change of subject, but she allowed it. "It won't be a scandal, not if everything goes as I intend."

He covered her hand where it rested on his arm. "You've taken many risks lately."

She stiffened. "Not really." Situations had been thrust upon her—she wasn't that reckless, thoughtless young girl anymore.

He arched a brow, disbelief evident in his expression. "Posing nude for a painting, dressing as a boy to steal it back, now pretending an engagement. My head is reeling from seeing all these different sides of you." He lowered his voice. "I enjoyed seeing one side above all others."

She knew he referred to the painting, and although embarrassment lingered within her, she forced it down. "I have done what was necessary. And is this strange discussion simply to show all our curious friends that you're fascinated with me?"

"Or to get the appropriate response out of you. I'm quite enjoying your blush. Perhaps we'll truly throw caution to the wind and dance together a third time."

"No, that is too much for one night," she said, stepping away when he would have pulled her back into the center of the drawing room.

"I must show my new devotion somehow. I could sneak into your bedroom . . ."

She laughed, knowing her reaction was what he

wanted to project to the room. "As if anyone would know. Shall we go for a carriage ride tomorrow morning? I understand you have a new phaeton, displaying your wealth in the typical way of a bachelor."

"I am so predictable, then?"

"Some men are. Your courtship of me will prove you're a radical."

"A romantic idealist. That's what everyone else will say."

She smiled. "A foolish optimist."

He met her amused eyes with his own. "You mean a foolish dreamer."

They looked at each other for a moment. Even after all the craziness of the last few days, her disappointment in him, her mistrust, it was still so easy to talk to him. She'd forgotten that these last few years since her coming out. Even more proof that, regardless of their teasing or their partnership in deception, they were not meant for more.

"So you will ride beside me tomorrow and look giddy with happiness," he said.

She nodded, telling herself that Thomas would soon be a thing of the past. She just had to be patient.

"And then you shall come to call upon my mother," she said firmly.

"So soon? Shouldn't we show our new devotion for at least a day or two?"

His eyes had become suspicious, watchful, and she knew she'd revealed too much haste.

"You're right," she said. "I was just thinking to get on with the engagement, the sooner for it to be finished."

"And then . . . what will happen?"

She glanced at him out of the corner of her eye. "None of your business."

"Ah, but I'm the love of your life," he said, smiling wickedly, even as he squeezed his elbow to his side, trapping her hand against him.

She had a fleeting impression of warmth, and the steely muscles of an active man, before he was forced by propriety to loosen his hold.

"How can you keep secrets from me?" he continued.

"Even husbands and wives aren't supposed to share everything."

"They're not?"

"Of course not. Such sharing is for friendships, like we used to have." For just a moment she let him see her seriousness. "I never thought you would wager over something so personal to me, Peter." She was still hurt, and didn't care if he knew it.

"And I never thought you would keep such reckless secrets. With your behavior, I can't even imagine the things you're hiding. You've been so insistent that you've changed."

The edge of her annoyance was sharp and brittle. "I

am not reckless. Everything I do is perfectly thought out."

"You'll have to prove that to me."

"Gladly. I will see you in the morning." She spoke stiffly, between smiling lips.

"You're not convincing anyone of your infatuation with me," he chided, letting her go as another man approached.

She lifted her nose in the air and turned away.

As Peter drove his pair of matched gray geldings through the London traffic the next morning, he couldn't forget the look on Elizabeth's face when she'd left him at Lady Marlowe's dinner party. As she'd allowed another man to take her hand and lead her into the dance, he could have sworn she seemed . . . afraid.

Before that, she'd put on such a show for the guests, being sweet and shy and beguiling in her innocent flirtation. Even he'd almost been fooled.

A barouche took a corner too quickly, and only his reflexes saved the two carriages from disaster. He glared at the coachman, who shook a fist, but Peter knew he should concentrate more on his driving and less on the mystery of Elizabeth.

And she was a mystery, even to his family. His mother already seemed suspicious about why he wasn't spending every moment trying to help Mary Anne. He was attempting to regroup where his sister was concerned, to think of a new plan to make her see the error of her ways. He'd had to tell them both that he was taking Elizabeth for a drive. Mary Anne had rolled her eyes and snickered, even as their mother allowed a flicker of hope to show in her gaze before she remembered their place in Society.

And what would Mary Anne think when he was engaged—and then it was broken? It would hardly convince her that she'd underestimated the appeal of marriage. But he would ford that stream later, and allay his mother's curiosity.

Perhaps he was growing too used to making excuses for himself, he thought, frowning.

At Madingley House, he left his groom holding the bridle of one of his horses and took the stairs to the front door with easy enthusiasm. After he rang the bell, the butler guided him through the ostentatious entrance hall and upstairs into a smaller drawing room. To his surprise, the Dowager Duchess of Madingley stepped inside. Where once her expression would have lit with fondness, now she smiled with a hint of concern.

"Good morning, Mr. Derby," she said, gliding into the room.

He bowed to her. "You look radiant as always, Your Grace." Once she'd settled herself onto the sofa, he sat down across from her.

"I understand you're taking Elizabeth out for a ride this morning," the duchess said.

"So I am. She expressed interest in my new phaeton."

"How kind of you to amuse her." Though she continued to smile at him, her black eyes seemed shadowed with curiosity and confusion. "And how is your mother?"

"She is well, thank you. Dealing with my sister, of course, although surely you are familiar with the travails of young ladies."

She nodded, but he sensed she had more on her mind than polite conversation.

"Mr. Derby . . . Peter."

She used his Christian name, smiling faintly, knowing she'd earned the right long ago.

"Forgive my prying," she continued, "but . . . I am curious about this recent attention to Elizabeth. I heard from friends that last night you danced several times together."

"We did." He continued to politely smile. "Elizabeth and I have always gotten along well together."

"Yes, but . . ." Her smile was fond, yet almost sad. "You know she thinks of you as a friend," she said in a low voice.

"Of course." He felt a slight surge of guilt. He knew things about her daughter . . . was doing improper things *with* her daughter.

Yet he wouldn't stop, couldn't, not after these last few years of dawning realization that Elizabeth was a special woman.

# Chapter 6

**E**lizabeth came to a stop outside the small drawing room, hearing Peter's voice—and her mother's. She winced and held still, listening, avoiding the gaze of the footmen, who pretended they didn't know what she was doing.

"Peter," the duchess continued, "forgive my curiosity, but I need to protect my daughter. After all, years ago, you showed interest in my niece, Susanna."

Elizabeth held her breath. Had something happened between them she didn't know about?

"There was a summer when I wondered if Miss Leland and I would be more than friends," Peter said, "but it was not meant to be."

Elizabeth had a brief memory of Susanna crying—over Peter? Perhaps there was more to the story. And then she remembered the ball celebrating Matthew's return home last autumn—she'd seen Peter and Susanna leaving the dance floor together. At the time she'd thought nothing of it, but now her curiosity was heightened. Had he tried to make Susanna . . . one of his women? How could she think of Peter as such a rogue? Except somehow, for some reason, he seemed to have become one.

Her mother continued to probe Peter's past. "And then you courted Emily Leland, when we thought she was Matthew's widow."

"And do you blame me for that, Your Grace?" he asked.

"Of course not, Peter. You were not the only man to show interest when she emerged from mourning. You even spent time at Madingley Court right after he returned from India. That was not awkward, between you and Emily?"

"Only at first, Your Grace," he said smoothly—too smoothly. "Emily made certain that I would feel at ease."

Elizabeth could not let this interrogation go on. It was time to play her new part, freshly "in love" with Peter Derby. She would use the memory of the portrait to make herself blush. But when she swept into the room, and Peter rose quickly to his feet, the way he looked at her made her stumble as she came to a stop. Those blue eyes glowed with admiration, and instead of thinking of the portrait, she found herself remembering being alone with him in the library, their arms about each other, their mouths so close to a kiss.

She smiled at him, aiming for enthusiasm. "Good morning, Peter."

He took her hand and bowed over it, giving it a special squeeze. "You look radiant, Elizabeth."

She tried not to look at her mother, who watched them closely and could usually read her mind. *She* would be the most difficult person of all to convince.

Elizabeth linked her hands when he released her. "Thank you, sir. Perhaps my radiance will drive away the chance of rain."

"A cloud would not dare show itself today," he said.

She laughed, then looked to the duchess. "Mama, we'll be off, then. I'll take my maid with me."

"And I have a groom with me as well," Peter assured her mother.

The duchess nodded, looking from Peter to Elizabeth. "I am certain you've both thought of everything."

What did that mean? Elizabeth wondered, not daring to exchange a glance with Peter. Oh, she was feeling so guilty she was reading hidden meanings everywhere. After donning her bonnet, she lifted her light summer shawl, but Peter took it from her hand and draped it around her shoulders.

"Thank you," she murmured, peering up at him from beneath her lashes with exaggerated admiration. She glanced at her mother. "I'll be back soon!" Putting her hand on Peter's arm, she allowed him to lead her outside, knowing that Teresa, her maid, followed. When the footman closed the door behind them, she let out a heavy sigh as they went down the stairs to the pavement.

Peter chuckled and said for her ears only, "Misleading your mother was not as easy as you thought it would be."

"It was manageable," she insisted lightly. "And for you? I overheard a bit of your conversation."

Though she watched him carefully, he betrayed no uneasiness as he said, "I believe she's worried I'm so desperate to be attached to your family, I'm going through every eligible relation one at a time."

"Then you skipped Rebecca."

"Give me time."

Elizabeth's laugh faded as he turned to help her into the carriage. She put a hand on his chest and looked into his eyes. They stood too close together on the public street, but he didn't move away.

"Peter, what if—"

"Stop worrying, Elizabeth. I saw a mother trying to protect her child. She thinks I'll hurt you," he said, grinning.

He didn't allow her to climb into the phaeton; instead he lifted her right off the ground, his hands strong about her waist. She sank onto her seat a bit breathlessly, then held on as he climbed aboard from the far side, rocking the carriage. Behind them, his eager young groom assisted Teresa into the lower rear seat.

They began their journey sedately enough, heading

into the heavier London traffic. The noise was raucous, from costermongers calling out their wares to performers on stilts shouting for a coin. They wanted to be seen, just like she did, but she was grateful the distraction made private her discussion with Peter, even from the servants behind them.

"My mother received a visitor this morning," Elizabeth said, "and I didn't think a thing of it—until I later heard her interrogating you. She must have heard that we spent an inordinate amount of time together last night."

"Ah, then we succeeded in attracting notice right from the beginning. That will work out well for you, for . . . whatever reason you want this engagement to seem real."

Smiling, she said nothing. She could take care of her own problems, without more complications from him.

"But then again," he continued, "the *ton* is always interested in whatever you do—especially when it involves a lowly gentleman such as myself."

She nudged him with her elbow playfully, feeling almost as if she had her friend back. Almost.

"I heard other things you were discussing with my mother. So tell me about your feelings for Susanna."

He held the reins loosely threaded through his fingers, and if he felt any tension at her words, the reins did not transfer it to the horses. They trotted along sprightly, gathering many an admiring or envious stare, while Peter considered her request.

"You know we briefly exchanged a flirtation," he said.

She tilted her bonnet to see him better, and was surprised that his smile had given way to a thoughtful frown.

"I was young, and very foolish, newly conscious of my limited status in our world."

She sobered. "Peter—"

"It was long ago, and I was far too immature. At the time, I truly considered that we might enjoy each other's company, two people who studied too hard, who tried to fit in." He gave her an ironic smile. "You've never had that problem, but Susanna and I both did. My father, obsessed with bettering our connections, had been pressing me and James to find highly born wives. And there you all were, next door. But right in the middle of our new flirtation was a crowd of revelers that I wanted to be a part of. They didn't care for Susanna's bluestocking ways, and made fun of her behind her back. I didn't defend her; I laughed along with them."

"Oh Peter," she said, touching his arm. "How old were you?"

"Eighteen."

"Surely you have forgiven yourself by now."

He shrugged. "I didn't even know she'd overheard. I

only knew that she'd decided anything beyond friendship was over."

"I saw you together last autumn at Madingley Court."

His smile was grim. "That's when I discovered she'd known all along that I hadn't defended her. In some ways I feel a part of her retreat from Society. I apologized, but it didn't go well at first. We are on better terms now."

"You mean until you confronted us over the painting." She spoke softly, just in case the servants behind them were listening. She glanced over her shoulder, but Teresa was holding on for dear life, and the groom was pointing something out to her and speaking in her ear.

Peter shook his head ruefully. "All my mended fences blasted apart."

"It was your choice," she reminded him.

"And yours. You're just upset I didn't openly come to your rescue that night."

She could not deny it. "You put yourself against me, Peter. I never thought you would."

He looked at her through narrowed eyes. "Did you ever think that my participation in the wager might save you from worse exposure?"

"No. And I disagree."

They were quiet for several minutes as he negotiated the turn into Hyde Park. They drove down the lane until he pulled up next to a wide expanse of lawn bordered by flowering roses.

"What are we doing?" she asked.

He reached behind their seat, treating her to a close view of his face in profile as the groom handed him a large basket.

"A picnic?" she said in surprise.

He only grinned.

She wanted to look at his handsome face, imagine they were courting, knowing that many people in the park were watching them. She had to play her part, so that every man here would know she was taken.

When Peter helped her down, she let her hands linger on his shoulders, and looked up at him wishing her bonnet didn't hide her love-struck expression from much of their audience.

Peter only smiled, and set about laying out a large blanket. Behind them, his groom and her maid stood talking as the groom watered the horses.

Elizabeth knelt down on the blanket, then sat back, allowing her blue flowered skirts to pool around her. She saw Peter stop what he was doing to stare at her. It seemed a long moment, and she was uncomfortable with the scrutiny, for she'd had too much of that the last few days. But it was all a performance for a tonnish audience.

She couldn't help saying, "You're very good at this. But then you've had practice."

"Your curiosity is showing, my dear." His gaze came back to her face, and wearing a self-deprecating smile, he knelt down and began to unpack the basket. Soon her plate overflowed with chicken and ham, jam puffs, late strawberries, and wedges of cheese. "Perhaps food is the way to a woman's heart."

She groaned and shook her head, but wondered how many women had softened to his attentiveness. He opened a corked bottle and poured lemonade into a glass before handing it to her.

"Not champagne?" she teased. "Shouldn't we be celebrating our partnership?"

"Celebrating our deceptions, you mean?" he countered mildly.

"You are too literal, Peter."

He sat down beside her, leaning back on one arm. "And you are surprising."

"What do you mean?" she asked, before taking a bite of ham.

"I thought you had put such deceptions behind you." He toasted her silently with his lemonade and drank.

To her surprise, she found herself watching the way his throat worked as he swallowed. She caught herself, embarrassed, then gave him a smile. "So you thought you knew everything there was to know about me."

"I can't say that," he mused, watching her openly. "We have not exactly been close confidantes these last few years. But that painting . . . I never would have guessed it of you."

"We keep coming back to that, do we?"

She popped a strawberry into her mouth and enjoyed the sweet burst of flavor. Even watching her eat seemed to distract him. He must be easily distracted by women.

"You'd become such a good girl, Elizabeth. Did you grow tired of it?"

"No," she said truthfully. "I discovered I wanted the feminine things in life, a home, a family."

"But since you didn't yet have them, you decided to once again be . . . wild?"

His voice deepened with intimacy, and seemed to stir up something forbidden inside her. What was wrong that now even his voice affected her?

"I'm not wild," she said crossly, then took a bite of cheese.

"When you take off your clothes for a strange man, I'd call that wild. Now if you took off your clothes for me . . ."

A blush heated her face immediately. "This must be the reaction you want," she said too quickly, not wanting to think about the image his words painted. There was only one man who deserved such intimacy—her husband, the one she freely chose. "I hope everyone sees my face."

He was watching her too closely. "Everyone sees . . . ?

Oh, your blush," he said, nodding. "You want them to believe I'm making love to you."

"Peter!" She wanted to throw something at him.

"And there is your new habit of thievery."

Back to the original subject—was she relieved or not? "Trying to take the painting? That was an act of desperation."

"Like our soon-to-be-announced engagement?"

She took a bite of chicken and didn't answer.

"Why are you so desperate, Elizabeth?" he asked softly.

"Tell me about Emily Leland."

He narrowed his eyes. "You're changing the subject."

"I've already told you that my reasons are my own. I didn't change my mind in less than twenty-four hours."

"But I can help."

"You *are* helping. And I'm grateful. So tell me about Emily."

"There's even less to talk about than my flirtation with Susanna."

But Elizabeth had seen him standing beside Emily, her cousin Matthew's wife, just the other night. They had seemed . . . awkward together, and she'd written it off as uneasiness because he'd tried to court a widow who wasn't truly a widow.

But after listening to him discuss Emily with her mother, she had to wonder if there was a story there.

"And you're accusing *me* of deception," she said, hoping for a response.

"The pot and the kettle, that's us." He took another long drink of lemonade.

The sun was blazing today, a rare hot day in London, burning off the fog and the usual haze of coal dust. She'd let her shawl lie in a heap behind her, but her bonnet protected her face from the direct sun.

She couldn't let the conversation go. "Then you're saying you can be deceptive, too?"

"What do you call our engagement?"

She rolled her eyes. "I'm talking about Emily."

"There's no deception, Elizabeth," he said.

Though a smile lingered about his mouth, her curiosity heightened instead of fading.

"Did you know that Emily is with child?" she asked, watching closely for his reaction.

He smiled with genuine pleasure. "How wonderful for them. They will make fine parents."

Well, *that* revealed nothing.

And then he reached into the basket and brought out a small tart. Instead of setting it on her plate, he held it to her mouth, his expression full of challenge.

She should take it from him, she knew. It was surely indecent to allow a man to feed her from his fingertips. But holding his gaze, she leaned forward and took a bite. His eyes narrowed, and without questioning her instinct, she lingered a moment, her lips close to his fingers. He might know how to court a woman, but she had some ideas of her own.

He laughed as he withdrew the tart, and there was a wickedness in his gaze that said he could answer her challenge.

Suddenly, she felt a strange tickling on her leg. She brushed at her skirts, Peter arched a questioning brow— and then she saw an ant on her plate. With a cry she slapped at her skirts.

"What is it?" he demanded, coming to his knees.

"Ants!" It suddenly seemed as if hundreds of them could be crawling on her legs. It was all she could do not to shriek her outrage. "Do something, Peter!"

"You know I'm at your service, but I doubt you want my hands beneath your skirts in Hyde Park. Try standing up."

"Ooh!" she cried in frustration, jumping to her feet. She shook her skirts repeatedly, swishing them across her legs.

Grateful for the turn of events, Peter relaxed back on one elbow, watching the show, enjoying her discomfort—anything to minimize his reaction to their flirtation. Feeding her the tart had been a way to distract her from questions about Emily he didn't want to answer. But when Elizabeth had leaned toward him, her mouth so close to his hand, her eyes full of innocent challenge, he could have easily startled all of Hyde Park by kissing her. The ants had been divine intervention.

He squinted up, watching her haloed by the sun. Its brilliance glittered across her white dress scattered with blue flowers like someone had thrown a bouquet in the air. Matching blue and white silk flowers decorated her bonnet, blue ribbons dangling. She was a confection of summer, and he wanted to taste her.

Patience, he told himself. He wanted more than winning a bet as his reward for this false engagement. He needed to understand her—he needed to help her. Why he needed so much, he didn't want to examine too closely.

At last she stopped moving, her face full of concentration.

"Feel any more ants?" he asked lazily.

She shook her head. "Why aren't you packing the basket? We certainly can't linger *here*. Don't you want to show me how fast you can drive your carriage?"

"At your service, Lady Elizabeth."

He put away their picnic lunch. When he tried to hand her the basket so he could fold the blanket, she looked at it like it was an ant colony, then shuddered and refused. She'd become such a girl.

And he liked it.

He escorted her back to the phaeton, saw her look

sharpen as she waved at a passing carriage. "Who was that?" he asked.

"Lucy Gibson and her brother," she said lightly. "Let's hurry and catch up with them."

While he was putting the basket on the floor of the back seat, she climbed into the phaeton without his help.

"You should have waited for me," he said as he sat beside her. The groom and maid climbed in behind them.

"Why?" she asked, not looking at him. She leaned forward, as if urging the horses with her very posture.

Peter took up the reins and guided the horses out into the lane. "We could have made a touching show of romance as I handed you up into the seat, my hands trembling with your nearness."

"You should write a romantic novel," she said absently, not looking at him.

He'd lost her attention, and he didn't know why, considering that she wanted to advertise their supposed engagement. But he went along with her request, guiding the horses out onto the lane, easing them into a trot then a canter to gain ground. They caught up with the Gibson carriage, and the two young ladies waved at each other. Peter knew of the young baron, but not personally. Yet Gibson eyed Peter's new phaeton, then urged his horses into a gallop, pulling ahead.

"Faster, Peter!" Elizabeth cried, holding onto the rail behind her.

Peter glanced over his shoulder, and although both the groom and maid were holding on with both hands, the maid didn't look frightened. So he went faster, enjoying the competition and Elizabeth's eagerness. Her bonnet fell back onto her neck, held on only by the ribbons. Several strands of her dark hair flew about her face, and her smile was full of excited eagerness. Meeting his eyes, she laughed aloud.

If he kept watching her, he'd lose control of the phaeton, so he concentrated on his driving, reaching the far end of the park before Gibson. At last he pulled up, letting the horses walk to cool down. Gibson pulled alongside him, and the two carriages took the turn, meandering slowly.

"That was so exciting!" Elizabeth called.

Her friend Miss Gibson sank against her brother and closed her eyes.

"I don't believe we've met," Gibson called.

"Forgive me," Elizabeth said. "William, allow me to present Mr. Peter Derby. Peter, this is Lord Gibson. You know his sister Miss Lucinda Gibson."

"Lord Gibson." Peter nodded. "Miss Gibson, I never would have believed you enjoyed a dangerous race."

Miss Gibson shuddered. " 'Enjoyed' is not the right word, Mr. Derby. I thought I would be flung from the carriage." She elbowed her brother hard. "You can be surprisingly competitive sometimes."

Gibson grinned.

"I enjoy a good competition, too." Elizabeth tried to tame some of her windblown hair with her fingers.

She had missed a curl, so Peter reached to tuck it behind her ear. Her eyes widened at his touch, but she didn't duck away from him. So her engagement act was also for the Gibsons. He wondered if she'd confided anything in her friend. He would have to find out, the better to question Miss Gibson about Elizabeth's secrets before it was too late.

Gibson touched the brim of his hat. "We're late for an engagement. A pleasure to meet you, Derby."

Peter nodded back, and as the pair drove off, Elizabeth smiled up at him in complete pleasure.

"I enjoyed that immensely," she said. "You know how to court a young lady, Peter Derby."

"If the young lady enjoys competitions and picnics."

"And that's me. Now you can take me home, because I'm certain my mother is waiting to talk with me. You made quite the impression on her so far."

"I assumed that's what you wanted."

"I'll let you know."

# Chapter 7

When Elizabeth and Peter returned to Madingley House, she allowed him to help her from the carriage, even though her mind could not focus on projecting her newfound love.

William had seen her with Peter—William had wanted to race them. Was he already jealous? If it was so easy to arouse that emotion in him, why hadn't she been able to do it sooner? Of course, he hadn't often attended events meant to show off eligible young ladies.

As Peter accompanied her to the door, she glanced up at him, almost ready to thank him for his help—but no, he had his own motives for helping her. Besides the wager, she suspected he might be along simply for amusement, as if it were a game. Was that how he treated women now? Perhaps his failed relationships with Susanna and Emily had sent him to the safety of a certain kind of woman who wasn't interested in marriage. As close as she had felt to Peter when she was young, she could not claim to know him well now that he was a man.

"It was a lovely ride, Peter. Thank you."

He bowed. "You're welcome."

"I'm sorry I cannot invite you in."

"I understand. I couldn't anyway. I have a meeting."

"An infamous railway meeting?"

"Infamous already? That was easy." He smiled. "But yes, business calls."

"We'll have to discuss what you do with the railway, Peter."

"I'm not just investing?"

She narrowed her eyes, watching his serene expression. "I don't think so."

"Perhaps I can match you secret for secret, Elizabeth." He bent low over her gloved hand and kissed it.

It would have been a harmless courtesy—until he lifted his warm gaze to hers. His eyes were warm, intimate, too knowing.

Just as she pulled away with haste, the butler opened the door.

Peter stepped back. "Good day, Lady Elizabeth."

Swallowing hard, she said, "Come to see me soon, Peter," adding a trace of wistfulness. She watched him walk away, realizing it wasn't difficult to show a bit of longing—longing for the truth about Peter, anyway.

Then she squared her shoulders and prepared to

face her mother. It happened more quickly than she'd guessed, for the duchess was waiting in Elizabeth's bedroom, reading a book as she reclined on a chaise beneath the sunny window.

Elizabeth shut the door. "Mama, what a surprise. Now I can tell you all about my picnic with Peter!"

"Picnic?" her mother said, lowering her book to read Elizabeth instead.

"Isn't he thoughtful?" Elizabeth gushed, then turned away, warning herself not to go too far. She set down her bonnet and shawl on the bed. "We even raced Lucy and her brother through the park."

"And did Peter win?" her mother asked dryly.

Elizabeth gave an uncertain blink. "Of course. He has a new phaeton, after all."

"And he wants to impress you."

Blushing was becoming too easy. "I think so."

"I never thought he needed to, before." Her mother sat up on the chaise but didn't stand. "My sweet Elizabeth, is there a reason Peter believes he must impress you? Have you given him . . . encouragement?"

Elizabeth walked to her mother and sat down on the chaise beside her. "Mama, what are you trying to say?" she asked carefully.

The duchess sighed and took her hand to rub it between her own. "I know you expected more . . . excitement as a young lady in London."

Her mother had no idea how much excitement she'd truly had. "It has been everything I imagined it would be, Mama."

The duchess shook her head. "No, I believe you've somehow been disappointed, and I worry that you are turning to Peter because he's . . . familiar."

"Familiar?" Elizabeth echoed. She was about to perpetrate a lie on her mother, her whole family—yet was offended that her mother would think something else that wasn't complimentary.

"You haven't received some attention that you wanted," her mother continued.

"I do believe you're wrong," Elizabeth said, removing her hand and trying to smile. "I'm growing to know him in a different way than I thought possible."

The duchess nodded. "Then promise me you'll be careful."

"I am being careful." In a softer voice, she said, "I have discovered feelings for Peter that go beyond friendship." She needed to allay her mother's suspicions, yet still prepare her for the revelation of the engagement.

Instead of smiling, her mother only studied her face more carefully. "Be patient with those feelings, Elizabeth. Make certain they are real."

"I will, Mama, I promise." She hugged her then, because she loved her mother's concern—but also giving her mother less chance to read her expression.

* * *

The invitation to dinner at Madingley House arrived not an hour after Peter returned home. He was sitting at the desk in the corner of his bedroom, going through his mail, when Mary Anne burst in without knocking, striding toward him wearing a frown.

Peter leaned back in his chair. "Good thing I wasn't changing."

His sister Mary Anne dropped an envelope on his desk, on which his name was written in a lovely feminine hand.

"Hand-delivered," she said with a sniff.

He couldn't help noticing that her gown was a dark brown. She could have been an unobtrusive governess. But there was a chalk smear on her skirt, and it hadn't come from a child's slate. Now if she'd added some red and yellow ribbons, perhaps sewed little fabric flowers across the bodice, the gown would have highlighted her light hair and pretty blue eyes.

But he would not say those things to her. His mother had done that enough, he was certain. So he only grinned at her and opened the envelope. Inside was a dinner invitation from the Dowager Duchess of Madingley—for that night. He arched an eyebrow, considering the implications.

"It's from Lady Elizabeth?" Mary Anne said coolly.

"No, from her mother. I've been invited to dinner."

Mary Anne leaned her palms against the desk, whitening her knuckles.

"Don't worry, you haven't been invited."

Her demeanor brightened. "I don't know whether I'm truly relieved."

"Since when?"

"I imagine their billiard table is exquisite."

He shook his head.

"Ah well, brother mine, you can brave that lair yourself." She considered him as she toyed with a chunk of sealing wax. "Why invite you at the last minute?"

He tilted his head as if considering her question. "A last minute guest sent regrets and they need their numbers rounded?"

He expected her to laugh, but instead she scowled. "They're using you."

"Not the duchess," he said. "I don't believe she's filling out her table. No, this is about Elizabeth."

There, he might as well broach a subject that would soon arise more often. He felt the need to prepare his sister—but he was preparing her for a lie. Rubbing his forehead with one hand, he reminded himself that something was so wrong that Elizabeth couldn't tell him about it. She needed his help.

But so did his sister, and lies were not a good answer.

Yet . . . the way he desired Elizabeth was not a lie.

Before he could speak, Mary Anne said, "I don't like her, you know."

"Mary Anne, how can you not like her?"

"She doesn't seem human! I have never met anyone who thought herself so perfect."

"She's never done anything to give that impression. She is a beautiful woman, born into a powerful family. Those things are more luck than anything else."

"Luck? Fine, maybe that's why she's always smiling—no one with bad luck could ever be that happy. It's like she's a doll with only one emotion."

"Perhaps the two of you never got on well enough for you to see another side of her. And that is her fault as much as yours." Then another thought made him regard his sister with worry. "I've always considered her my friend, although until recently we did not socialize as much as we used to. Did you believe that kept me away from you?"

Mary Anne sighed and rested her hip on the edge of the desk. "No, of course not."

"You're my sister, and nothing comes before that."

"A woman will come before that soon—perhaps she already has."

Peter turned the invitation over and over in his hands, watching her.

"You don't have to marry, just like I don't," she continued. "Only James's marriage matters at all."

"But someday I want a wife to love, my own house-hold, and children," he said softly. "Don't you?"

She wouldn't meet his eyes. "I don't see why it's so important, but then I can't dictate my beliefs to you. Go ahead and woo Elizabeth, but remember that they're above us, Peter—too far above us. You'll never be one of them."

Surely she was suffering some sort of crisis of faith in herself. He understood it well, for it had once afflicted him, and caused him to make a terrible misjudgment. He'd learned his lesson. She would do the same.

"Mary Anne, I don't need to feel like a Cabot. I'm proud of being a Derby."

"That's all well and good. But the duke will never allow Elizabeth to marry into our family."

Mary Anne let her fingers run along the green baize of the billiard table. She was alone with her thoughts, which she preferred. It took absolute concentration to be the best, and hours of practice, all of which required solitude.

But as she positioned the red and white balls, she could not stop thinking about Peter and his relationships with women.

She turned away from the table in disgust, rubbing her hands tiredly over her face. Oh, she wasn't fool enough to require both her brothers' absolute attention.

They had lives, she knew. Her own faults could not be ascribed to them. Yet they'd never shown the slightest inclination toward marriage either, and somehow she'd thought they'd all just go on living as they were.

Peter was about to change things, and this invitation only confirmed it. She'd lied to him earlier in the day, told him what he wanted to hear—that she didn't think his friendship with Elizabeth had taken him from her.

It had. And everything had changed in her life because she felt she was on her own.

That mistake was in the past, and she was no longer allowing it to affect her. Peter was her brother, and he loved her.

But Lady Elizabeth Cabot? Was intelligent, sensible Peter truly so blind?


Peter was shown to the drawing room at Madingley House, and at first he thought he was alone. With a frescoed ceiling and huge paintings between carved archways decorating the walls, it was easy to be distracted and not notice a solitary figure sitting on a sofa in the corner.

"Hello, Mr. Derby."

He turned to find Miss Gibson giving him a friendly smile. She rose to curtsy to him, and after he approached, he bowed.

"Good evening, Miss Gibson," he said, realizing that

he could not have manipulated the evening better if he'd tried.

"Are we both early?" she asked.

"I believe the family is late. Not an unusual occurrence for an informal evening."

"Of course not. I'm used to waiting for Elizabeth."

Though they'd known each other for several years, Lucille Gibson stood with her hands twisted awkwardly together, watching him in a direct manner, leaving him even more convinced that she surely knew something about Elizabeth's problems and was leery of talking to him.

But she probably didn't know about the painting, which Elizabeth seemed far too embarrassed and furious about.

"Please sit down," he said.

She did so, and he took the chair perpendicular to her. There was no use chatting about the weather; he thought being forthright might work the best.

"Miss Gibson, I am worried about Elizabeth."

Her eyes briefly went wide, then fixed on his face. "I . . . I don't understand."

"Surely she has told you about"—he looked at the door as if concerned about being interrupted—"our arrangement."

Miss Gibson studied him. "I'm not certain that she did . . ."

She drew her words out, as if she, too, didn't know what to reveal. They were both trying to determine what the other knew.

"Not certain?" he countered. "So you didn't understand what she told you?"

"Of course I did, but—"

He interrupted, saying, "I know she feels desperate. And we both want to help her."

Miss Gibson said nothing.

"And neither of us wants to betray her confidence. But I don't think she's telling me everything. And how can I help her—protect her—if she's withholding something from me?"

"You need to talk to her about this, Mr. Derby," Miss Gibson said in a low voice, leaning toward him.

"I have been—constantly. And she won't tell me why. I don't know if she's protecting someone—"

There was a definite widening of her eyes before she looked away.

"Whom is she protecting?" he demanded. "It can't be one of her cousins—no one is here to protect, and our engagement would hardly matter to them."

"You're . . . engaged?" she said weakly.

"That was a halfhearted effort at surprise, Miss Gibson. You'll have to do better with other people. So you know about the engagement, and you know she's protecting someone. It's certainly not me. There is her mother, of course, if Elizabeth somehow wants to protect her from knowledge. Knowledge of the truth, perhaps?"

Miss Gibson only swallowed and kept her gaze averted.

"No, I don't think that's it," he mused, as if they were carrying on an actual conversation. "Elizabeth is so desperate as to pretend an engagement she plans to break. It sounds to me as if she's protecting *herself*. Who's hurt her, Miss Gibson? I won't stand for it."

She leaned back against the sofa cushions, and he realized he'd spoken more forcefully than he'd meant to.

"Is she in danger?" he continued. "How can I protect her if you won't tell me?"

"I don't think she's in danger . . . exactly. But she *was*, and this engagement solved the problem." She spoke brightly, as if she'd answered with the truth.

"Then it's only temporarily solving the problem, because she plans to end our engagement eventually."

"But that will be long enough . . . she thinks." Then she winced, as if she'd revealed too much.

"Ah," he said, hiding his triumph, "so she's not certain how this issue will resolve."

"Nothing in life is certain, Mr. Derby. But you're helping her, and she's grateful."

"What is she frightened of? What does an engagement stop except . . . other men?" he said slowly, the realization overtaking him.

Miss Gibson sighed.

"That's it, isn't it? She's afraid of another man—or men." It couldn't be because of the wager. An engagement would not affect that one way or another. But had another man found out about the painting? "Has a man been pressuring her, perhaps in an attempt to win her favor?"

Heaving a sigh, Miss Gibson leaned forward and spoke in a low voice. "Elizabeth trusts you enough to ask for a false engagement. It's only fair that you understand the ramifications. There was . . . a man who tried to force her to be alone with him, who made advances upon her person. And not in the pursuit of marriage." Her cheeks reddened, but she resolutely held his gaze. "It was as if he felt free to do as he wished. I was frightened for her, though she believes this engagement will protect her until her brother's return. She will be upset that we've discussed this, so I ask you not to tell her what I've told you. But there comes a time when one friend must look out for another, and that's what I'm doing. Be watchful, Mr. Derby."

They heard voices in the hall, and she stiffened and donned a false smile.

"You can trust me, Miss Gibson," he said softly. "I've only ever wanted the best for her."

She seemed to relax, and her smile became more natural just as Elizabeth entered the room. She was followed by the ladies in her family who were residing in the Madingley town house for the Season—the dowager duchess; Lady Rosa, who was one of her sisters by marriage and the mother of Susanna and Rebecca; Abigail, the current duchess, who was a lady journalist; and Emily Leland.

Emily smiled at Peter, and he returned her smile. He wondered if he'd ever feel at ease with her again, but he was determined to try. She made it so obvious that she'd forgiven him—why could he not leave their shared past where it belonged?

Elizabeth, never lacking in intelligence, looked back and forth between himself and Miss Gibson, but all she said was, "Peter, good evening! I am so glad you could join us on such short notice." She pointedly stared at her mother.

The duchess smiled. "Since you and Peter have been spending time together, I thought you both would appreciate another opportunity."

"Of course I do, Mama, but I'm not certain Peter realized he would be the only man at a table of nosy women."

Peter grinned at the ladies. "I feel privileged indeed, Lady Elizabeth, so have no concern for me." He openly held out his arm to Elizabeth, who set her hand there. If she was tense, she did not show it. He smiled at the dowager duchess. "Unless, Your Grace, you'd like me to escort you down to the dining room?"

"Of course not, Mr. Derby. We'll follow you both down."

As they went out into the hall, which opened all the way up to the stained glass dome in the ceiling, Elizabeth spoke quietly through her smile. "My mother is very suspicious, Peter. We will not be able to wait long before announcing our engagement."

"After I ask her permission to marry you," he answered softly. "There's no guarantee she'll give it. Surely you've thought of that. This is a scandalous match that not many families would support. And your brother is the head of the family."

Elizabeth eyed him, but he knew she was too confident in herself to doubt her mother's acceptance. As she walked serenely at his side, he thought of the painting. Only a confident woman would dare reveal herself, even if she thought the painting would be sold out of the country. Only a confident woman would try to solve her own problems—like dissuading men much larger and stronger than she was—without asking directly for help.

But it was growing more and more obvious that she no longer trusted him to the same extent she once had.

Had she connected her problems to the painting? Did she have regrets? But she was not the sort of woman to live in the past. What was done, was done, and he was certain she planned to make everything right in her world.

But he planned to protect her, and he would need information to do so. Miss Gibson had told him all she probably intended to; but there were others to question. It would serve Elizabeth right if he made her uncomfortable, for she was keeping dangerous secrets, and that made him angry.

Though the dining table was long, they all sat at one end, with the dowager duchess presiding, her daughter on her right, and Peter on her left. The other four ladies filled in, and as they dined, Peter felt more than one curious glance his way, but he ignored them. Instead he played his part, looking at Elizabeth as a smitten suitor. He would see her safe—and he would enjoy every moment of her attention.

He listened to the feminine gossip they shared, the discussion of friends and follies, wistful longing for absent husbands, and the coordination of calendars for the week's events. Abigail mentioned an article she was writing for the newspaper about a children's charity that Emily was active in. He wondered if Emily, so bold when she needed to be, would ignore the fashion to retreat from Society during her time of confinement. But a man could not ask a lady such an intimate question. At last there was a lull in the conversation, and since several pairs of eyes considered him again, he decided to accept the unspoken invitation to speak.

"Lady Rosa," he began, "Lady Elizabeth tells me that both of your daughters have left London."

Elizabeth's gaze sharpened on him.

Lady Rosa smiled. "I know it seems strange," she said to him from across the table, "but I have a dear old aunt who's been unable to come to London due to illness. Rebecca volunteered to visit her."

Volunteered to visit, Peter thought, amused. "Is that not surprising, considering it's the Season?"

"Yes, but Aunt Rianette is elderly and frail. Putting off such a visit for even a few months was not advisable."

"I will hope for her continued health. Where does she live?"

Elizabeth kicked him under the table, but he didn't look at her.

"The Lake District. Rebecca took the train. She so loves to travel, especially since she did not have the chance much in childhood."

He wondered if Julian took the same train. It amused him to imagine both of them matching wits over the painting. "Did Susanna journey with her?" he asked, even though Elizabeth had said her cousins went their separate ways.

Elizabeth continued to eat her roasted mutton, looking back and forth between him and her aunt.

Lady Rosa's face brightened. "No, she accepted a house party invitation in nearby Hertfordshire. And Peter, you know her well enough to understand why I am so happy that she chose to attend without me coercing her."

He laughed. "Yes, my lady, I do understand. Why did she decide to leave?"

Another kick under the table, but the question was already asked.

"She said she felt a need for the fresh air of the countryside, but she did bring her painting supplies as well." Lady Rosa sighed, giving him a rueful smile. "I don't hold out hope that there is a young man involved, but since I'm her mother, I never give up."

A man had followed Susanna, but Peter wasn't certain that Lady Rosa meant someone with Leo Wade's reputation.

But he had all the answers he was going to get. He didn't imagine he'd go chasing off after the Leland sisters, although it wouldn't hurt to keep Elizabeth guessing. Instead, he stirred his mashed turnips and watched her, waiting for the next step in his plan for the evening.

When the ladies rose at the end of the meal, Peter did the same.

Abigail, the duchess, said, "I don't believe we need to stand on ceremony and leave you alone, Mr. Derby."

He grinned. "My thanks, Your Grace." Then he

turned to the dowager duchess. "Madam, if you have a moment, Elizabeth and I would like to speak to you privately."

Everyone seemed to freeze, the rustling of skirts trailing off into silence. Feminine eyes focused on Elizabeth, who blushed and looked at Peter with the perfect amount of excitement.

Though the dowager duchess smiled, he detected the faintest hesitation. Was she only worried about the suddenness of his relationship to Elizabeth—or did she suspect something else?

# Chapter 8

Elizabeth hadn't imagined she would feel so very self-conscious. Even if her relatives had not guessed about her relationship with Peter, they certainly knew what it meant when a young man asked for privacy with a woman's mother.

Her blush could certainly be attributed to the suffusion of shame she hadn't expected. Though she told herself that she would right this problem soon enough, lying to her entire family still bothered her.

And there was Peter, looking at her with the proper amount of devotion and certainty. She would never have imagined him so capable of deception.

She wouldn't have imagined it of herself either, she thought wryly.

But it was too late to change her mind now. Memories of Thomas made her shudder. He would not maneuver her into marriage.

She met her mother's gaze but could read nothing but a pleasant interest.

The dowager duchess said, "You may both accompany me to the morning room. That should be sufficiently private"—she glanced at the rest of their relatives—"and though there is curiosity, I'm certain we won't be disturbed."

Abigail rubbed her hands together. "I'd better hear a story quickly, or I might have to come discover it."

"There's nothing to write about here," Elizabeth said, then realized she spoke too quickly, perhaps too defensively. "My life would bore your newspaper readers."

Luckily, Abigail only laughed. "Our Society writer would disagree. But I can be patient."

Peter held out his arm, and once again Elizabeth rested her hand there. He smiled down at her with a softness that made her catch her breath. What was wrong with her? All she wanted was one certain man to look at her like that.

The morning room was a place of privacy for the duchesses, with a very feminine writing desk where together they coordinated the complicated business of overseeing the running of an immense household with a staff of forty. But now the duchess didn't seat herself at the desk, only walked slowly toward the windows as if she could see out over the dark gardens below.

Then she turned to face the two of them, wearing a faint but welcoming smile. Elizabeth felt some of her tension drain away.

Peter covered Elizabeth's hand with his own, where it rested on his arm. "Your Grace, you certainly must know what I am here to ask you."

"But she wants to hear it anyway, Peter," Elizabeth urged.

He smiled down at her, and again she found herself overcome by the warmth in his deep blue eyes. Memories were suddenly stealing over her—leaning toward her as if he would kiss her, his strong hands on her waist as he lifted her into the carriage. Those memories raised an awareness she hadn't expected to feel with Peter—and she didn't know what to think about it.

Now there was a rakish set to his brows that made her believe he was enjoying himself, unlike her—she was so nervous that her mouth was too dry to swallow.

"You've suddenly become very impatient, my daughter," the duchess said.

She smiled at her mother, then was mortified that her lips started to tremble. Oh dear, couldn't this be over with?

"Your Grace," Peter said, "you know that I have spent much of my life in the company of your family."

*Just ask her!* Elizabeth thought with desperation.

"I have looked upon Elizabeth as a friend, but part of me always wished for more. And I didn't think I could ever have such a preposterous wish."

His voice was solemn and low, yet with an earnestness that made it sound so convincing. Elizabeth found herself watching his face, stunned and amazed at how believable he was.

"But lately, Your Grace," he continued, "I began to hope that perhaps Elizabeth returned my feelings after all. And now that my financial situation is settled, I can take care of her. All of which leads me to ask your permission for Elizabeth's hand in marriage."

It was done, Elizabeth thought, feeling light-headed. She had linked herself in her mother's eyes to Peter, who wasn't the man she'd thought he was, who had secrets—but so did she. How could she find out his without revealing her own?

The duchess inhaled slowly, then sank onto a sofa, motioning them toward her. They sat side by side on another sofa, across a low table from her. To Elizabeth's surprise, Peter sat so his thigh just touched hers, hidden beneath her voluminous skirts. She wanted to move away, once again too aware of him. Why was such a simple touch so distracting?

The duchess smiled at them at last, but Elizabeth wasn't fooled.

"My dear children," her mother said, "this seems very sudden."

"But is it, Your Grace?" Peter asked. "Elizabeth and I have been drawn together our whole lives. It seemed only natural to allow these feelings to develop at last."

"You mean since your situation has improved," the duchess said.

"I will be happy to discuss it with you."

"You and my son may discuss a marriage settlement when he returns, Peter. That is not what concerns me now."

She paused, as if giving her words careful consideration, a trait Elizabeth had tried to emulate these last few years.

"My concern is that perhaps one or both of you simply *wants* your friendship to be more than it is."

The duchess looked directly at her, and Elizabeth realized it was she at whom the comment was aimed.

"Mama, I know why I want to marry Peter," she said earnestly, for it was the truth. "I am not settling because I haven't found the right man. Surely you know that I have met scores of men"—*and been pressured by some of them*—"and never have I felt for even one of them the way I feel about Peter." Which was again the truth.

"And what is that, my child?" the duchess asked kindly.

"I love him, Mama." She slid her hand into Peter's and held his gaze a moment. She felt almost dizzy with the intensity he showed her. She gathered her composure to continue. "I think I always have loved him, but I just didn't realize it. I want to marry him."

Her mother's smile widened gradually, but concern

still lingered. "Then I am happy for you, Elizabeth, for I know Peter to be a good man. I grant my permission."

Elizabeth glanced again at Peter, but he wasn't smiling now, only watching her mother solemnly. She knew she had trapped him in her lie, and she imagined it did not come easily to him, when he'd always respected her family.

But at last he turned to her and gripped both her hands in his, smiling as he said, "This is the happiest day of my life."

"Mine, too," she whispered, grateful for his help. She had cleared one obstacle to her happiness, and now she could work on the rest, she told herself.

"Did you have a date in mind?" the duchess asked.

Elizabeth spoke before Peter could. "We've decided to give it some thought, Mama. After all, we're not certain when Chris will return. We'll need to consult with him."

Peter only smiled his agreement.

"That is good, Elizabeth," her mother said. "The wedding of a duke's sister is not an easy event to plan. I imagine the guest list will be extensive."

"Do you think so, madam?" Peter asked. "Or do you think there will be some who choose not to attend?"

Elizabeth caught her breath, but her mother seemed to understand exactly.

"It will be an unusual event," the duchess agreed, her expression wistful. "I remember well what it is like to marry into such a powerful, wealthy family. There will be many who disagree with Elizabeth's choice."

"I can accept that," Peter said evenly. "Can you, Elizabeth?"

"You make me happy, Peter," she said, reaching up to touch his face, surprised to find a faint roughness of stubble. It reminded her that he was a man, not just a friend.

"There will be newspaper articles that question your sanity," he said.

"And my sister-in-law is a journalist who can be trusted to print the truth."

"You would do well to speak with Abigail, Peter," the duchess said. "Not just as a journalist, but as one who recently married into the aristocracy."

"I will do that, Your Grace," Peter said.

"Until you decide on a wedding date," the duchess said, "I will need something more immediate to plan. Will you permit me to give you an engagement party?"

Elizabeth wanted to refuse, or at least delay her.

But Peter grinned. "Thank you. I will enjoy showing off my future bride." He glanced at Elizabeth. "I will be happy to help you and your mother with any or all of the plans."

"All of them?" Elizabeth asked sweetly. "Shall I consult you on the flower arrangements?"

He laughed. "If you wish. I do have opinions, you

know. And my mother would, too, if you wish to consult her."

"Have you told your family?" the duchess asked.

"Not yet. I wanted to wait for your permission, Your Grace."

"And did you doubt it?" She raised an eyebrow.

Elizabeth winced, although she could see that her mother teased him.

He lifted Elizabeth's hand and kissed her bare fingers. "I knew Elizabeth could persuade you of the sincerity of our feelings, madam."

She stared at the moist spot where his mouth had touched. Her hand had been kissed by dozens of men—but never soft lips on bare flesh. It felt too good.

"Shall we tell the rest of your family?" Peter asked, pulling her to her feet.

"Only if you wish." Elizabeth smiled.

"Biddable already," he said to the duchess. "I like that."

Elizabeth watched her mother laugh, even as the woman came around to take Peter's other arm with easy familiarity. Peter escorted them both into the smaller drawing room, where the family usually gathered in the evening. There was no denying that they all awaited the news with excitement, for each of them rose to their feet when the three came through the door.

Elizabeth was amused at their various comical expressions of anticipation and decided not to draw out the suspense. "Peter asked me to marry him," she said.

With a happy cry, they surrounded Peter and her. She accepted their kisses and congratulations, and watched Peter surreptitiously as he did the same. One would never know he was lying. She'd been feeling relieved at how her plans had flowed smoothly so far, but now her mood dampened.

"Congratulations, Elizabeth," Lucy said, kissing her cheek.

"Thank you." Elizabeth met her gaze but didn't hold it long, afraid that Lucy might not be as accomplished an actor as Peter.

Abigail shook her head as she looked up at Peter. "You are a brave man, Mr. Derby. This announcement will affect all who know you. Many will be disbelieving; many will be jealous."

"And well they should be," he said, hugging Elizabeth to his side with an arm around her shoulders. "I am marrying the sweetest girl in all of England."

No one said "and the wealthiest," but Elizabeth knew many would. Her dowry could transform the life of any man.

She found herself watching Emily, though she tried not to. Had Emily been attracted to Peter when she thought her husband dead? Was that why Peter wouldn't discuss their courtship?

But Emily seemed genuinely happy for Peter, her eyes sparkling as she spoke to her mother-in-law. Obviously, she had come to terms with whatever had happened between Peter and her.

Had Peter?

Oh, what did it matter? she reminded herself. She wasn't marrying Peter. She was burying herself so deeply in the charade that she was forgetting the truth.

The questions about their secret courtship began to flow, and Elizabeth realized she hadn't settled on a story with Peter. She answered with the truth, that she'd always thought of him as a friend but had only recently begun to understand that there was more.

"Did something in particular make you realize that you loved him?" Abigail asked. "Oh, I do love romance."

"Enough," Elizabeth said, holding up her hands. "Peter has yet to tell his family, so he cannot spend all evening answering your questions. I'll walk him to the door."

They smiled and called their good-byes, and Peter clearly enjoyed every minute of the feminine attention. At last she had him in the hall, but before they even reached the central split staircase, he pulled her through an open door into the library.

"Peter!" she cried softly, reproachfully.

"I won't shut the door," he said. "This is perfectly respectable for an engaged couple."

"We should have a chaperone," she said, releasing his arm.

"We don't need one in our homes any longer. Out on the street it is a different matter, but now, here, we have an understanding."

He grinned and arched an eyebrow, looking devilish. She suspected he wanted her to laugh, but there was something intimidating and . . . exciting . . . about being alone with him. She didn't know what to make of it.

"Why did you bring me here?" she asked unsteadily.

"Would not an eager bridegroom want to be alone with his future bride?" he asked softly, his smile fading as he looked down on her. "I'm only doing what you want me to, Elizabeth."

She hesitated, caught up in the blue of his eyes, the determination she read there. "You are taking advantage of this situation."

"The situation you created for a purpose you won't divulge?"

"I'm not one of your smitten women, Peter."

"Smitten women?" he echoed. "Barely engaged, and your jealousy is already showing."

She ignored the teasing. "I know you were questioning Lucy about me earlier tonight."

He smiled with satisfaction. "To keep you safe, I'll do what I must. She is worried about you, too."

"What did she say?"

He was no longer smiling. "That more than one man has tried to force himself on you."

"That sounds positively sinister," she said, trying to make her voice light. It didn't work, even to her own ears.

He took her shoulders in his hands. "But you were afraid of them, Elizabeth. Why wouldn't you tell me that?"

She looked away. "I don't want to be afraid." Her voice was low, strained. "I've never had to be before."

"You weren't even afraid when I found you stuck halfway down as you climbed a bluff."

She gave a faint smile. "I just need . . . help, until my brother arrives."

"And you trusted me to help you."

"And I don't know that I should have," she said, raising her chin. "Look at your behavior tonight—boldly asking Aunt Rosa about Susanna and Rebecca. As you can see, you learned nothing that would help you win your wager."

"Perhaps I was simply showing you that you cannot lead me about without suffering the consequences, Elizabeth."

"You're angry that I'm not falling into your arms like a helpless girl needing to be rescued."

"Aren't you?" He pulled her up against his body.

She gasped, but didn't struggle. She didn't like how

his proximity affected her. It made her feel . . . delicate, feminine. He suddenly seemed so much larger and stronger than she was, his chest a hard wall against her breasts.

"Peter, anyone could walk in here," she said. Her voice sounded too breathless, not her own anymore.

He was leaning over her, overwhelming her, and he'd never made her feel that way before.

"That is the point, Elizabeth, my sweet."

He leaned down until his lips were only a breath away from her own.

"This mustn't happen," she whispered, "not even to prove—"

"Be quiet, Elizabeth."

And then his lips touched hers. She didn't know what she'd expected, but now she knew why she should have resisted. The feeling of his mouth on hers was sublimely sweet, unbearably powerful. It wasn't a simple meeting of lips. He kissed her repeatedly, tilting her head, nibbling on her lower lip until she moaned. The sound gave him entrance, and to her shock, his tongue invaded her mouth. She shuddered as excitement and pleasure and confusion all churned inside her. She hadn't imagined a kiss from a man could be so powerful, so compelling.

As if he knew her sinful weakness, he put his arms about her and lifted her clear onto her toes, molding her to him. She didn't want to hold him, but when at last she needed some touch with reality, she slid her hands up his shoulders. He groaned against her mouth, startling her, even as he deepened the kiss. His mouth, hot and open, played with her, teasing her tongue until at last she met him in return. Pleasure was a dark, overwhelming sin that took away her resolve, whispered that nothing else mattered. It curled low in her belly, giving a throb of need that fascinated her.

She could not be this person so easily overcome; and she could not stop the transformation. It was as if her years working so hard to control herself had never happened. She had no idea how long they stood thus, wrapped in each other's arms. Mouths mating, hands roving along backs and sliding into hair. His lips were softer than she'd imagined, his body harder than hers. She almost whispered *Yes!* when his hands slid up her sides. Though she wore a corset, she could feel the edge of his palms just touch the outside of her breasts.

It was that forbidden touch that forced her to remember who she was—who they were to each other.

She reared her head back, put her hand in front of his mouth when he would have captured her lips in another melting kiss.

"Peter, thank you very much for the lesson!" she cried unsteadily.

He frowned, his darkly shadowed eyes still on her mouth. He pulled her hips tight against his, and the pressure of their bodies together threatened to pull her under his wicked spell again.

"What are you talking about?" he rasped.

"I can use everything you just showed me to woo the man I intend to marry."

# Chapter 9

**P**eter was certainly dazed, overcome by the kiss. He didn't think he'd understood her words, for they'd taken so long to get to his lust-addled brain.

"What did you say?" he asked, trying to concentrate, when all his body wanted to do was press her down on a sofa and finish what they'd begun.

She pushed at his chest, and he had no choice but to let her go. Stepping back, she looked at him too brightly, her face flushed, her mouth moist and pinkened from his kisses. He found himself reaching for her hand, but she eluded him, stepping farther away.

"I've been very sheltered, you know," she said conspiratorially. She looked over her shoulder as if to make sure no one had come to the doorway. "I didn't know *where* I was going to learn what I needed to make a certain man realize we're perfect for each other. Now, thanks to you, Peter—"

"Wait a minute." He lifted his hands to stop her chatter. "You have a 'certain man'?"

"Yes! Didn't I tell you?"

She tilted her head, smiling up at him as if they hadn't just kissed each other senseless. Or maybe he was the only senseless one.

"No, you didn't," he said, frowning. She was only saying something so brazen because she'd been overcome by what they'd just shared. Surely she now realized there was more than friendship between them.

"It's difficult to talk to one man about another, Peter—even though you are a friend." She seemed to add the last as an afterthought.

"How long have you been partial to this man?"

Something in her eyes softened as she seemed to look inward. "For many years, even in my girlhood. I was too embarrassed to tell you then, and as an adult, I would hardly run tell you about him. Don't ask me his name, since I won't divulge it. It shouldn't concern you," she added sweetly.

The tender look on her face made him realize at last that she wasn't just putting off his romantic overtures. She was telling the truth. He wanted to shake this nonsense out of her, but he had a sinking feeling that it wouldn't work.

"It feels so good to finally admit this to you," she continued with sigh. "You've been helping me with the engagement—surely you won't mind if I use everything you teach me?"

"He obviously doesn't deserve you if he needs to be persuaded," he said in a cool voice.

"He is young and unattached. Surely you understand that he is not ready to marry, although he did imply to me that I would be his perfect choice for a wife. I've been patient, and I'll continue to be. But at least now I'll know what to expect, how to react, when at last he and I kiss."

"Was he why you posed for that painting?" he asked softly. "Were you preparing yourself to pursue him?"

"He doesn't know anything about it!" she cried, then covered her mouth and glanced guiltily over her shoulder at the open door.

"So he wouldn't like that reckless side of you."

"I am not reckless, Peter Derby!"

"Go ahead and tell yourself that." He advanced on her slowly, and felt dark satisfaction when she backed up another step. "But you're talking to the man who saw that side of you for many years, who knows the signs. And now you want one man, have been pursued by many, and you've gotten yourself engaged to another."

Anger and worry passed through her expression swiftly. "I've had no choice!"

He straightened. "Very well. I have no choice either. I've promised to help you, and I will, however you need me to, using whatever methods we must to convince everyone we're in love."

He deepened his voice, and was surprised when her gaze dropped to his mouth. She might say the kiss meant nothing, but she was lying to herself.

"Should I kiss you again, Elizabeth?"

He reached for her, and she let him draw her against him. He felt her trembling, watched her delicate eyelids close as her head tipped back. She desired him but would not admit it to herself.

Breathlessly, she whispered, "Surely you've . . . taught me all I need to know."

"Oh no, your suitor will expect much more."

He laughed against her mouth, taking her breath, her tongue, inside him. Kissing her made every thought leave his head but his need for her, his desire that had simmered these last several years. He would enjoy what he could of her, knowing she would have another. He told himself to be content with awakening her passion.

She moaned, and he felt her hands clutching his back, gripping his coat as if her legs would no longer hold her. He spread kisses across her cheek, down her neck, reveling in the scent that was only Elizabeth. Bending her backward over his arm, he suckled her skin, dipping his tongue into the hollow at the base of her throat. He could hear her quick pants, felt her fingers flexing in the folds of his coat. Unable to stop himself, he moved lower, penetrating the silky valley between her breasts with his tongue.

Somehow he put her away from him and watched her sway, dazed, as her wide eyes gaped at him.

"You're sensitive between your breasts, Elizabeth."

She flinched.

"Make sure you tell your suitor that. I'll see you again tomorrow."

He turned and walked out of the library, barely seeing the stairs he took or remembering to nod to the butler who opened the door. The night air fanned across his face but did not cool his ardor—or his disappointment.

Elizabeth didn't remember the long walk to her bedroom. She felt like a ghost of herself, and was grateful that she avoided being seen. When at last she looked into her dressing table mirror, she stared at herself, appalled. Her face was flushed, her lips puffy. There was a faint red mark on her chin from Peter's whiskers. She . . . tasted like him.

What was happening to her? She covered her face with her trembling hands. Surely she wasn't supposed to feel this way, all confused and overwhelmed and on the verge of tears. She'd thought kisses would be sweet and sedate, showing a depth of love.

Instead her emotions had been searing, violent, shocking with intensity.

Somehow she'd managed to take some control by

telling Peter that she could use his kissing lessons. She'd wanted him to know the truth, that she considered herself another man's future wife.

But he'd kissed her again anyway, making all her certainty about her future go up like smoke.

Moaning, she tried not to shudder. She'd invited this on herself. Everything had begun to fall apart with that foolish painting, leading Thomas to her. She'd fallen back on Peter as a safe choice—her mother had been right about that, she thought bitterly—and then he'd kissed her.

What was she supposed to think?

Of course he had to kiss her—to prove that they had fallen deeply, quickly, in love.

And to her, all he'd proven was that she was not the woman she'd worked so hard to become, the sensible one, unlike her brother, who'd only left his thoughtless, foolish youth behind after tragedy. But what was inside her? How did one learn to temper it with control and good sense?

But she would try. And she would succeed. She knew what she wanted in life: a good, sensible marriage with a man she loved. She wanted nothing to do with this wildness that made her question everything she'd believed about herself.

Yet . . . she dreaded facing Peter Derby again.

* * *

Peter found himself at his club, standing beneath the nude painting of Elizabeth. This was certainly not the way to cool his passion, but he couldn't help himself. The woman who'd bared her body for a stranger's canvas had kissed him with innocence, then growing arousal—but not love.

She loved another man.

But he had marked her with his mouth, as if she could be his.

Why was he letting her revelation affect him so? He had a good life, and women when he wanted them. He'd only joined the wager to try to help her, to make her see him as something other than a friend—had kissed her for the same reasons. And her shocked gaze announced his success. He couldn't expect anything else.

Yet to have her say to his face she would use his methods of seduction on another man—it made him so furious, he was glad he didn't know the man's name, didn't know what he'd do to him out of jealousy.

A servant brought him a brandy and he downed some of it, grateful for the burn in his throat.

He wasn't going to stop this dance with Elizabeth—he'd promised to help her, and came here tonight to take the next step in discovering her secrets.

The "lessons" would continue. Let her learn how he could make her feel.

His hungry gaze roamed the painting one last time, as if he hadn't already memorized the pale curves of her breasts—the breasts he'd almost touched tonight—and the dark valley of her thighs.

When he felt that his emotions were sufficiently under his control, he turned and began to circulate among the members who were enjoying themselves with excellent drink and good conversation.

He gave advice on the railways—it was a theme for the gentlemen of his acquaintance lately—debated the horse destined to win at the Ascot, and talked about the newest crop of debutantes. The painting was also still a frequent topic, the identity of the model discussed, but no one seemed to have a clue—which was a relief.

So perhaps that wasn't a motive in the stalking of Elizabeth by several men of Society.

He let some time pass, watched as others drank more deeply, and listened for Elizabeth's name. At last he overheard it, and seated himself with three gentlemen, all closer to her age than his own. They laughed with brash arrogance over their conquests of women, not mentioning Elizabeth again until Peter brought her up. He had already realized that once everyone knew of his engagement, they'd never talk about her in front of him again.

Seton and Dekker elbowed each other and guffawed, while the third man, Bowes, only smiled.

"You know her, Derby," said Dekker, his teeth too big for his smile. "You know what she's like."

Peter looked between them, pretending good-natured confusion. "What she's like? She's the highest prize of the *ton*."

"Always thought she was," Seton said, shaking his shaggy head. "Or at least that's how she makes a man feel."

They shared snickering laughter.

"Maybe she's not the innocent she appears." Dekker downed the last of his drink, then leaned forward as if to speak privately, but his drunken voice was still too loud. "I almost got her alone on a terrace a couple days ago, but another man took her away from me. Never thought I'd stand a chance at touching her. Still don't know if I do, but if she likes me—you never know."

"Did you hurt her?" Peter asked coolly. It took everything in him not to haul Dekker up by the throat, as he imagined how Elizabeth might feel at being manhandled.

"Hurt her? We were *dancing*!" Dekker said in confusion. "Even my *mother* was there—not about to do anything stupid."

Bowes looked at Peter, narrowing his eyes as if he couldn't quite see him. "Why do you care, Derby? Or do you think you can have her?"

They looked at each other and shared a laugh, even

as they staggered to their feet and went off to join another group.

If Dekker had frightened Elizabeth, the man himself didn't think he'd done anything wrong. And although Peter spent another hour moving from group to group, bringing up Elizabeth where he could, he learned nothing else.

When he went home that night he found himself pacing his room, unable to sleep at the thought of Elizabeth being hurt because he couldn't protect her. But when he was finally exhausted, it wasn't Elizabeth who haunted his night, but Emily Leland, another woman hurt because of him. His dreams were full of rushing waters and her scream.

Peter awoke before dawn, breathing hard, the sheets clinging to his perspiring skin. After Emily, he'd sworn not to involve himself again in something so personal. He'd turned to the sort of women who didn't demand anything of him but pleasure. And everything had been going well—until Elizabeth had needed to be rescued again.

At breakfast Peter looked at his mother, brother, and sister, who ate as if it were any other day. He was about to change that.

"Mother, I'm getting married," he said.

She coughed on a piece of toast, and he patted her

back, while across the table Mary Anne rolled her eyes. James gave him a scowl, then hid it before their mother could see.

James was an older, darker-haired version of Peter, and they usually got on well together. As the heir, James had received the education and the property, and always felt badly that there was little for his younger brother. Peter had never resented him for something not in his control. Before venturing into the railways, Peter had spent much of his time helping James oversee the family property. He didn't have as much time for that these days, and James hadn't seemed to resent his new luck.

But marriage? When their mother had been pressing James for years to find a wife and beget an heir? Peter knew that his brother wasn't going to take his supposed defection from bachelorhood well.

After several restorative sips of her morning coffee, their mother faced him in shock and delight. "Peter? How can this be? You've said nothing to me! I've seen you courting no particular young lady."

"That's because she's been there all along," Mary Anne muttered.

Mrs. Derby looked at her daughter in confusion, then turned to James, who only shrugged his ignorance.

"Mary Anne, dear, what are you saying?" Mrs. Derby demanded.

"Don't you want to hear it from Peter?" Mary Anne asked, nodding her head toward him.

"Well of course!" Mrs. Derby cried, turning in her chair to face Peter. "If you've known the young lady a long time, then surely I do, too."

"You do, Mother. Elizabeth Cabot has agreed to marry me."

James's jaw dropped and he didn't bother to mask his surprise. Mary Anne simply sighed and shook her head, as if she'd known Peter would make this terrible mistake.

But his mother cried out her delight. "Lady Elizabeth? Surely not . . . *Lady Elizabeth*?"

She sounded as if he were betrothed to a princess of the realm. Elizabeth was almost that royal. But he understood his mother's disbelief.

"Yes, Mother, Lady Elizabeth," he said dryly.

James leaned forward as if he, too, wanted to hear about this miraculous event.

"But . . . but . . ." Mrs. Derby practically sputtered with shock. "Of course we've known her and the Cabots for many years, but . . . but . . ."

"She is the daughter of a duke," James said, his voice laced with both amazement and dismay. "Peter, however did you accomplish such a thing?"

"I have always remained a friend of the family," Peter said with a shrug. "I never thought to aspire to more. But the last few weeks we've been seeing each other at the same dinners and balls, and there's been something . . . new growing between us. We went for a carriage ride yesterday, and had a wonderful time together. I knew then that I felt more for her than simple friendship."

It was James's turn to roll his eyes. "As if we all didn't know that. I remember your surprised expression at her coming out."

Peter stared at him. "Really? I was that obvious?"

"To those who know you well," James answered. "But I never thought . . ." His words died away as he stared again at Peter.

Peter chuckled. "I never thought either. But yesterday I impulsively asked her to marry me, and she agreed."

As his mother began to cry, his guilt taunted him.

"Oh Peter, I never thought to see you so well settled, so happy."

It was a shame his mother could only tie happiness with marriage; he was satisfied with his own life.

"He's not happy yet," Mary Anne said.

Peter shot her a look, and she folded her arms over her chest and sank into silence.

"We'll have to put the announcement in the paper," Mrs. Derby said.

"Of course. I'll discuss the wording with Elizabeth." He hadn't even thought of details like that. And that was an important detail for Elizabeth. She wanted all of Society to know that she was taken—protected. "Her mother is planning an engagement party," he added.

"Oh, my," Mrs. Derby breathed. "I can only imagine how splendid that will be."

"They aren't gods on Mount Olympus, Mama," Mary Anne said.

Peter ignored her. "We won't set a date until her brother returns from Scotland."

"Oh, of course. You'll have to discuss the marriage settlement," she murmured.

James sighed. "You'll certainly have more to invest."

Peter nodded and returned to his eggs and toast. But he couldn't help glancing at his sister. She had some kind of negative fixation on Elizabeth, and it couldn't be healthy. He would have to bring the two women together regularly—

And that sparked an idea for a way to help Mary Anne and stay near Elizabeth all at the same time.

# Chapter 10

**E**lizabeth had gone to bed without a visit from her mother. She'd been surprised, then relieved, over-whelmed by the events of the day. Perhaps her mother had been as well, since she was still recovering from a recent fever.

But after breakfast, before Elizabeth could escape the house, her mother asked to meet in the morning room. When Elizabeth arrived, the duchess took her arm and drew her to her side so they could sit together on a brocade sofa.

"So," the duchess began thoughtfully, "you're be-trothed."

Elizabeth smiled.

"Thank you for giving me at least a day to prepare for Peter's request."

Elizabeth winced. "It all happened rather quickly, I know."

Her mother watched her thoughtfully. "Is there a reason it had to happen so quickly?"

Elizabeth's first jumbled thoughts were of the painting and Thomas and a zealous suitor—and then she realized what her mother meant. "No! Good gracious, no. Peter has always been a gentleman." *Until last night.*

Her mother's smile widened with relief. "I assumed so, but wanted to be certain." She took a deep breath. "I am not so certain about your brother's reaction."

Elizabeth sobered. "I know my marriage was supposed to bring the dukedom powerful connections. I tried to see my suitors with that in mind, but . . ." She let her voice trail off, praying that her mother wasn't just placating her when she taught her that love mattered above all.

"I cannot complain about the speed with which one falls in love," the duchess said, a smile on her lips, her eyes focused far away. "When I met your father, I knew almost instantly that I would fall in love with him. I could not believe he felt the same about me, a common girl from another country. But then I imagine Peter understands how I felt."

"Your story is so romantic," Elizabeth said with a sigh. "Swept away by love from the moment you met."

She'd felt that way about William—but what had she felt when Peter kissed her? How could she compare the two men when she'd never been lucky enough to kiss William?

"Christopher will be happier knowing that Peter has become a man of independent wealth."

"Is money so important, Mama?" Elizabeth asked, surprised.

"No, of course not. But it will be easier for Peter to hold his head up amidst the coming gossip. Men value their pride, you know."

She did understand that, especially where Thomas was concerned. His pride had been damaged when she'd rejected him the first time, and now she believed he was trying to rebuild it however he could.

"Do you know much about Peter's investments?" the duchess asked.

"Only that it has to do with the railways."

"Ah, good, then he has not been secretive."

"Secretive?" she echoed in surprise.

The duchess shook her head. "Lady Rosa said that last autumn, when Matthew returned home and Peter was invited to stay with them, he was . . . not himself."

"Did she say how?"

Her mother waved a hand. "Only that he seemed distracted, ill at ease—"

"He had been attempting to court Matthew's wife. I imagine it was very awkward to be at Madingley Court when the couple was newly reunited."

"True. And from what I understand it was just after that that he began to take an active part in growing his investments. Ignore my concerns, my child. I am simply an old woman who wants to see you happy. Christopher only wants the same. He will not care that Peter is a commoner, since he himself married a journalist!"

Elizabeth smiled, but her thoughts were of Peter's explanation that he and Susanna had tried to work out their past disagreements last autumn. Had there been something more going on?

At last Elizabeth was anticipating receiving visitors. She would be able to tell any bold men that she was now engaged, and they'd best leave her alone—especially Lord Thomas Wythorne, the smug . . . bounder. His plan to force her to choose him as her husband had failed, thanks to Peter.

Even though she'd looked forward all day to the event, she barely made it home in time. She'd spent much of the day in the offices of one of the charities she supported. She was particularly drawn to a young woman from the country, a respectable girl who was supposed to marry a vicar—until an obsessed young man had taken her away and ruined her name.

The woman had been rather dazed as she talked to Elizabeth—dazed with her good fortune. Thrown out by her family, she'd been desperate enough to look for work in London, and almost ruined for good until the Society for the Rescue of Young Women and Children secured her a sewing position with a modiste. Elizabeth was there to help with the paperwork, to soothe the young women by listening to their stories and offering comfort.

The girl had lost her family, her friends, the people she'd grown up with—all because of a man. Much as Elizabeth was grateful that her own situation was not so desperate, if she'd been truly ruined by one of her bold suitors, she might never have been welcomed into the homes of friends again, even if she married. She could have been forced to live in the country so that she wouldn't infringe on her brother's political life. A man who would hurt her reputation could also be a man who would beat her. And what could she have done about that? In her work with the charity, she'd met more than one woman who suffered such a fate.

That wouldn't be her. She'd taken steps to solve her problems. True, she'd needed Peter's help, but he was a partner, and would be compensated after all. Defeating two men was more important to him than her friendship, so he should be satisfied.

During the day's at-home, another group of men paid their calls. She had to force herself not to wonder who knew about the painting, who'd revealed it to Thomas. He'd promised to stop his friend from spreading the rumor, but had it worked? She could almost swear that men laughed behind her back when she passed, but she could never catch anyone.

Almost a dozen suitors had arrived when Thomas

Wythorne sauntered in. His smile was easy with confidence, and he touched his brow to her in a show of supposed respect that made her grit her teeth. He didn't approach her, simply watched from afar, daring her to produce what he thought was a fictitious fiancé.

She would be happy to do so.

In the middle of a discussion with two men about a new Society marriage, she was able to blush prettily and say, "I am so thrilled that soon I, too, will be making an important announcement."

The men glanced at each other in surprise.

She covered her mouth, eyes wide. "Oh dear, I was supposed to wait for the official announcement, but I can't seem to stop my good news. I'm engaged to be married!"

She said the last sentence rather loudly, and heard rumbles of male conversation from behind her. Thomas arched a dark brow as if to say he'd heard this before and still didn't believe it.

And then Peter arrived, his hair disheveled from the outdoors. When he spotted her, his smile fairly beamed with pride and adoration. She felt a jolt of warm pleasure before reminding herself what they were to each other.

She reached her gloved hands to him, and he brought them to his lips.

"Elizabeth."

He murmured her name as if just seeing her put a

shine on his day. Several men glanced at each other at his informal use of her Christian name.

"Peter," she breathed quietly, smiling up at him. "I hope you don't mind, but I could not keep quiet about our news."

No one bothered to pretend a conversation; she had every man's attention.

Peter grinned and surveyed the other men. "Elizabeth has done me the great honor of agreeing to become my wife."

Elizabeth watched the shock and whispers sweep the room. More than one man looked at Peter with astonishment as if there had to be a mistake—he was a commoner, she was the daughter of a duke. Their families certainly wouldn't have arranged such a match. Love could be the only reason—except for scandal or ruination, all of which she hoped to prevent. The scandal of marrying a commoner seemed minor to her. If only William had been here to see it!

For a short while the men mingled and talked and watched them. Peter never left her side, playing his part to perfection. One by one the guests politely congratulated them and took their leave. Even Thomas did so, although when Peter looked aside to speak to someone, Thomas raised an eyebrow at her and grinned. She desperately wished she could give him a smug look, but she didn't want to antagonize him. He still knew about the painting. Surely he wouldn't say anything . . .

Thomas's last unreadable look was for Peter, and then he left. Elizabeth told herself to calm down, to wait and see if Thomas made a counter move.

When it was just she and Peter, they shared a long glance as the footmen departed. Peter looked at her as if the kiss was still on his mind—it certainly was on hers. It was wrong of her to remember the wildly exciting feelings he had stirred inside her. He kept watching her mouth, his eyes smoldering with memories. She put a table between them.

"Peter, please sit down. Would you care for tea? Oh dear, I should have asked the footmen before they left."

His grin was arrogant, as if he knew she was flustered and regretful but didn't care. He waited while she stepped into the hall to speak with a footman, rather than pull the bell for another servant. When she came back to sit across from him, he slid a folded piece of paper from his pocket and handed it to her.

At her puzzled glance, he said, "It's from my mother. She knew you would be putting an engagement announcement in the paper, and these are her suggestions."

She read through it, as well as the lovely words of congratulations. Though she was well acquainted with Mrs. Derby, of course, there had always been a reserve about the woman that Elizabeth knew was because of the Cabot family's noble status.

"Give her my thanks, Peter. Promise her I will have this to the newspapers later this afternoon. Do you wish to add your own advice on the wording?"

He grinned. "I trust you. I know you want this out in public as quickly as possible. With the men who called on you today, word will have spread by nightfall."

Again he was looking directly at her mouth, instead of into her eyes. It made her feel fluttery and nervous inside. In a low voice, she said, "You do not have to look at me so . . . intently when we are alone."

He leaned forward, elbows resting on his knees. "It would be a mistake to act differently in private, Elizabeth."

Pressing her lips together, she nodded.

"You don't like me looking at you?"

She hesitated.

"Men have looked at you for years, even before you emerged from the schoolroom. Surely you are used to it."

"But it's . . . *you*, Peter. I am not used to that."

They said nothing as a maid entered with a tea tray and left it for Elizabeth. She poured silently, preparing Peter's tea as he liked it, then handing it to him. She met his amused gaze and responded with a faint smile, reminding herself that she'd asked for this.

After he took a sip, his smile faded and he considered his china cup for a moment. "Elizabeth, I have a favor to ask."

"We seem to be asking much of each other lately."

"Friends often do."

She didn't answer, and that seemed to amuse him.

"You have never been close to my sister, Mary Anne," he began.

Surprised, she said, "She and I both tried for a deeper friendship. But we seemed to have nothing in common."

He smiled. "Believe me, I do not blame you. As a child, Mary Anne was always more interested in tree forts and reptiles than the gentle pursuits of a young lady."

"I seem to recall an occasional fascination with reptiles myself," she said dryly. Her escapades were more about dares and challenges.

"But your interests matured," Peter said.

Her interests, perhaps, but she was feeling far less than mature, with the crazy direction her life had taken.

"Mary Anne's interests turned from reptiles to billiards," he continued.

Elizabeth blinked at him. "Billiards?"

"She even won money from several friends the other night."

"She wagered on her game?" Elizabeth asked, then added pointedly, "I wonder where she comes by that trait."

He ignored her taunt. "You don't understand. She deliberately misled them about her skill and lured them into a game."

"Oh dear," she murmured in understanding.

"If she continues in such a way, she'll be ruined. And although she promised me she would no longer play for money, she is obsessed with the game, playing for hours every day. She tells me she values her independence and doesn't want to marry. But I think something else is at the heart of her rebellion, and she has not yet found a way to confide in me, nor our mother. As for another female relative, we only have a distant aunt, and she's not a close relation. Would you consider taking her under your wing, perhaps guiding her through the shoals of Society in a way that two brothers cannot?"

"Billiards," Elizabeth mused, setting down her teacup and studying Peter. The knowing smile he'd been sporting for too many days was gone. She knew he loved his sister. "Who taught her the game?"

He sighed. "You probably know, or you wouldn't ask. I did, several years ago. She enjoyed watching me practice, and soon she was asking intelligent questions. Before I knew it, she was handling the cue with talent. But misrepresenting herself to men, trying to take their money—"

"Yes, that is a different thing. I will admit your dilemma intrigues me."

To her surprise, he rose suddenly and came around

the table to sit beside her. She leaned back, but all he did was lift her hand.

"No man would believe that I could sit for long without touching you," he murmured, squeezing her fingers gently.

She looked down at their joined hands, now resting on her knee. His was larger, rougher than hers, and she remembered it on her waist, pulling her against him. She'd had no choice, had never imagined that Peter would need strength to force her to do anything. But soon she'd wanted to be within his arms, she thought with guilt. Soon his kiss had made her forget their mistrust, and worse, her love of another man. What did that say about her?

"Do you need more time to consider?" he asked sharply.

"Of course not," she assured him. "Mary Anne is important to you. I would be grateful for the chance to do something for you in return—even though I've already promised you the truth about the painting."

"I haven't forgotten," he said. "That is something between men, where Mary Anne is close to my heart. What do you think we should do?"

"We? I do believe you've asked *me* to guide Mary Anne. I do not believe it wise for you to be a part of it, or she might suspect your involvement."

"But—"

"For now she thinks I am to be her new sister by marriage. That will give me the chance to begin a closer friendship."

Peter looked away.

"Peter, what's wrong?"

He sighed. "Mary Anne might have her own impediment to your deepening the friendship. She is not happy that I'm marrying you."

Elizabeth straightened. "Excuse me?" She tried to pull her hand away, but he didn't allow it.

"She is concerned that I am setting my sights too high, that a marriage between two such different social classes will never work."

"You're not a chimney sweep, Peter," she said, feeling cross and even offended. "Does she believe I cannot love you for the man you are, that I'd prefer a title?"

"I don't know—do you need a title?"

"The man I love has a very minor one," she said coolly. "It is unimportant to me."

He looked at her without speaking, and she knew he was considering her words as a clue. Of course Peter would be curious about William Gibson. He was curious about the painting—curious about everything. She had never imagined it would be so difficult to keep things from him.

But there was also the mystery of why she had never

been able to befriend Mary Anne, when she usually got on well with everyone. There was always an awkwardness when they were together. Had she avoided Peter's sister deliberately, as her one failure?

"You know how important my father considered a title," Peter said. "It bothered him so much that your father was a duke that he couldn't even be civil. His attitude was a source of pain for my mother."

"Was it because of my mother's heritage?" Elizabeth asked. "There were many who did not agree with the marriage."

"I don't believe so. I think my father simply felt there was a competition for respect in the countryside, and that he was always the loser. His own fault, of course."

"I'm sorry, Peter. Do you think Mary Anne feels the same?"

"I don't know. She doesn't say so, but frames her objection as caring about me."

"Then you should assume that's what it is. She's always been blunt and outspoken."

"She used to be," Peter said musingly. "Something has changed."

Was the problem of Mary Anne even larger than he was letting on?

"I thank you for agreeing to help," he said.

He raised her gloved hand to his mouth and kissed the back, looking at her as he did so. He'd always had laughing eyes, and sometimes she still glimpsed the old Peter. But long ago she would have been sharing his amusement, and now she felt like she didn't understand him anymore. Something had changed him.

He gave her his easygoing smile. "My mother would like you to come for luncheon tomorrow morning. Mary Anne will be there."

"Then I accept." Again she tried to remove her hand from his, but although he lowered it again, this time their hands rested on *his* knee.

"I have something else we need to discuss. After I left here last night, I went to my club."

She stiffened, and he gripped her hand even more tightly.

"I can see your mind working," he continued in a chiding voice. "Much as I stood beneath the painting for a long while to admire it—"

"Ooh!" She pulled harder but she couldn't escape him.

"—the painting was not my purpose there. I went because of the men pursuing you."

She froze, and her every fear threatened to materialize. What would happen if Peter discovered Thomas's manipulations? What if they confronted each other—would someone be hurt, all because of her?

# Chapter 11

"**G**ood, now I have your attention," Peter said, trying not to show his satisfaction.

"Peter—"

"Did you think once I knew your fears, I wouldn't try to uncover the truth?"

"But it doesn't matter anymore. I am engaged to you, and the news of that will protect me."

Peter studied her beautiful face, willing her to tell him the truth. There was more she wasn't saying; she was forcing him to pull secrets, one at a time, from that clever brain of hers. If she wanted to play this game, he would do so.

"I heard one man claim he tried to be alone with you on a terrace."

"We were dancing," she said tightly.

"That's all I could uncover. I heard no one mention the painting in connection with you. But I will keep searching."

"Peter, what if you're making things worse?"

"But as your fiancé, it would be expected of me to protect you."

She could not dispute that, he realized, although she obviously wanted to. She must think she'd defeated . . . someone . . . with her false engagement. But Dekker? He seemed harmless, but perhaps Elizabeth hadn't felt that way. There must be more he didn't know.

But he let it go, allowing her to think she'd solved all her own problems. He could not force her trust, but wanted her to grant it willingly.

"Thank you for informing me of what you're doing," she said, rising to her feet.

He did the same.

"I have a dinner engagement to prepare for."

"And since I do not, then I will only see you tonight in my dreams?"

She rolled her eyes, then glanced at the door. "Really, Peter, who would even overhear such—"

He cupped her face in his hands and kissed her. He ran his tongue along her lips, which tasted of sweetened tea with cream. To his surprise, she didn't push him away, but parted her mouth in invitation. Did she crave his kisses the way he now craved hers?

"Sweet dreams, Elizabeth," he murmured against her mouth. Then he stepped back. "I will call for you at eleven o'clock tomorrow morning."

She nodded, pressing her wet lips together, saying nothing. She looked a bit dazed, he thought with satisfaction.

He bowed to her and left the drawing room.

Elizabeth wrote a letter to Mary Anne, inviting her on a shopping expedition, and had it hand delivered. Surely they would become better acquainted as they roamed Bond Street. All women had the love of such a pastime in common.

She then put Peter, his kisses, and his closeness to discovering Thomas's deeds, out of her mind—though she found it surprisingly difficult. She was having dinner at the Gibson home, and Lucy had assured her that William would be in attendance. It was time to see his reaction to the announcement of her engagement. She took extra care with her toilette, having her maid style her hair to look its best. She wanted William to see what he was missing.

In the Gibson drawing room, small but cozy, with warmly colored paintings and family knickknacks scattered across every table, Elizabeth stood with Lucy and Lady Gibson, awaiting the arrival of the Gibson brothers.

"William had business in the city," said Lady Gibson, a plump woman whose blond hair had gone white.

Lucy rolled her eyes where her mother couldn't see. She mouthed the word "horses," and Elizabeth smothered a laugh. She had always enjoyed William's devotion to the equine world, even if it meant watching a race to determine the next horse he meant to invest in. But obviously he wasn't as good at racing them, for Peter had beaten him in Hyde Park. For a moment she was back at Peter's side, the wind in her hair, the horses stretching out gloriously in front of them. She and Peter had exchanged eager smiles.

Realizing where her mind had drifted, she pulled her attention back to the Gibson drawing room. William liked racing horses, too, she reminded herself.

At last William and his younger brother Bernard came through the doors, their hair windblown, their faces wide with smiles. Elizabeth softened as she looked at William, who took such joy in life. His light hair only set off the devilish green gleam in his eyes.

Both young men bowed to her before regaling their family with the horse they hoped to purchase soon. They didn't mention why they were waiting to pursue the sale, but it wasn't her business.

Before they went down to dinner, Lucy gave Elizabeth an excited glance, then cleared her throat to capture her family's attention.

"Got a frog in there?" Bernard taunted, elbowing William.

Lucy made a face. "For your information, Elizabeth has exciting news."

They all turned to her expectantly, and she found herself blushing again. "Although the announcement will be in the papers tomorrow, I cannot keep my silence tonight. I'm engaged to be married."

She could not help glancing at William first. He studied her—was that a gleam of shock in his green eyes?

"Congratulations, Lady Elizabeth!" Lady Gibson said before William could speak.

The older woman enveloped her in a hug.

"Congratulations," William said, while his brother off-handedly mumbled the same. "Who's the lucky man?"

*That* made her feel better. "Mr. Peter Derby."

She immediately realized that she had better become used to the reactions of Society, for Lady Gibson's smile faded a bit and Bernard openly gaped. William only continued to smile, and she wasn't certain whether to take that as disinterest or trust in her judgment. He *should* trust her, for after all, Peter was a perfectly fine man who would make any woman hap—

What was wrong with her mind? It was as if this false engagement had rattled everything she believed for her future.

Lucy's words rushed out. "They've known each other all their lives. Isn't it romantic?"

Lady Gibson succeeded in hiding any more doubt. "How wonderful, Lady Elizabeth. I hope you will be very happy."

And then they all went in to dinner, where the discussion went back to horses. Elizabeth knew the subject well and was able to ask knowledgeable questions about the breed William was looking for. Soon they were carrying on a spirited conversation about men's saddles versus ladies' saddles. Elizabeth made him laugh more than once, and told herself that the day was a success.

It unnerved her, however, that she almost had to *convince* herself.

By late the next morning, after the newspapers had been devoured, the invitations began to arrive. Elizabeth knew everyone was interested in the reasons for her engagement and that she would be the focus of all the gossip for a while.

Let them talk, she thought with satisfaction. The more they believed, the more *Thomas* would believe he should leave her alone.

One of the letters, hand delivered, was Mary Anne Derby's polite rejection of the shopping invitation, without even a suggestion of a date that would be more suitable for her. But the battle to win over Mary Anne was hardly over, Elizabeth thought, not after only one brief engagement of their forces.

Peter called for her, and she was disappointed that a rain shower caused them to ride in his family carriage rather than the phaeton. When they were seated across from each other, she told him so.

"Nonsense," he said. "This only gives us an opportunity to continue your lessons."

She studied him warily. "What do you mean?"

"Have you ever ridden in a carriage with the man you admire?"

"I have."

"And did he look only at you?"

"We weren't alone," she said tightly. This conversation felt wrong on so many levels.

"But what would you do if you were?"

She hesitated.

"You would smile and make polite conversation, as you've been taught."

"Make your point, Peter. It will not be long before we arrive at your town house. And I would never be alone with him, unless we were riding in an open carriage, with servants just behind us. The only reason *we're* alone is that everyone thinks we're engaged." Her words and voice sounded defensive, flustered, and she hated appearing so before him.

"If you can't be alone with him," he murmured in a husky voice, "you must make him *wish* you were."

Her mouth sagged open; then she gave a start when

she felt the toe of his boot touch her slipper. "Peter—"

"Just hear me out. Imagine his surprise when you touch him. He'll think you did it accidentally, and then when you do it again, he'll know it was on purpose."

"I cannot possibly do something so . . . obvious."

"Has subtlety worked up to now?"

She hesitated, then murmured thoughtfully, "No, it hasn't. But he'll think me too free with my affections."

"Wouldn't you rather take the chance?"

He kept his boot beneath her skirts, rubbing along the outside length of her slipper, then along the top. She had her feet pressed tightly together, but instead of wedging them apart, he began to trail his boot up the line between her calves, bunching her skirts over his lower leg.

"Peter!" she hissed, disturbed by the way her pulse beat loudly in her ears at the cool touch of leather on her silk stockings.

"Aren't you forced to consider me?" he asked. "Then he'll think about what he'd do if you were alone, how he'd come to sit beside you"—he rose above her, then sank onto the bench at her side—"how you might welcome him."

"Welcome?"

Though she leaned away from him, it only allowed him to bend over her. He braced himself with his arm on the far side of her legs. With the windows closed against the rain, the carriage felt overheated and damp, making her skin flushed and her mouth parched. She looked away, unable to meet his gaze, trying to pretend she could see out the rain-streaked window. When she felt the faintest touch along her temple, she realized he was nuzzling her there with his nose.

And then the carriage slowed to a stop. "You can move away now," she said.

She gave him a push, and he laughed and fell back on the bench.

"I can feel it all tight inside you, Elizabeth," he said softly, his eyes gleaming. "All that wildness, longing to be free."

She was glad a footman opened the door, or she would surely have hit him with her reticule. She was suddenly feeling so overwhelmed by this charade, necessary though it was.

Mrs. Derby met them in the entrance hall, sinking into a deep curtsy that was so humble as to be embarrassing.

Elizabeth raised her up. "Please, Mrs. Derby, there is no need for such formality. Soon I will be another daughter to you."

Though Mrs. Derby blushed and smiled, Mary Anne, standing in the doorway to the drawing room beside her brother James, looked anything but pleased. Elizabeth wanted to sigh. She was not winning over Peter's sister.

And a small, guilty voice inside her said that Mary Anne had the right of it.

This engagement was only for a few weeks until Christopher returned, she told herself. By then she might have some answers for Peter about Mary Anne's behavior—and then Mary Anne could go back to hating her, this time for supposedly breaking Peter's heart.

Elizabeth glanced up at him, remembering to give him her sweetest smile. She was beginning to wonder if he even had a heart to break.

Mrs. Derby looked at her in confusion, as if she suddenly didn't know how to treat her. Elizabeth took the older woman's arm and walked with her side by side into the drawing room.

"I simply never saw this coming," Mrs. Derby said, shaking her head.

"And I neither, ma'am. For all those years, I saw Peter only as a friend."

"What changed your mind?" Mary Anne asked.

Elizabeth ignored the faint air of belligerence as she smiled up at Peter. "Now that I've been out for several years, I felt that I'd met most of the men. None of them seemed to compare at all to Peter."

James gave a faint snort, and Peter smiled wickedly at his brother. Mrs. Derby sniffed and dabbed at her tears with a handkerchief.

Mary Anne was only suspicious. "But what about

when the duke returns? Certainly he might want a say in your plans."

"My mother has approved the match," Elizabeth responded happily. "And I'm certain Peter can handle himself when he and my brother discuss the marriage settlement. I can barely wait until then, so we can set a date."

"In a hurry?" Mary Anne asked.

"Mary Anne!" Mrs. Derby scolded. "That is too forward, young lady."

"No, please, I understand," Elizabeth hastened to say. "Mary Anne, you have every right to question me. Perhaps I can settle your fears if you go for a ride with me." If she could help Peter with his sister, her guilt might not be such a heavy burden.

Mary Anne opened her mouth, probably to decline, but Mrs. Derby clapped her hands together.

"How wonderful, Lady Elizabeth! Mary Anne will be happy to attend."

Elizabeth waited for Mary Anne to protest, but both her brothers were watching her, and her hesitation lengthened into acquiescence.

"I'll call for you at nine tomorrow morning," Elizabeth said.

Mary Anne gave a single nod.

Mrs. Derby turned back to Elizabeth. "Peter tells me that your mother has graciously offered to host your engagement party. I would like to offer my help in any way."

"Of course! My mother has just begun to make guest lists, and she would appreciate a list of your relatives."

"Oh, they'll all want to come," Mrs. Derby gushed. "We have several living farther to the north, so with some notice, I do believe even they'll travel for the wonderful event."

"You mean Aunt Virginia and Uncle Cecil?" James asked. "It has been a long time since we've seen them."

Elizabeth had been watching Mary Anne as much as possible and seemed to be the only one who saw her stiffen and look away at this discussion. It disturbed her that Mary Anne was so reluctant to have her as a sister-in-law. Although they weren't good friends, she had thought they'd always been easy with one another. This was simply more proof that she had been far too ignorant about the emotions of others, too wrapped up in her own hard-won complacency.

For several minutes before dinner, the conversation revolved around the engagement party, until at last the meal was served. Elizabeth had to try hard to effect an expression of enjoyment, and she sensed that lying to his family wasn't so easy for Peter either.

After dinner, rather than separating, the men returned to the drawing room with the women. Mary Anne soon excused herself, and Elizabeth murmured to Peter that she needed a moment of privacy. Instead, she followed

Mary Anne, and found her right where she imagined she would be—in the billiard room.

Mary Anne was already deep in concentration as she studied the table. Elizabeth remained in the corridor, peering in to watch her. Each shot was a study in precise, calculated movements. Her face showed no emotion, as if she could immerse herself in the game and put aside what she didn't want to think about.

Elizabeth gave a start when she felt a hand on her elbow. She looked up to find Peter watching her, then gesturing with his head down the corridor. She followed him into a small parlor where needlework bags rested beside the sofa and a deck of cards waited in the center of a small table by the window.

"Did you think I misled you about the billiards?" he asked dryly.

"Of course not. I simply wanted to confirm that her frustration with me tonight led her to play the game. Have you noticed that pattern?"

"No, but then I have not thought to study it before these last few days. It makes sense. When one is concentrating on an objective, one can forget unpleasant emotions."

"Speaking from experience?" It was her turn to affect a dry tone.

"The only thing I'm concentrating on right now is you."

"And perhaps that is what's bothering Mary Anne."

His smile faded. "Yes, I've wondered the same thing. I haven't been able to spend as much time with her—and that started before our engagement," he added.

"Your railway investments."

He nodded.

"Matthew helped you somehow?" she asked.

"Who told you that?"

"Emily, I believe. She mentioned that you and he were in discussion together about investing." She hesitated, feeling as if he'd somehow retreated from her, though he hadn't moved a step. "Surely it wasn't supposed to be a secret."

"No. Or else everyone would think I had not earned the right to marry you." He let his finger trail along her cheek.

He was already changing the direction of the conversation back to their false engagement, back to the caresses that so aroused her. It wasn't her place to interrogate him—she didn't want to be interrogated herself, but . . .

"If your working with Matthew wasn't a secret, then why are you so remote about it?"

"Remote?"

He kept touching her, sliding a wayward curl back behind her ear, making her shiver.

"I just admitted I'd worked with him," he continued.

"I had much to learn about the railways, and he put me in touch with friends who could help. There's no special meaning here, Elizabeth."

She didn't like how strange he could make her feel now, with just a look or a touch. He confused her, made her skin sensitive and hot, made her long for things she shouldn't. She was determined to have a safe, easy marriage, without all these riotous sensations that made her doubt her sanity, that made her think she wasn't the proper girl she'd molded herself into.

# Chapter 12

**T**hat night, as Peter stood at the entrance to Lord Ludlow's ballroom with Elizabeth at his side, everything felt a bit unreal. Never had the *ton* noticed his introduction at such affairs, until his name was linked with hers. He'd been anonymous, his liaisons with women his own business. From now on everything he did would be fodder for gossip—even everything he'd done in the recent past.

And if the gossips wanted more, they could dig deeper—but he knew no one involved would talk about that sensitive time. He hated having those secrets on his soul, the bitterness at his own behavior that seemed to be lingering too long.

As their names were announced, Peter focused on the night and the part he played. He glanced at Elizabeth and exchanged smiles. She looked radiant in white satin tonight, her black hair exotic and darkly enticing, her gown like the stars to the darkness of the night sky. He felt natural and right at her side.

He reminded himself that it was all temporary, that he could only enjoy her kisses briefly. But he'd understood that from the beginning. He found it wasn't so easy to accept anymore.

It was his worry that went deeper. She had posed for that nude painting for some reason she couldn't—wouldn't—discuss. It altered everything he thought about her. He wanted her happy, not worried about a man's threats. Much as she thought their false engagement would protect her until her brother's return, he didn't think it would be that easy.

As they descended the wide, curved staircase into the ballroom, Elizabeth was immediately surrounded by excited young ladies. Peter stood on the outside, smiling when any of them sent shocked glances his way. They chattered so quickly he couldn't tell who was speaking.

"You never even mentioned Mr. Derby!"

"Wasn't he only a friend?"

"Didn't you once try to interest him in Miss Alden?"

At that, Elizabeth sent him rueful smile and a shrug, before saying, "And then I realized I was terribly jealous, and I could not give him up."

Peter lost track of their conversation when a hand came down firmly on his shoulder. He turned to see several men, sometime suitors to Elizabeth, regarding him in amazement.

"However did you catch Lady Elizabeth Cabot?"

"She was supposed to marry the highest aristocrat!"

"How could you not tell us?"

He felt Elizabeth's hand slide underneath his arm, saw her sweet smile as she boldly leaned her head against his shoulder.

"I swore Mr. Derby to secrecy," she said, her smile wicked.

How easy it was to use the truth when one could. The men gaped at her.

"I wanted his attention all to myself," she continued. "I had to know if he shared my feelings."

"And since I do," Peter said, "I believe it is time to dance with my fiancée."

They left the young people behind, even as Elizabeth whispered to him, "That was fun!"

"Fun?" he asked in surprise.

"Doing the unexpected."

"Another sign of your returning recklessness," he teased.

"It is not reckless to hope that people realize that I want more from life than to marry exactly as expected."

"So your young man isn't in the usual noble group you were expected to choose from?"

She bit her lip, eyes evasive, and he laughed softly.

"You don't need to tell me his name," he said, sweeping her into his arms for a waltz. "At this rate, I'll deduce it myself."

She put her nose up in the air and didn't answer.

Any dance with Elizabeth was always exhilarating, but tonight felt . . . different. The crowds parted to watch them, other couples moved aside to allow them to dance through. She felt wonderful in his arms, delicate and lovely, strong and supple. He enjoyed the curve of her back beneath his hand, the way she took his lead without making him feel as if he dragged her along. He smiled down into her eyes, not needing to remind himself too much to look proud and humbled and love-struck all at the same time.

He didn't forget that she was wary about these new feelings they shared. But tonight no one could see that. Her smile was soft, yet dazzling, and she looked at no one else, as if she were drowning in his eyes.

Inwardly, he chastised himself for such romantic drivel, but he told himself it helped him maintain the illusion she was so desperate to portray.

At last he had to give her up and watch her dance with other men. He made sure to send each man a narrow-eyed warning as they claimed her, silently reminding them that she had a protector now.

There was no shortage of partners for him either. He usually danced much of an evening, for there were always women who appreciated a man's attention. But tonight he found himself interrogated by a line of young ladies who seemed to want to discover why the most eligible lady in the *ton* had settled for a fiancé so far beneath her. He enjoyed himself immensely as he flirted and flattered and teased.

At last he sought a glass of champagne, and briefly stood alone to watch Elizabeth. If any of the men dancing with her had threatened her recently, she didn't show it. She only displayed confidence and happiness, and more than once he saw her laughing.

"You picked the best flower in the garden."

Peter turned around, then had to look far down, to an elderly lady who barely reached his shoulder. She wore a turban that allowed wisps of white hair to escape. She clutched a shawl about her shoulders—though it felt like a desert at noon in the ballroom—but Peter did not make the mistake of thinking this lady frail.

"Good evening, Miss Bury—forgive me, it's now Mrs. Fitzwilliam."

The old woman chuckled. "I left Mr. Fitzwilliam home tonight. He tends to sleep through such things—and he's still exhausted from the elopement!"

Peter chuckled. "You stayed single a long time, ma'am. I applaud your insistence on waiting for the best."

"I waited until I knew my own mind, young man. I knew Mr. Fitzwilliam in my youth, but did not think I loved him enough to marry. He needed some settling down first."

Peter thought of Fitzwilliam, whom he always saw

sleeping in a wing-back chair when he entered the reading room at their club. It was difficult to imagine that the old man was once high-spirited.

"I take pride in predicting who will end up with whom," Mrs. Fitzwilliam was saying.

"I imagine you did not lay money on me as Lady Elizabeth's husband."

Her laugh was a dry cackle. "I thought for certain that your young miss would end up with Lord Bakewell."

"The heir to the Marquess of Ashborne," Peter said, wondering if this was the man Elizabeth loved from afar. "Perfect for a duke's daughter." But no, Elizabeth said that the man she wanted had only a minor title—so he had already inherited.

"And then there was Lord Dekker."

The one who'd confessed that he tried to get Elizabeth alone outside. Surely not the man she professed love for.

A bit too coldly, Peter said, "He made it clear that he was interested in her."

Mrs. Fitzwilliam looked up at him, her lids drooping as she narrowed her eyes. "You're a proprietary boy. I like that."

Before she could say more, two elderly ladies joined them, and Peter felt like a tree amidst shrubbery. They boldly questioned him about his surprise engagement and discussed the various men who'd "flitted about"

Elizabeth, without ever once making him feel as if he didn't deserve her.

When he had the chance to escape, he did so, but remained near enough that he could listen to them talk in confidence. He didn't feel guilty, for they were talking loudly enough into each other's ears to be overheard by anyone within a ten yard radius. He learned nothing of significance, however, except that there were many young men who thought they had a chance with Elizabeth. None had stood out—which he had assumed from his own experience.

So who was this man Elizabeth fancied herself in love with?

"You're the toast of the ball," Thomas said.

Elizabeth tried to smile up at him, but it was difficult, since he had claimed her for the next waltz. Peter had been talking to a bevy of elderly ladies, and she knew if she tried to catch his eye, she would only have drawn attention to herself. So she'd been forced to accept Thomas's hand.

He was a good dancer, but she'd already known that. She tried to pretend she was concentrating on the steps, on the press of the crowd, as he led her effortlessly.

"Surely you planned to attract such attention," Thomas continued. "Peter Derby is one of the most unsuitable men you could have chosen. Everyone is aghast and disbelieving."

"I did not choose him—I fell in love with him," she corrected, striving for the mildest of tones. "The heart doesn't consider the opinions of the *ton*."

He chuckled. "But the Duke of Madingley will. Your brother returns soon—you can't fool him as easily as you've fooled the rest of Society."

"He knows my attachment to Peter."

"Attachment. What an interesting word."

She tried not to grit her teeth. "Lord Thomas, what is the point of annoying me? I'm engaged; you cannot have me as your wife."

"I already told you I don't give up that easily. Does Peter Derby know the real woman inside?"

"You don't know the real woman," she shot back through a false smile. "The painting is only one facet of me. And Peter knows it all."

One of Thomas's eyebrows arched. "I should not be surprised, but I am. So Mr. Derby knows what you've done. And he approves?"

"It is not for him to approve or disapprove. I made my own decision, before I was his fiancée."

"I like this side of you more and more, Lady Elizabeth."

He bent over her, whirling her through a turn until her breath caught, wondering if they'd fall.

Thomas laughed softly. "You will go far to have what you want."

Startled, she met his mocking gaze.

"It's a side of you I empathize with—and find very exciting. And it only makes me more determined to have you. Don't worry. I'll protect your good name until you realize we're perfect for each other."

He let her go then, and she realized that the dance had ended. She sank into a curtsy and moved away, not wanting to look into his face. She was unsettled and confused by his words—and his conclusions.

"I thought I'd never have you to myself."

This voice she recognized, and she turned to Peter with relief and gladness.

He studied her face for a moment, and she prayed that he would not question her, not now.

But he simply smiled. "Shall I take you away from here?"

"Ah, if only you could," she murmured, feeling tired and not very triumphant. "But my mother will be here soon, and she wishes to show off her almost married daughter."

"More pressure you don't need. I promise to have you back within the half hour." He took her hand and pulled.

She didn't want to resist, so she let him lead her through the crowd. When they'd gone past a decorative grouping of potted ferns and shrubbery, he pulled her behind them and down a corridor.

"Where are we going?" she asked, now moving more quickly to keep up with him.

"I couldn't very well lead you right onto the terrace."

"We are engaged, or so you keep reminding me."

"But I want to take you beyond the terrace."

"Even that is tolerated for couples in our situation."

He smiled back at her, teeth gleaming. She made the decision to forget everything else, to enjoy the night, to think about her problems tomorrow. He was just Peter, and she was just Elizabeth, off on an adventure. She thought she'd given up adventures—why did sharing one with him now make her feel so much yearning?

He pulled her downstairs and through a door into a library, softly lit with several low lamps scattered across the tables.

Did everything have to happen to her in a library?

But he kept on going, through a set of double doors and out into the night.

Elizabeth caught her breath, and the magnificent smell of azaleas filled her nostrils. There were torches to the left, where the terrace spilled off from the ballroom, but here, on a lower level, there was only darkness, the light of a half moon, and the faint glow of Peter's face as he looked back at her. He brought her down marble stairs, and gravel crunched beneath her feet.

When she pulled on his arm, he swung back to her, his hands settling easily onto her hips.

"Do you know where you're going?" she asked. "It's rather dark."

"I spent time here with Lady Ludlow's daughter."

A gasp escaped before she could stop it. "I thought it was a different sort of woman you consorted with."

"Consorted with? Was I the subject of rumors?"

"A few."

"Then we're well matched." He lowered his voice and murmured, "Did you think I saved myself for you?"

She hit him on the arm, then let him continue to pull her along. The music and laughter faded away behind her, and although they were in London, it almost felt like another world, as leaves brushed her wide skirts, the moon hung wild above them, and the scents of so many flowers overpowered her. She'd walked in a night garden a time or two, but somehow this was different. She wasn't the one in control, and instead of being frightened, she was excited and intrigued.

The moon was suddenly blocked out, except for pinpricks of light.

"An arbor," Peter said. "It's beautiful during the day, covered in vines and flowers."

His face was invisible, his deep voice a caress. She felt mesmerized, her problems somewhere else, only her body alive in the night.

"But its true purpose is to keep things hidden," he

said, and gathered her against him. "I had forgotten it was here."

He was tall and solid, his legs on either side of hers, her skirts bunching toward the back. She closed her eyes as he suckled her lower lip. With a soft moan, she gave herself to his kisses, to the swipe of his tongue as he sought entrance, to the thrust deep into her mouth that made her shudder. Twining her arms about his neck, she held on, squirming as he rubbed his hands down her back, arching on a gasp as he cupped her backside and pulled her even harder against him.

Was she like a man now, taking her pleasure with no plans for anything more serious? His kisses overpowered and devoured, his hands moved lower, separating her thighs so that she felt the pressure of him even more intimately. They were separated by layers of garments, but it didn't seem to matter to her excited body. He rolled against her, again and again, long and slow and maddening as her body reacted in a wild, uninhibited way.

And then he pulled back, and she almost staggered. Taking her hand once again, he spoke in a hoarse voice that almost didn't sound like him.

"Come, it's too risky here."

She couldn't speak, could barely keep up with his long strides. After the darkness of the vine-covered arbor, the half moon seemed almost too revealing, and she wanted to hide in the night shadows. Soon walls loomed above her, an inkier blackness against the night sky. He followed a turn in the path that took them to a far corner.

"It's a grotto," he said with satisfaction. "Lord Ludlow had it made, rock walls inside and out. Come inside, but duck first."

She didn't have to keep low for long. She heard the running water echo off the stone, the sound gurgling and peaceful in the sudden stillness. Next, she heard them both breathing, and she felt suddenly self-conscious, alone with him, far removed from family or servants.

Again she felt his hands on her shoulders, as he gently pushed her backward. "There's a bench," he said, just as one hit the back of her knees.

She abruptly sat down. "You are very familiar with this place," she said dryly.

He sat down at her side. "To be honest, I played here as a little boy."

Though she had no claim on him, the fact that he hadn't come here with Lady Ludlow's daughter made her feel better.

His voice lower, he murmured, "By day, the water seems to gush out from tumbled rocks until it reaches the small pool. Shells and bright rocks line the bottom, and light glitters with the effect. Even the walls have brilliant stones in them. I can imagine the shimmer across your skin."

She didn't know what to say, how to respond. His words sank into her, around her, like a warm blanket on a cold day. They were almost like poetry—she'd never suspected that Peter had a romantic soul. And then he was kissing her again. She heard a moan and knew it was hers, could not control her response to such unexpected pleasure. It swept over and around her, drawing her down to where passion and heat and touch all merged into one.

He spread kisses down her neck, nibbling behind her ear, grazing with his teeth. It felt wicked and animalistic—and so very good. Her head fell back and her arms dropped from his shoulders so that she hung from the support of his hands at her back. When his open mouth slid from her neck and down the bare expanse of her upper chest, she shuddered, remembering what he'd done to her with his tongue. He didn't disappoint, giving deep kisses to her cleavage, then trailing his tongue along her neckline.

She moaned his name and held his head to her, wanting him to continue rousing this pleasurable rising, this need for more.

And then his hand slid up from her waist and cupped her breast. Even through her low corset she could feel the delicious pressure as he kneaded her.

With an oath, he put his fingers on the rim of her corset and pushed down. It didn't give much, but it was enough, for his bare hand cupped her warm breast down inside her gown. She cried out, and he covered her mouth with his own. Her head swam in confusion, with his tongue in her mouth and his fingers caressing her. When he rubbed over the top of her puckered nipple, the shot of sensation went clear down into her belly, making her squirm and pant. His mouth left her and he bent his head, lifting her breast like an offering.

His tongue lapped at her nipple and she convulsed, moaning and shaking. When she didn't think she could bear more, he drew her into his mouth, suckling hard. She wanted to press herself against him, to wrap herself about him, to pull her clothes off and be free of constraint. The wildness rose higher inside her, urged on by the feel of his other hand sliding under her skirts, parting her legs, sliding up the sensitive skin between her thighs—

And then the rational part of herself, fading fast beneath the rising improper girl she used to be, called out a warning that she was forced to heed.

She put her hand down hard on her thighs, stopping his exploration. "Peter, no!" she cried, breathing so hard she felt faint.

His hands immediately left her, and she fell back on her elbows on the cold stone bench. The draft of air across her damp breast made her shudder. She sat up and turned her back—as if he could see—and tried to right her clothing.

"Elizabeth." He spoke her name in a low, husky voice. "Do not use this on your mystery suitor, who might not be able to stop himself once he tastes you."

"Who?" For a crazy moment she couldn't even remember whom he meant. *William*, she suddenly thought, mortification seeping over her. Peter had made her forget all about the man she thought she loved. How could that be? Did that mean . . . were her feelings for Peter stronger than . . . No. It was William she wanted.

She'd lost all sense, all reason, writhing in Peter's arms, letting him do . . . everything. How would she even face him in the light of day? She felt embarrassed at her weakness, when he was only trying to show her what to expect with a man.

And all her old habits, her risks just for the sake of excitement, were returning with a vengeance.

"Why didn't you prepare me?" she blurted out.

# Chapter 13

**P**eter heard all the hurt and confusion in her trembling voice. He reminded himself of her innocence, the trust she'd shown coming to him for help—her desperation. He told himself she'd agreed to all his terms, had *wanted* to learn how to please her secret suitor, he thought darkly.

Damn, but he wasn't going to do this—wasn't going to have his fun with her, then gift her to another man, who might crush the very spirit that he so admired in Elizabeth. How could she not see how right they were in each other's arms? He'd spent the last few years imagining exploring her body, and the wonder of it exceeded every forbidden expectation.

He wasn't going to go along with them using each other—he was going to convince her that she belonged with him. This false engagement had become far too real in his own heart.

He heard the sound of her troubled breathing, knew

how upset she was. He put a hand on her knee, and although she stiffened, she didn't pull away.

"Elizabeth, one can never be prepared for passion—not the first time. You agreed to all of this."

Her voice was low, bewildered. "I know, but . . . I had no idea what it would *feel* like."

"Overpowering," he murmured.

She said nothing, and he felt the haze of desire suffuse him again.

"Wicked." His voice didn't sound like his own.

She was trembling now, and he wondered if she hugged herself, as she always did under duress. He leaned toward her again, and she shot to her feet, leaving him to brace himself on the bench, now warmed by her body.

"Take me back to the house, Peter."

He stood up, adjusting his trousers in the dark. He took her hand, and her trembling disturbed the vow he'd just made to himself.

"Elizabeth—"

"I think our absence has displayed the right amount of longing for each other, don't you think?"

Reluctantly, he turned in the darkness to the faint light outside. "Don't forget to duck."

"And don't forget your gloves. You took them off."

He found his gloves on the ground beside the bench. His bare hands on her bare flesh were something he wouldn't soon forget.

\* \* \*

Elizabeth felt . . . dazed as she moved through the crowd at Peter's side. The ballroom was hot, and once again she was the subject of so many stares. And it wasn't because she was disheveled. On the terrace she was able to check her décolletage, and everything had been back in its place—

But she couldn't think about that. She couldn't remember the shock of Peter's hand on her breast, or his mouth—

No, she definitely wasn't thinking about *that*.

She felt a tug at her elbow and turned to find Lucy smiling and wide-eyed as she looked between Peter and her.

"Good evening, Miss Gibson," Peter said, bowing to her. "Have you by chance seen my sister?"

She pointed to the far wall, and with his height, he looked over many of the guests.

"Ah, I see her. Would you like to accompany me, Elizabeth?"

Elizabeth thought that if she had to smile nicely at his family, after the sinful things they'd just done together, she would be a quivering wreck. "Would you mind if I join you later? I'd like to speak with Lucy."

He nodded, kissing the back of her hand, his eyes smoldering. Another hot wave of weakness swept over her. She couldn't even pretend it was caused by too many people packed into one small ballroom. He smiled winningly at Lucy before disappearing into the crowd.

Lucy plucked at her skirt and Elizabeth frowned. "What are you doing?"

"I found a leaf caught in your beading!" her friend whispered.

Elizabeth briefly closed her eyes. She wanted to seem desperately in love with Peter, but this was too much.

"You were outside with him?" Lucy asked into her ear.

Elizabeth looked about. "We can't talk here."

"Since the card games are in the drawing room, let's try the library for privacy."

"The library," Elizabeth said grimly. "Of course."

Once inside the empty room, Lucy locked the door. Elizabeth stood awkwardly, trying not to twist her fingers together. She'd already clutched the front of her skirts, perhaps damaging the delicate satin.

Why was she worried? she thought bitterly. Any damage had already been done on a stone bench, under Peter's hands.

When she at last looked into her friend's expectant face, her guilt seemed to sit in the pit of her stomach. Why did she feel this way? After all, Lucy knew almost everything—except about the painting and Thomas's threats—and had approved of her using Peter's courtship methods on William.

But . . . surely Lucy was just as ignorant as she herself

had been about the intimacies between men and women, or she would have argued against Elizabeth's plan.

"How does it go?" Lucy asked. "You were outside with Mr. Derby?" She held up the leaf.

Elizabeth crumpled it and tossed it into the bare hearth. "I was."

"And . . . ?"

"Do you see any other leaves or twigs?"

Lucy circled her. "What were you doing, falling onto the lawn?"

"No, I was on a bench. And I was letting Peter kiss me."

"Oooh! How exciting!"

"Lucy, I am not marrying Peter, remember?"

"I know, but you're not engaged to my brother either. There is no reason to feel embarrassed for kissing a man."

"Being found kissing a man can make a woman engaged very quickly."

"But you're already engaged," Lucy said in a confused voice. "Or so they all think. Why is kissing always taken so seriously?"

"Because of where it leads," Elizabeth whispered, hugging herself.

Lucy's smile faded. "Where did it lead, Elizabeth?"

"Too far. Men like to . . . touch a woman. And it feels far too good. Do you remember how wonderful it felt the first time you danced in a man's arms?"

Lucy nodded uncertainly.

"It is so much better than that."

"But . . . you're not in love with Mr. Derby."

"And he's not in love with me. But that doesn't seem to matter. It's like . . . my body had its own mind, and I wasn't in charge."

Lucy's eyes widened in sudden horror. "Did he . . . ruin you?"

"No! Heavens, no! I stopped it before it went too far. But at least now I know something of what men like."

"And William will like this?"

"I'm certain he will."

Lucy grimaced. "I can't picture my brothers alone with women. It's unnatural."

A reluctant laugh escaped Elizabeth. "Thank you for that distraction. You want William alone with me, don't you?"

"Well, yes, but I don't have to think about it, do I?"

"I don't want to think about it either."

"It was so terrible?"

"Oh no—and that was the problem. How will I face Peter again, remembering the scandalous way he touched me—and the forbidden way he made me feel?"

Peter had gone to bed late and frustrated—and not just out of aching desire for Elizabeth. Yet he'd still awoken early, and was already dressed for riding.

Having learned nothing new about her secrets, at

least he now knew she was not indifferent to his touch. He had known she enjoyed his kisses, of course, but that was far different than sharing the intimacies they had last night. She'd been so responsive, so wonderful—how could she not see that she belonged with him?

He'd had too much experience with women this past year, as he'd striven to change himself, to forget. Being with Elizabeth was like opening a window on the first day of spring—he felt like he'd come back to life, or perhaps found the life he was always meant to have.

But she was innocent; it was up to him to show her the truth. And the only way to do that was to spend even more time together. Elizabeth and Mary Anne were driving in the park this morning. He would "accidentally" meet up with them.

It rained during the night, but the mist had burned off by the time he reached Hyde Park. There were not many carriages, so he thought it would be easy to spot them, but none looked familiar. Had they argued and gone already?

And then in the distance he saw two horses thundering toward him. Two women rode sidesaddle, one with her light hair streaming back—Mary Anne—and one with a jaunty hat perched on her dark hair. Elizabeth. He only briefly glimpsed her expression, but he could not miss her exhilaration, her joy. She'd forgotten her worries with this ride, and he was glad for her.

As they shot past him at a gallop, he lifted a hand, but wasn't sure they even saw him until they gradually slowed the animals to a walk. They circled back toward him, their horses blowing with exertion, their own breathing quickened.

"Couldn't leave us alone for even a morning?" Mary Anne demanded lightly.

Peter shrugged. "I thought you might come to blows."

Rolling her eyes, she asked, "Who won?" then glanced almost haughtily at Elizabeth.

"I didn't really notice," Peter said, finding that he couldn't stop watching Elizabeth, that hat tied with a ribbon beneath her chin making her look so adorable. *Adorable*? What kind of word was that? Hardly masculine vocabulary. "Ravishing" was clearly a better word. There was a flushed glow to her face, and her black eyes gleamed.

"You didn't notice?" Mary Anne said, then followed his gaze to Elizabeth. "Lovesick men," she grumbled.

Elizabeth held his gaze, and her blush only heightened. Her horse nervously danced to the side, and he saw her relief as she looked away to control the animal.

"I think you won, Mary Anne," Elizabeth said.

Mary Anne sighed her frustration. "Don't be so conciliatory."

Elizabeth glanced with more interest at his sister. "You didn't want to win? You're the one who suggested we ride." She looked at Peter, smiling. "I thought we would be driving in a carriage so we could talk."

And then she blushed and couldn't look at him anymore. He knew exactly what she was remembering.

"Too boring," Mary Anne said. "And even you have to admit that was thrilling."

Elizabeth's sparkling eyes gave her away. "It has been some time since I raced."

She'd raced against him in her youth, Peter remembered, sometimes regardless of his protest that the path was too dangerous or the fence too high. She'd been fearless then. Like most adults, she'd learned caution—perhaps too much. And then all her buried wildness had burst forth with that painting.

"You're not bad." Mary Anne's compliment was grudging but seemed sincere.

Peter grinned. "I think she's rather reckless on a horse. Always was."

Elizabeth frowned at him.

Mary Anne didn't notice as she said, "Reckless? She had superb control. Women don't have to sedately walk a horse. I never thought a brother of mine wouldn't understand that."

"I didn't say anything of the kind," Peter answered.

"I imagine you want to ride with her yourself," Mary Anne continued.

Elizabeth straightened, hastily saying, "Oh, no, please

ride with us. It's been a very enjoyable morning."

"Thank you, but I can see true love needs time together. My groom is here somewhere. Have a good day, Lady Elizabeth."

"Call me Elizabeth," Elizabeth said to her retreating back. Then she sighed.

Peter studied her. "That seemed to go well."

Elizabeth shrugged and turned her horse, about to continue walking down the path. "We didn't talk much."

"But she respects your horsemanship."

"I imagine it's a start."

She looked straight ahead as she rode, and although her horse gradually cooled down, she did not, for the blush still lightly touched her face.

Hesitantly, she said, "I was hoping to talk about—"

"You looked magnificent as you galloped toward me," Peter said.

She stiffened so much her horse danced sideways and bumped into his.

"Peter—"

"Your Spanish eyes were alight with fire. You enjoy letting go of your control."

"It was only a race! You and I must have done the same thing dozens of times."

"You always were competitive."

"But I didn't know how very competitive Mary Anne felt toward me," she said glumly. "Not much of a basis for friendship. Especially since I trapped her into accepting my company."

"As you said, it was a start. We can't discover Mary Anne's problem and help her in a day or two."

"We don't have all that much time, Peter. When we break the engagement, any relationship she and I have will be finished."

He didn't intend to break the engagement, but he couldn't very well tell her that.

"We did talk a bit while we waited for the grooms to saddle two horses," Elizabeth said. "Strangely enough, we talked about you."

"Much as you two grew up as neighbors, I seem to be the only common link between you," he said wryly.

"We talked about your businesses again."

"Businesses?"

"I understand you've branched out from railways to shipping. You never told me that."

"It is a natural progression, two different methods of shipping goods. The investment is sound."

"And attending a dinner tonight with the Southern Railway board of directors is part of your investment strategy?"

He hesitated, watching her profile until at last she met his gaze. She was interested, concerned, as if he were hiding a dark secret from her. "Yes."

"Mary Anne says the directors and their wives are attending. She seemed to be very interested that you chose not to invite your fiancée. She was a tad . . . smug."

He winced. "I'm sorry. You know she's not taking this well."

"And she's competitive," Elizabeth added, smiling faintly. "But if I'm pretending to be your fiancée, wouldn't I be invited tonight?"

"I didn't think it would matter to you."

"Won't everyone believe I hold myself above them, that I didn't deign to attend a meeting of industrialists and their wives?"

"I would assure them—"

"I would like to attend, Peter."

"Even after last night?" he asked softly, at last allowing his gaze to travel down her body, to those breasts he'd held and worshipped.

She seemed to stop breathing, then indignantly said, "You're trying to distract me!"

"Elizabeth—"

"Will you take me with you?"

When they were only friends, he would have thought nothing of it. But now his very future with her might ride on this night.

"Very well," he said. "I will call for you at six."

It was her turn to give a smug smile. "I'm looking forward to it."

"But I have one condition."

Her expression turned wary. "And what is that?"

"You wear a gown and corset that are easily removed."

Her mouth dropped open, red flooded her face, and she drew her horse to an uneasy stop. "What kind of wicked condition is that?"

"I'm not finished with your lessons, Elizabeth," he said with quiet firmness.

"I think last night I learned all I want to know!" But her voice was breathless, hesitant.

"Really? You think you know everything? I've taught you how to please a woman, but I don't think that lesson will do you much good."

"But—"

"Doesn't this reluctant mystery suitor of yours need persuasion?"

"I—I—" She practically sputtered, and no coherent words formed.

He leaned an elbow on the pommel and gave her a knowing look. "I promise to wear something equally easy to remove. Now why don't I escort you back to my town house, so you can take your carriage home."

Her lips practically slammed together in a straight, prim line as she nodded and rode ahead of him.

# Chapter 14

That night, Peter sat across from Elizabeth in the carriage and watched her squirm. She didn't meet his eyes, only looked out the window as if she'd never seen Mayfair before and was fascinated. But she must have been very aware of him, for every time he adjusted his position, she flinched. He didn't try to make conversation, didn't try to seduce her—that would come later.

The deep green gown she wore was elegant, but without elaborate decorations. He was almost tempted to ask her to show him the fastenings, but decided that would make her too nervous. Let her think he was only teasing her this morning.

When the carriage stopped after a very short time, she at last gave him an astonished look. "We're here already?"

"Mr. Bannaster has a fashionable town house. He's made himself a very wealthy man."

As they waited for the footman to open the door, she said, "He is married, yes?"

He nodded.

"And how many people will be here tonight?"

"I would think less than twenty, but I'm not certain of the exact amount. Other people might bring guests, just like I'm bringing you."

"You didn't tell them I was accompanying you?" she demanded, her expression aghast.

"I only decided this morning."

"But—But—Mrs. Bannaster will have worked out the seating arrangements, and now my presence will change all of her plans!"

"I'm certain she'll be fine with it," he said, surprised at her reaction.

"Oh—you men!" She flounced back in her seat and folded her arms across her chest. "Do you think a dinner party just magically happens?"

He frowned. "No, it looks like there is some effort involved."

"And *seating arrangements*!"

She would have said more, but the door was opened from the outside, the step lowered, and a white-wigged footman bowed and reached to help her descend. Peter followed, then offered her his arm as they walked up the stairs.

In the gilded entrance hall, Elizabeth lagged behind to hand her wrap to the butler, so Peter faced their host and hostess first.

"Bannaster," he said, nodding as he shook the older man's hand and smiled at his wife. "Mrs. Bannaster, thank you so much for offering us your home for the evening."

They were both middle-aged and stout, but with a vitality that seemed to come along with being a part of a new industry transforming the world.

Elizabeth appeared at his side, smiling and lovely. Mrs. Bannaster arched a brow at Peter even as she smiled back.

Peter cleared his throat. "Please forgive me for failing to notify you in advance, but I've brought my fiancée. Mr. and Mrs. Bannaster, this is Lady Elizabeth Cabot."

Mr. Bannaster's bushy brows rose halfway up his forehead, while Mrs. Bannaster's face paled and her mouth briefly fell open. Peter felt Elizabeth's hand tense on his arm, and he knew she feared that her worries were coming true.

Then Mrs. Bannaster burst into a silly grin and sank into a curtsy. "Milady, what an honor ye do me!"

Mrs. Bannaster's accent betrayed her humble East London beginnings, but to Peter it was a testament to her determination.

Elizabeth blinked for a moment at the effusive greeting, then her smile returned, although to Peter's trained eye she still appeared worried.

Elizabeth curtsied back. "Please, Mrs. Bannaster,

the honor is all mine. I hope I have not inconvenienced you."

"Oh, my dear, of course not! Do come in and allow me to introduce ye." As she took Elizabeth's arm to lead her forward, she looked back at Peter. "What a devil you are, Mr. Derby, snarin' yourself a lady."

He exchanged a laugh with her husband, but he wished he could have seen Elizabeth's expression.

Mrs. Bannaster led Elizabeth about the drawing room, introducing her to the Staplehills, the Perries, the Huttons, and the Wiltons. The husbands were all directors of the Southern Railway. One by one the ladies curtsied and the men bowed, and Elizabeth responded to each. Whenever she moved from one group to the next, the women she left behind reacted the same way, gaping at each other behind her back as if royalty were in their midst. The men had one identical reaction as well—an approving grin for Peter.

"And of course you must know Lord and Lady Thurlow," Mrs. Bannaster said last.

Viscount Thurlow, heir to the Earl of Banstead, was a tall, powerfully built man with pale blue eyes that gleamed with intelligent amusement. His wife was small and plump, with hair so blond as to look like a halo about her head.

"Lady Elizabeth, it is good to see you again," Lord Thurlow said.

She curtsied to him. "Good evening, Lord Thurlow."
Then she smiled at his wife. "Lady Thurlow, I am so
sorry I was unable to attend your last reception for the
arts. It is the favorite event of my cousin, Miss Susanna
Leland."

"We missed her this week, Lady Elizabeth. Her
knowledge of painting has helped so many students."

"She is away from London temporarily," Elizabeth
admitted.

Peter wondered if Leo was having any luck chasing
Susanna back to town. He imagined they were close to
killing each other by now.

"And how is your son?" Elizabeth asked.

"The little baron is the joy of our lives," Lady Thurlow said, glancing up into the soft eyes of her husband.

He cleared his throat. "That is her pet name for him.
I firmly believe using his honorary title like this will
only give him airs."

"Nonsense," said Lady Thurlow. "He understands
subtleties."

"At one year old," Lord Thurlow said dryly.

"He is very intelligent," Lady Thurlow confided to a
smiling Elizabeth.

As the ladies continued to talk, and several other
women joined them, Peter found himself standing
beside Lord Thurlow.

"I hear Lady Elizabeth was a last minute addition to

the party," Thurlow commented, eyeing him. "You've been engaged for several days, yet you didn't intend to bring her tonight?"

Peter sighed. "I am not certain how her family will take my involvement in Southern Railway."

"She doesn't know the details?"

Peter shook his head. "Up until now, people assume I'm simply investing capital, and I haven't needed to explain." He eyed the viscount. "You don't feel the need to hide your directorship?"

Thurlow smiled. "Once, I did, but I have gotten over caring how Society views me. You will, too."

"But you will be an earl, and I will never be other than a gentleman."

"But your brother-in-law will be a duke," Thurlow said dryly. "And you know him very well. Surely that connection matters."

"But marrying his sister—then embarrassing the family—could easily make me his enemy."

"I don't think Madingley embarrasses easily. Tell your lady what you're doing. If she's involved with *you*, she'll be proud."

Peter nodded, but he wasn't convinced.

Not long after, as the crowd shifted again, Elizabeth found herself alone with Peter, watching the railway directors and their wives mingle. She felt a bit more at ease after Mrs. Bannaster's enthusiastic welcome, but to her bemusement, she was almost underdressed, as the ladies' gowns were quite stylish. She hadn't wanted to make a haughty impression for Peter's business associates.

For a moment she wondered what they would think of her when she ended her engagement to Peter. But she didn't let herself think of the future often. It was difficult enough to manage the present.

"Everyone is very generous with their welcome," she said to Peter. "I like them."

"I'm glad."

"Did you think I wouldn't?"

He chuckled. "You can't believe that. You like everyone, and everyone likes you."

"Except—"

"Except my sister, but she'll come around."

Her gaze roamed the guests, all of an older generation except the Staplehills and the Thurlows. "So these men are railway directors?"

He nodded without elaborating. She could see she was going to have to pry more details out of him, glad she had something to occupy her mind so she wouldn't have to think about what he had planned for the carriage ride home.

"Do they regularly invite investors to dinner parties?" she asked, gesturing toward Lord Thurlow.

"Thurlow is not just an investor. He owns the majority shares, and is a director on the board."

Surprised, Elizabeth glanced up at Peter. "He's in trade? I had no idea."

"It isn't a secret. And it's not quite the same thing as being in trade. He is an industrialist. Being heir to an earldom helps a man overcome Society's disapproval. Julian is a director as well."

"Julian?" she asked in surprise. "Lord Parkhurst, who's even now chasing my cousin Rebecca?"

He grinned. "The very one."

"So if all of these men are directors . . ." She let her words trail off, not breaking her gaze with Peter.

"So am I."

He wasn't smiling, and she knew he awaited her opinion. She almost spoke flippantly, reminding him that it wouldn't affect her because she wasn't really engaged to him.

But . . . it was obvious he had withheld the depth of his involvement because he cared about her opinion. It saddened her to think he couldn't confide in her.

But of course she wasn't confiding in him either. The ache inside her rose up again, but she battled it down.

"Congratulations, Peter," she said softly. "You've taken the little money you had and accomplished so much."

He smiled. "Thank you. The rewards for me have been about more than money."

"I can see that. I know it was difficult being a younger son, thinking you'd never have much. Instead, like these people, who also didn't inherit their wealth, you've worked hard to reinvent yourself. And now you're a railway director."

"You don't have to say that loudly at *ton* events," he said. "I don't want to embarrass you."

"You could never do that, Peter."

"I admit, I've been swept up in this new industry."

His voice took on a depth of enthusiasm and excitement she'd never seen in him before. And she liked it.

"Every industry will soon be controlled by those of us moving the goods and services. It's a future we never imagined. Our railway corridors are lined with the wires of the new electric telegraph—instant communication across the country."

She laughed. "I can see why you're so excited."

"It's more than that. You've ridden on the railways, haven't you?"

She nodded. "It's thrilling to move so fast, to see the scenery fly by. But perhaps you can do something about the cold drafts that lift my skirts."

Grinning, he said, "In good time. The way to accomplish a broad change is to consolidate the railways. In the last few years we've acquired several other railroads, standardizing the tracks, so every train runs on every rail. It's ridiculous that when you reach the end of one railway, owned by one company, you sometimes have to drive across town to reach the beginning of the next. We've even begun to build new lines into Cornwall, once so remote—" He broke off. "I'm boring you."

Elizabeth put her hand on his arm and squeezed. "Never think that. I am fascinated by your interest and your passion."

They looked at each other.

"For railways," she quickly said.

His smile faded into quiet intimacy and his gaze dropped from her eyes to her mouth.

"Keep telling me about Cornwall!" she said brightly.

"Perhaps I now want to tell you about my more personal plans."

And then the butler announced that dinner was served, and Elizabeth felt she'd escaped just in time. But she wouldn't be able to put off Peter for long.

Elizabeth lingered in the drawing room after dinner until they were almost the last couple to leave the party.

Mrs. Bannaster said, "Ye've enlivened this dull old gatherin', Lady Elizabeth. We'll certainly talk again about the Society for the Rescue of Young Women and Children."

"We are always in need of help, Mrs. Bannaster. Thank you for your interest."

"And thank you for attendin' tonight. I would have

thought ladies like you were very . . . different."

Mr. Bannaster rolled his eyes and winced.

Elizabeth laughed. "I hope you see we're not very different after all." Then Peter took her arm, and tension crept up her back.

"It's time for me to return my lady to her home," he said.

She couldn't resist, she couldn't retreat, so she merely followed him down to the entrance hall and waited for her wrap and the summoning of the carriage. Peter and Mr. Bannaster discussed an imminent contract, but she could not concentrate on their discussion.

Why was she so nervous? All she had to do was say no to whatever he had planned for their carriage ride, and Peter would abide by her wishes.

But . . . *could* she say no? She'd tossed and turned all the previous night reliving the steamy darkness of the grotto and Peter's hands and mouth upon her. It had been exciting and terrifying all at the same time. To think her body had been capable of flowering like a new blossom, unfurling, reaching—

Reaching for what? Certainly there must be more, besides the actual act of procreation. But she was afraid to find out.

And desperate to find out at the same time.

It wasn't Peter she didn't trust—it was herself. These sensations were new and overpowering—and forbidden for a reason. She didn't want to feel like this, yet was lured to it as if pulled by an invisible rope. Her old longings to explore what she didn't understand rose unbidden.

The night was dark and warm, gaslights gleaming in the distance. Lamps hung from the front and rear of the carriage, and the coachman gave her a smile, as if reassuring her. Oh, that was her imagination.

But then she realized that the coachman was nodding to Peter. A signal of some kind?

The interior of the carriage was lit by another small lamp hung in the corner. She sat down, spreading her skirts wide, and Peter must have taken the hint, for he sat across from her.

The door closed, and she coolly met his stare, lifting her chin. She shouldn't antagonize him, but she couldn't help it. This morning's race had proven just how competitive she could be. Let him try—

He lowered the blinds on both windows as the carriage jerked into motion.

"I like to look outside," she said defiantly.

"I don't want anyone looking *inside*. The coachman has instructions not to return to Madingley House until I give the signal."

His voice was low and seemed to etch its way through her, as if she were raw with expectancy.

She gaped at him. "But—"

"You wanted lessons. Where else but in a carriage will we find enough privacy to explore everything you need to know?"

Shakily, she said, "There cannot be *that* much to tell me."

"*Tell*? Telling is for mothers as they inform brides about the wedding night. Have you already had that speech?"

She gulped, but nodded, thinking of her mother telling her the truth so she wouldn't be afraid. Elizabeth had eagerly listened to the unveiling of the mystery. At her mother's explanation of a man putting part of himself inside her, she'd tried to think of William's face looking into hers, but damn him, it was Peter's knowing gaze, his haunting smile, his body on top of hers. She squeezed her eyes shut. And there had been something about caresses and preparation, but it had already fled her mind.

"Peter . . . have you . . ." Oh, how could she even ask it? "Do you have . . . a mistress?"

"Not now." His eyes were hooded, serious. "I'm too busy with you."

She couldn't look away from him, didn't want to. Was she really going to let him show her more?

"Last night I gave you a glimpse of a woman's pleasure," he continued softly. "But you need to know how to seduce a man—"

"I'm not seducing—him." Heavens, she'd almost said William's name!

Peter's eyes narrowed but he didn't press her. She was frankly surprised he hadn't interrogated her more, but always thought he was respecting her privacy about such a sensitive issue. But perhaps he didn't want to know William's name. The realization was surprising, intriguing. Could Peter be . . . jealous?

"Seduction is about making a man want you," he said softly. "This man has to be blind not to be attracted to you, but since you insist on moving forward, you need to know how to persuade a man."

"Are you attracted to me, Peter?" Then she covered her mouth—where had that come from?

He gave her a wry half smile. "Again, a man would have to be blind not to be attracted to you. You're a beautiful woman, Elizabeth, with a lively intelligence and a good heart."

She felt a pang that her "good heart" was keeping secrets, but it was for Peter's protection, too.

"So, what lesson did you learn in the grotto last night?" he asked.

She blinked at him, her skin too hot, her nerves flickering wildly. "Lesson?" she croaked. "We're going to . . . discuss it?"

A faint smile playing at the corners of his mouth, he said nothing more.

"A lesson learned," she muttered, trying to force her brain to work. "Touch . . . is very important."

"So if *you* like to be touched, what is the conclusion?" he asked, tilting his head.

"That a man likes to be touched," she whispered.

His grin was slow and steamy, half in shadow, half in flickering lamplight. He spread his arms wide, as if presenting himself.

She looked at his broad chest and swallowed. "Can't you just . . . tell me what to do?"

He tsked, shaking his head. "Elizabeth, Elizabeth, what would you learn from that? I think you need to experiment and see what I like. Trust me; men are the same about this. Come here—or should I come to you?"

Biting her lip, she let her shawl drop. It was a warm night, too warm inside the carriage. She already felt overheated, overdressed—and he'd threatened to take care of that problem. But he couldn't if she was in charge.

As she studied him, she thought of his own whispered words of passion last night. He'd been just as affected as she was, and he'd been doing all the touching. But she'd kissed him back, too, and now she knew some of what he liked.

As the carriage rocked rhythmically, she half stood, then slid onto the bench next to him, pushing down her skirts as best she could. His arms now rested wide against the back of the seat, as if to give her access to more of him. He looked down on her, his blue eyes gleaming, that infuriating smile on his mouth, but he seemed suddenly too watchful.

His coat was unbuttoned, and she remembered being held against the solid wall of his chest. She'd seen nude statues in the Madingley gallery, of course, but hadn't imagined that Peter might look like that beneath his proper garments. She reached forward and slid her hand beneath his coat, across his chest. He inhaled and didn't let his breath out, but when she looked quickly up into his face, he was still smiling. She wanted to wipe the superiority right off his face. Staring into his eyes, she moved her hand across his chest, feeling the hills and valleys of muscle. And then she began to unbutton his waistcoat.

Still, he had no other reaction. Once the garment was loose, her hand drifted across the fine linen of his shirt, molding him, feeling his chest. To her surprise, she felt the pucker of his nipple, and he gave a jerk. She looked back up into his face. At least that smile was gone. Remembering what he'd done to her, she let her thumb brush over and over the tight point.

His hand suddenly cupped the back of her head, and he drew her mouth toward his.

"No!" She resisted, and at his baffled look, she said, "I'm touching you, remember. I'll do what I want."

And then he shuddered, but he did release her. This

feeling of power actually felt good. She could affect him.

And then her skirts escaped from beneath her elbow and pushed up between them.

"Take off your petticoats," he ordered. "You're surely wearing dozens of them."

True, they *were* in her way, and she positively wasn't removing anything else. Sliding to the edge of the bench, she pulled up the back of her skirt, where Peter couldn't see, and fumbled for the laces on the first petticoat. She felt ridiculous lifting her hips up two separate times, especially for the inner petticoat, which was made of stiffened horsehair to hold the shape of her skirt. She tugged and tugged, but Peter never laughed at her.

At last she tossed both petticoats on the opposite bench. She was able to turn toward him much easier now, even though her knees bumped his thigh.

"Straddle me. You'll be able to reach anything you want."

"And so will you!"

"You're seducing *me*, remember?"

"I'm *learning* from you." She knew very well it was indecent. She knew where . . . that part of a man's anatomy was supposed to go.

But she had gone along with him, and there was an imp inside her that urged her to try, to see what would happen, what she could learn. *He had all his clothes on*, the imp whispered in her ear.

So before she could second-guess herself, she got up on one knee and slid the other over his thighs, folding her skirt down between them even as she settled near his knees. He still kept his arms wide on the bench, not threatening her, and she was even with his face now.

They looked at each other, both of them breathing more rapidly than normal. Feeling his hard thighs along the inside of hers made her feel vulnerable, too open to him. But she couldn't stop thinking of those statues, so she spread his waistcoat and coat wide on his chest. "Take these off," he said.

He leaned forward, his head bent near her face— with a view down her cleavage, she was sure—and she pushed his coat off his shoulders. There was almost as much tugging as she'd done with her petticoats, but at least the sleeveless waistcoat was easier.

And then she started to explore, putting both hands on his chest, feeling his nipples in her palms, his muscles flexing and tensing beneath her hands. He dropped his head back on the bench and closed his eyes as she slipped her hands up his shoulders and down his arms. It was amazing how different an arm could be on a man, no softness, nothing but long lengths of hard muscle. She remembered watching him fence once, and knew he still exercised that way.

She tugged at his cravat, ruining the starch as she pulled it from around his neck. There were three little buttons below, and she undid them one by one to see the hollow of his throat—and a few curls of light brown hair.

"You have hair on your chest?" she asked in surprise.

His voice sounded tight. "I imagine there are a few other differences between us."

So she tugged the shirt out of his waistband and let her hands slide up underneath. She was rewarded with another shudder. She felt the ridges of muscle, then the tickle of hair along her fingers.

"Just kiss me," he murmured. "A man needs to be kissed."

Her hands sliding around his waist, she leaned in and kissed him over and over, her lips slightly parted, meeting with his as she turned her head this way and that. She licked his chin and felt the rasp deliciously along her tongue. With her mouth she traced the tendons of his throat, moving lower, even as she lifted his shirt. She was trembling with excitement, no longer nervous. Her body felt hot and yearning and tingling, especially down low between her spread thighs. She wanted to press herself against him, remembering how he'd done that last night. But then there had been so many more clothes between them.

She kissed the center of his bare chest, then hovered above his nipple. With a wicked glance up at him, she whispered, "Should I? This touch certainly felt good."

"God, yes." His voice was hoarse and unrecognizable.

She leaned forward and licked his nipple, slow strokes, then tickling little strokes, until she drew the little bit into her mouth. With a groan, he put his arms around her. She straightened in surprise at the way he took over, about to protest. Then he pulled her hard against him. Her open thighs straddled his hips, and she gasped as her softness met a long hard length.

"Is that the part of a man that goes inside a wife?" she asked.

"And it can do other miraculous things. No more questions."

And then he was kissing her, deep, throat-touching kisses that explored her mouth. She met his tongue, played with it, suckled it. And all the while he moved between her legs, rolling against her as he had last night.

But this time—this time it felt even better.

# Chapter 15

**P**eter was dazed with lust, overcome by the knowledge that at last he held a very willing Elizabeth in his arms. Why ever she had agreed to this playing, he didn't care. There was no other man between them now—she held nothing back.

And the feel of her hot depths cradling his erection, even through his trousers, almost made him come. But he thrust his tongue into her mouth instead, trying to hold her hips still, but she kept wiggling, kept pressing herself, her little moans lost between their lips. He had to have more of her.

Never breaking their kiss, he swiftly unhooked her gown to her waist. As the fabric fell forward, her arms became trapped and she could no longer hold him. He didn't even know if she realized that she pulled her arms from the short tight sleeves, but then her hands were on him again, up under his shirt in the back, caressing him as he'd imagined a thousand times during long sleepless nights.

The corset laces came free next, and he was able to pull the contraption right over her head. Before he could even gather her breasts in his hands, she groaned and leaned into him, rubbing herself all over him. Then he took her shoulders and laid her back on his thighs. He cupped her breasts through her chemise, and she moaned and arched into his hands, her hips pressing even harder against his erection, her head spilling back over his knees. He played with her nipples through the linen, but at last he bared her to his hungry gaze. Her breasts were perfect, darkly rouged at the tips, full enough that she wouldn't fit into his mouth.

But he was going to test that theory. He bent over the feast of her body and pressed his mouth between her breasts, moving back and forth to feel the sloping curves against his cheeks.

"Peter, oh Peter!"

That was *his* name on her lips, no other man's, thank God. He rewarded her by circling her nipple with his tongue, then taking it into his mouth. She cried out and held his head to her. She was rocking against him, he was rocking into her, and it would be so easy to unbutton his trousers, to give her what they each so desperately wanted—

But did he want *this* to be Elizabeth's first memory of lovemaking? Rushed and cramped in a carriage circling

London? This was the woman he wanted to marry, not some mistress to be treated so roughly.

He pulled her upright, and her dark, feverish eyes searched his face. "Please, Peter, please, don't stop."

"But I have to," he said, his own voice trembling. "You wouldn't forgive either of us otherwise."

Her eyes widened, invaded with her first regrets. He wanted to find some way to end this more playfully.

"Let me see you," he said.

"What?" she murmured, shaking her head.

He slid all the way to the left on the bench, then lay her out next to him, pulling her skirt down around her hips until he could just see the top of her dark pubic curls.

"Arch your body, Elizabeth. Lift your arms over your head. Show me the pose captured in the painting."

For the briefest moment she did so, and the lamplight caught the creamy skin of her breasts, the indentation of her navel, the erotic bones of her hips.

And then she started to cry.

"Elizabeth?"

He lifted her up and tried to hold her, but their bare flesh touching only seemed to make her cry harder, so he pulled her chemise up between them and readjusted her so she sat across his lap rather than straddling him.

"I'm sorry," she said, using the back of her forearm

to wipe her face, and her words continued to tumble out. "This isn't your fault, none of it's your fault. It's all because of me."

When she trembled in his arms, he pressed her head to his shoulder so he could kiss her soft hair. An ache built in the center of his chest, spreading outward, tightening his throat.

"Elizabeth—"

"No, don't find some excuse to hold me blameless. I'm the one who forced you into a public engagement; I'm the one who wanted to *practice* on you, for God's sake."

"And I haven't complained."

"But don't you see?" She tilted her head up, and the light caught the tears that streaked her face. "I'm behaving just like my brother!"

He knew he gaped at her, but he was dumbfounded. "Like Madingley? What does he have to do with us?"

"I have forgotten myself," she whispered. "Once I realized—realized how my antics affected my family, I tried to be so good, so level-headed, the one not attracted to scandal in any way."

"And you've been all of those things."

"Oh, I convinced myself it was true. But there's this—passion inside me, these emotions I obviously don't know how to control. You warned me—you said that underneath I was reckless and wild."

"But—"

"And I didn't believe you! I didn't *want* to believe you! Even though I had my brother's example to follow. He fought so hard to prove himself because he was half Spanish, thinking fighting made people forget his heritage."

"You've never had to prove yourself."

"No? Then what do you think I'm doing right now? Perhaps I'm proving that I'm desirable, that just because one man doesn't want me, another does."

"Elizabeth—"

"Peter, you know that Chris's temper was so uncontrollable that he fought a man, and the man lost the use of his legs!"

"It was an accident. Michael Preston hit his head. And he was the one provoking the fight. Don't forget that his medical condition has improved, I hear."

"It doesn't matter. It wasn't until Mr. Preston couldn't walk that Chris realized how out of control he was. Chris still has a difficult time living with the fact that our father died thinking he would destroy the dukedom with his irresponsible ways."

"That didn't happen."

"No, it didn't. But I was so smug—I never thought *I* had such problems! I had grown up, matured, become the perfect lady. But here I am, my passions out of control so much that I can't even stay true to one man!"

"You're not being fair to yourself, my sweet. This nameless man doesn't even know how you feel."

"I thought I was trying to show him," she whispered. "But I guess I can't trust myself."

She climbed off his lap and Peter didn't try to stop her. He wanted to hit something, to lash out because of his own stupidity—but that would only frighten her. Had he learned nothing from all his mistakes, his belief that he was always in the right? He obviously didn't know the depth of Elizabeth's pain. But he'd never been one to dwell on emotional pain.

Instead he began to pull his clothing back on as she did the same. After struggling into her corset, she was balanced on the end of the bench, trying to reach the laces, but wasn't having much success.

"Let me help," he said gently.

With a sigh and slump of her shoulders, she did. Soon he had her laced up, and then her gown hooked back together. She wrapped her shawl around herself so tightly that for a moment he felt as if she were guarding against his attack.

But he knew she didn't believe that of him. Holding back a sigh, he reached behind him and knocked on the ceiling, alerting the coachman.

Elizabeth gave a dispirited sigh. "If I would have known it was that easy, I would have tried it myself."

He only arched a brow.

"No, no, that's not true. I didn't try to get away from you at all."

"Perhaps you didn't want to get away from what we feel."

Wearing a bleak expression, she murmured, "It's wrong for our bodies to feel like that."

He thought she was deliberately misunderstanding him—or perhaps she really was such an innocent. He let it go.


Mary Anne knew she'd lost the horse race yesterday, so she accepted her punishment with determined grace—a shopping trip with Elizabeth. Peter had escorted her to Madingley House, then left her alone in a drawing room. There was a palace to explore, she realized—and a billiard room to find. It was all too easy, for the servants were happy to help.

In the doorway of the billiard room, she stopped in awe. There were *two* tables. The ceiling was carved in the most intricate designs, flowing about the set of lamps lighting the center of each table. The cues were lined in racks on the wall, and she reached for one, admiring the balanced weight of it, then began to place the balls on the table.

"You must be out of reading material."

She gave a start at the interruption, glad she wasn't about to make a shot. To her surprise, Lord Thomas

Wythorne leaned in the doorway, all lazy elegance. She'd first seen him dancing with Elizabeth at the Ludlow ball. He was handsome in that arrogant way of aristocrats, with brown waves of hair about sharp cheekbones. He'd looked down on Elizabeth with too much boldness, a rakish smile never leaving his face. A confident man, so sure of his place in the world. Mary Anne couldn't imagine how that felt.

Now, his knowing smile made it seem like he guessed everything about her, every weakness. She stiffened. No wonder Elizabeth had looked like she wanted to escape him.

Mary Anne lifted her chin and spoke coolly. "We haven't been introduced."

He walked toward her, his stride long and loose and graceful. Then he bowed, his eyes never leaving her face. "Thomas Wythorne."

"Don't forget the 'lord' at the beginning. It's right there in your voice."

He only chuckled. "So you know of me."

"I saw you dancing with Lady Elizabeth, and since she is to be my sister-in-law, I made it my business to know who you are."

Something flickered in his eyes. "Sister-in-law? Then you must be Peter Derby's sister."

"Brilliant deduction, my lord." Mary Anne never allowed herself to be alone with men—especially men who exuded danger from their very pores. She could feel a faint tremble thrum through her, but there was something about his sense of entitlement that annoyed her, that made her speak more freely than she usually did. She held the cue planted on the floor and looked him in the eyes. "And here's *my* brilliant deduction," she continued. "You're visiting here, just as I am."

"Passing the time while my mother and the dowager duchess gossip."

Gossip. That's all he thought women did. It infuriated her.

"Do you play?" he asked. "Or are you bedeviled by boredom?"

She let her demeanor soften into regret as she glanced at the table. "My brother taught me the rules, but he hasn't found the time to practice with me."

"I imagine Lady Elizabeth is a demanding fiancée."

There was the faintest question in his voice, and that made her curious enough to look into his handsome face again. "Demanding? They've only just announced the engagement. Both mothers certainly expect a lot from them right now."

"Defending them both. How admirable."

Defending her brother anyway. She looked at the door, hoping he would take the hint and leave.

"You're not surprised by this sudden engagement?" he persisted.

Whatever her feelings, they were none of his business. "Not at all. Peter accomplished what he wanted."

He frowned briefly, and she thought she would have to refuse to discuss her brother's private life, but Lord Thomas walked to the elegantly detailed racks on the wall and chose a cue.

"Since both of us are passing the time," he said, "shall we play a game?"

He'd stepped right into the trap she'd set for him, and all she had to do was close it tight.

"You will certainly beat me and won't enjoy it at all. You would do better to find men to bet with."

"I have money," he said.

She widened her eyes. "Really? You would play *me* for money? How wicked!" She hadn't come prepared for a game, but she did have several pounds in her purse. She pulled the coins out and set them on the baize cloth of the table.

He grinned. "Won't they be in the way there?"

"Of course you're right." She set them aside, then smiled at him. "Don't even bother producing your purse, my lord. We both know the outcome. Now you go ahead and go first."

He chalked the tip of his cue. "Do you know English billiards?"

She drew out her hesitation. "The one with the two white balls and the red?"

He nodded, and she reluctantly had to give him credit for not appearing too patronizing. Then the game was on, and he began to accumulate points. She was very good at playing confused and uncertain. And she'd mastered girlish giggling as if it were an art form.

When she put her ball right off the table, she gasped. "Oh, dear, that's a foul, isn't it? Two points for you."

She let him get comfortably in the lead, before she decided she'd made him out to be a fool long enough. She began to "accidentally" accumulate points, making one shot when she'd attempted another, acting quite excited and stunned when a ball sank into a pocket.

When it was his turn and she was only a few points behind him, Thomas leaned a hip against the table and studied her.

"Do you usually win the purse like this?" he asked casually.

She straightened and met his stare, her smile deliberately coy. "I don't know what you're talking about."

He didn't say anything, just continued to smile.

She finally couldn't help but laugh. "You caught me."

"You're a sharp," he said slowly, with even a bit of admiration.

"Compliments won't work with me. Why don't we finish the game, my lord?"

They did, and he won. She handed over her coins.

"I'm not certain I can take this from a lady. Shall we

play again? I am very impressed at your skill misdirecting shots that still score points. Perhaps you can teach me a trick or two."

She blinked at him. Men didn't usually like to lose to a woman—and he hadn't lost, although his temporary belief in her charade was a loss of sorts. But he didn't bluster about how she'd lied to him. He saw through her, not assuming she was stupid, as so many men did. She liked that.

But he was still a strange, intimidating man.

Elizabeth strode down Bond Street with Mary Anne at her side. The sun peaked through puffy white clouds, the temperature was pleasant, and other shoppers crowded the pavement. She told herself to enjoy the day, glad that Mary Anne didn't seem to mind looking in every shop window, which Elizabeth always enjoyed. It helped her forget about her embarrassing confession to Peter.

She was allowing herself to become distracted from her goals. Only two weeks remained before her brother returned for the Kelthorpe Masked Ball. If she didn't have her own life figured out, Christopher would do it for her—for her own good, he'd tell her.

She had to let go of her anxiety over every returning weakness she discovered in herself. No one was perfect. Why did she hold herself to a higher standard than anyone else? It was better to understand her faults and improve. Now that she knew she could lose control of her emotions again, she would do a better job of containing them. Her brother had mastered that skill; so could she. Peter had somehow brought them out of her, and she should thank him for showing her the truth.

But she knew she wasn't going to do that. When Peter had brought his sister to the house that afternoon, Elizabeth made sure she was never alone with him, although he tried to make that happen. He wanted to talk everything to death, trying to help her. He seemed very eager to talk, unless it was about his recent, mysterious past.

She told herself that she was getting swept away learning what might please William, when she should be spending more time in William's presence. That was the logical conclusion. Only . . . it was starting to seem pointless, even . . . uninteresting.

How could she think that? she wondered, aghast.

Lucy's note this morning, telling her that William would be attending the Royal Italian Opera at Covent Garden this night, was the perfect solution for her to refocus herself—on both of her goals.

"Mary Anne?"

Peter's sister must not have heard her, because she continued walking, her gaze unfocused.

"Mary Anne?"

The woman gave a start, her smile distracted. "Yes, Lady Elizabeth?"

Elizabeth touched her arm. "I wish you wouldn't use my title. We've never needed to be formal with each other."

Mary Anne nodded, saying nothing.

"Would you like to attend the opera tonight? It is the opening of *Benvenuto Cellini*."

"Will Peter be attending?"

"I mentioned it to him this morning, and he agreed to escort me."

"Then since my mother will insist I go anyway, I accept."

"Such eagerness for my company overwhelms me," Elizabeth said dryly.

Mary Anne's eyes focused on her at last. "Is that sarcasm from the perfect Lady Elizabeth?"

Elizabeth winced, but she understood. "I am capable of it. I try not to use it, but sometimes I'm provoked."

Mary Anne nodded slowly. "You're not usually competitive, but yesterday I provoked that response in you as well."

"You don't know me as well as you think. I'm very competitive."

They stopped at a dressmaker's window where colorful ribbons were on display. Elizabeth hoped Mary Anne would like them, but she only continued to regard her.

"If you're so competitive," Mary Anne said, "then you won't mind that while you made me wait today, I played billiards with one of your guests."

"A guest?" Elizabeth said with a frown, choosing not to respond to the goading about her tardiness.

"Lord Thomas."

She stiffened, but tried not to show it. "Yes, I saw him briefly. He'd arrived with his mother, but I was already running late, and I didn't want to keep you."

"So he came to see you?"

"No, he accompanied his mother to see my mother."

Mary Anne nodded thoughtfully and looked back at the window. Elizabeth suspected she wasn't really seeing it.

"I think that color blue would be lovely with your hair," Elizabeth said. "Shall we purchase a length?"

"I'm not fond of frills," Mary Anne said distractedly. Then her gaze turned keen. "You don't mind that I played billiards with him?"

"Mind? No, of course not. You have a passion for the game." Peter had already deduced that forbidding his sister would only make things worse. "Was anyone else playing with you both?"

It was Mary Anne's turn to stiffen; it was in her wary eyes, and in the way she fisted her hands before putting them behind her back. "Afraid I will embarrass you?"

Elizabeth touched the other woman's arm. "Of course

not! I only care about your reputation, since Lord Thomas has his own reputation as a rake."

"Really?" That deflated her defensiveness, and her voice turned curious. "He didn't seem that way to me."

"And that's another reason to make more friends in Society. You'll learn of whom to be wary."

Mary Anne shrugged and started walking again.

Elizabeth knew not to press her advice too hard. "My favorite dressmaker is just down the block. Do you mind if we stop in, so I can pick up a gown I just had made?"

Mary Anne nodded.

If Elizabeth hoped to have the woman try on a sample dress or two, those hopes died as Mary Anne remained seated and watched her being fawned over by the clerks. It was embarrassing, and certainly made her seem even more above a commoner like Mary Anne. Not the impression Elizabeth wanted to leave at the end of the afternoon.

She would have another chance at the opera to leave a better impression on Mary Anne—and William, she reminded herself quickly.

# Chapter 16

**P**eter walked the crowded corridors during intermission, Elizabeth displayed on his arm. The Royal Italian Opera House with its elaborately painted ceiling and immense chandelier hanging over the grand staircase was the place to be seen—and they were being very well seen.

Who wouldn't look upon Elizabeth? She wore blue and white striped silk, like a wrapped confection in a candy shop. Her shoulders were bare, palest peach, the top curves of her breasts well displayed. It was enough to make his mouth water. He hadn't nearly tasted enough last night—and he suspected, from the polite, reserved expression she wore, he would not get the chance tonight.

But when she'd first seen him, he thought for certain that her eyes softened, that she had actually looked forward to being with him. Not that she'd admit that, of course, but he could be patient.

More than one couple looked upon Elizabeth with

faint pity as they passed, as if something tragic must have happened for her to choose Peter as her husband. He had known this would happen, and so had she, but she seemed overly sensitive about it tonight.

She was overly sensitive about everything since their interlude in the carriage. Shadows of weariness darkened her eyes, and he imagined that the strain of the charade—and whatever else was bothering her—had begun to wear her down.

Yet still she didn't confide in him. And last night might have made that possibility even more remote.

Now as they stretched their legs at intermission, and again someone whispered to someone else as they passed, Elizabeth appeared to have reached a turning point.

"I just want to tell them all to mind their own concerns," she fumed.

"My sweet, to them, you *are* their concern. You're one of them, and I'm not."

"I was not raised with the absolute rule that a title was important in my choice of husband. But I also know that for romance to flourish, my husband should not be like a friend to me."

Peter wasn't certain she directed that at him, so he pretended not to take it that way. Giving her a bewildered look, he asked, "Why wouldn't you want your husband to be a friend? Don't you wish to get along?"

"But 'getting along' is different than confiding your

dreams and secrets, as to a friend. A husband is supposed to inspire romance and mystery, make a woman yearn to be with him. My parents had such a fairy-tale beginning, and it stood them well."

Was this crazy philosophy the reason she'd never even considered him in the first place? All he could do was speak huskily into her ear. "I made you yearn."

"You know that's not what I mean. Marital love is a delicate, romantic thing."

"And you know this from experience?"

"I've done my research."

"And what we did last night—"

"Isn't the same thing," she insisted, not meeting his eyes.

"So by denying passion, you can pretend it doesn't matter, that it didn't show you a side of yourself you'd never seen before."

"It was the wrong kind of passion," she hissed between smiling lips. "Uncontrollable."

"Wild."

Her hand clenched his arm. "Let's not talk about this anymore."

He went along with her because they were in public, but he wasn't finished with the topic. Instead, he turned his attention back to his other goal for the evening: watching Elizabeth's reaction to the people they met. Somewhere here might be the man threatening her—or the man she thought she wanted. So far this evening he'd seen no emotion betrayed in her eyes, but the night was young.

At the summoning for the second half, as they began to walk back toward the private Madingley box, he heard a woman call, "Lady Elizabeth!"

Through the crowd, he saw Miss Gibson and her brother, the baron. For one brief moment Elizabeth's unguarded expression softened into confusion.

His gaze shot back to the man who now stood at Lucy's side, and then he truly examined him. The man was several years younger than himself, tall and blond as a Norse god, with green eyes that passed right over Elizabeth, as if he were looking for whom else he knew.

Passed right over Elizabeth?

Her smile remained pleasant, but in that moment he knew: this man wasn't her enemy, the one who'd frightened her into a false engagement. This man was the one with whom she wanted to share her future—and her body. He was Peter's opponent in the ancient struggle; and apparently Gibson didn't even know it.

"Are you enjoying *Benvenuto Cellini*?" Miss Gibson asked. Then she giggled. "I worked hard on that pronunciation."

Peter nodded to the baron. "Gibson," he said.

Lucy showed more reaction, looking quickly, almost worriedly, between both men. So she knew, Peter thought. Of course, Gibson being her brother, after all, and Elizabeth her best friend.

Gibson bowed and then grinned. "Derby, since we last met I've heard a lot about your success in the railways."

"Thank you."

"I'd enjoy bending your ear about it."

"Any time." Then he decided to test the waters. "I do believe we're both members of the same club."

"We are. We'll talk there."

Peter tensed, wondering which of his escapades Gibson might have heard about, and if he'd bring them up. That wouldn't do in front of Elizabeth.

But Gibson only grinned and changed the subject— to something worse. "Some painting, isn't it?"

He'd lowered his voice, but the young fool could still be heard by the ladies. And then Gibson elbowed him.

If Gibson knew the truth about the painting, he certainly wouldn't bring it up in front of Elizabeth. Hell, if he knew the truth, he'd be paying a lot more attention to her.

Peter glanced at Elizabeth, and though she looked a shade paler, she was holding up admirably. But then, she must be used to Gibson's inattention. How could the man look at any other women when Elizabeth was right before him, so exotic and beautiful? She had the kind heart of a lady, the bravery of a woman who could accept a good challenge. She was curious and intelligent, always wanting to learn new things. Each conversation with her was different from the last—and yet Gibson still looked about as if someone else could be more interesting.

Much as Peter told himself it was better to know his enemy, he still felt frustrated. Elizabeth thought she loved this man, yet responded to his own caresses so wholeheartedly. She seemed to separate romance from passion, as if the two couldn't meet. Yet now he knew she was afraid of passion, afraid of being out of the control she'd worked so hard to win. He wasn't yet sure how to show her the truth about her feelings, except by spending as much time with her as possible, hoping she couldn't do without him.

Elizabeth felt as if her face were frozen in place, unmoving, while her brain frantically jumped from thought to thought. She'd known Peter and William would come face-to-face again, but William paid more attention to Peter, and to her shock, it made her want to laugh. Now the two men were talking about the railways while Lucy gave her sympathetic looks. She wished she could warn Lucy to be restrained, but there was nothing she could do.

Before the opera had begun, Lucy had stopped by the Madingley box and said she'd tried to persuade her brother to come visit with her, but complained that he never paid attention to what she said. During the first act, Elizabeth found herself watching Peter with his sister. He didn't ignore Mary Anne like William did Lucy—Peter was so concerned about her that he'd asked for Elizabeth's help. More than once during the show, he'd leaned toward his sister and said something to make her laugh, a light expression Elizabeth hadn't recently seen on the young woman's face.

Most men were more like William, focused on their own needs, rather than on the family they took for granted. She'd always told herself that under her influence, she could make William a better man, the one he was meant to be. But now as she watched him talk to Peter, she felt . . . exasperated.

And then she realized that William was speaking to her, and she smiled at him. "Forgive me, William, what did you say?"

"Could I have a private moment? My nosy sister can't hear this. It's a surprise."

Lucy stomped her foot as if upset at the exclusion, but Elizabeth saw that it was an act. Lucy was excited, and assumed that she was, too. But Elizabeth had learned never to assume she understood William's intentions.

Peter graciously distracted Lucy. "Miss Gibson, tell me what you thought of the first act."

And then William was drawing her a short distance away, and in the crowded corridor, few would hear them.

"Elizabeth, you're going to the Kelthorpe Masked Ball, are you not?"

Just the name of the event gave her a jolt. It was her self-imposed deadline—the return of her brother. "Of course I am," she said, hiding her bewilderment. William couldn't be asking to escort her when he'd just met her fiancé.

"Something important is happening that night, and I want you to be prepared. Stay with Lucy at the ball. I was worried if I didn't tell you now, I might not see you in time."

"Of course I'll do as you ask. But, William—"

"Good girl," he said, smiling at her.

He'd aroused her curiosity. Did he suspect that her engagement wasn't real? Could he want her for himself?

She tried to be thrilled at the thought, but it just wouldn't happen. That masked ball had felt like an anchor around her neck for too many days. Everything was coming to a head that night, and William's mysterious request only seemed like one more thing to worry about.

When they returned to the others, William took Lucy's arm. "Time to go, little sister. I have people to see."

Lucy waved at them as he towed her away. Elizabeth sighed, following at a slower pace as Peter moved to her side.

"My turn to speak with you privately," he said.

She glanced up at him with dismay, but he wore his usual polite, attentive expression—centered on her and no one else.

"The second act is about to begin," she said.

"Even better. We'll sit on the sofa outside your box, in plain sight, and wait until everyone has returned to their seats."

They did exactly that, until only servants roamed the corridors, politely avoiding looking at them. Elizabeth fussed with her skirt, spreading it out, trying to keep it from wrinkling.

Softly, Peter said, "You can avoid my gaze, but you can't avoid the truth."

She pasted on a smile and looked up at him. "What truth?"

"That at last you've given yourself away. Lord Gibson is the one you wanted."

She took a deep breath, telling herself this was inevitable. She'd tried her best to keep the two men apart, after all. Regardless of the other ways he'd changed, Peter still knew her too well.

"Why didn't you simply tell me?" he asked with exasperation.

He wasn't . . . angry? Jealous? she wondered, feeling confused.

"It's not as if he's so totally inappropriate you couldn't tell me his name," he continued.

"When I was younger," she began cautiously, "it was only something to whisper about with my cousins or with Lucy. And then when I was an adult, and the feelings hadn't gone away, it still felt like a private, feminine secret to me. Being unable to win his interest, I was frustrated and embarrassed and—" She stopped, searching his patient face. "At what point was I supposed to confess all of this?"

"When you asked for my help."

She pressed her lips together.

"And how does a"—he lowered his voice—"false engagement help?"

"William is not the reason I—" She cut herself off, realizing she'd once again almost confessed everything to Peter. She had an image of a bloody duel at dawn, Peter lying on the ground, Thomas standing over him. She shuddered.

Peter was watching her too closely. She tried to assemble some of the truth. "William is not the *only* reason I wanted to be engaged. You do remember those men pursuing me so aggressively."

"I remember, but you haven't answered my question. How does our engagement help you with Gibson?"

"Because he was supposed to realize I might be lost to him," she said stiffly. It sounded ridiculous now—a little pathetic.

Peter's expression remained neutral, and it bothered her that she couldn't read his emotions.

"So tell me what you see in him," he said.

She took a shaky breath. Had she truly convinced

him so easily? "He's handsome, of course, and I'm sure that's all I was drawn to when I was younger." It felt terribly awkward to talk about another man to her fiancé. "I liked his lightheartedness, and that he's always laughing. He doesn't need my dowry, of course, and nothing seems to bother him."

"He seems inhuman," Peter responded dryly.

"Is that how you see me?" she demanded.

"I don't understand."

"Nothing used to bother me either. Perfect Lady Elizabeth, as your sister is fond of saying." He squeezed her hand, but she didn't let him talk. "Well I'm not perfect," she insisted.

"Just because you have some things in common," he said, "doesn't mean you're in love. Being in love requires a reciprocal feeling from the person you want."

"One can't rush that reciprocal feeling."

"How many years will you give it, Elizabeth, before you realize—"

"Stop it, Peter. I don't need lectures from you."

Peter watched her stand up so hurriedly her blue and white skirts shimmied. She didn't look at him as she marched back inside the Madingley box. The second act had begun, the corridor was deserted, the music rising in crescendo—and he was wretched.

To think, he and Elizabeth suffered from the same flaw—both of them wanting a person who didn't return their feelings. No one could tell him not to love Elizabeth—so how could he say the same thing to her? And was he the one who was the bigger fool here? She could keep dreaming that Gibson would someday notice her, but he himself couldn't give up.

Because he loved her.

The other man now had a face. The merest thought of Elizabeth trying to seduce Gibson made his blood boil. She had planned that before she even knew what passion was, he thought, and changed her mind about risking herself in so uncontrollable a way.

But how could he be sure? He loved her—but did she only want to study his methods of seduction?

For the first time in several days Peter did not come to call. Elizabeth kept busy, making house calls, doing some work for her charity, and coordinating engagement party details with her mother.

But every time she had a moment to think, her thoughts went to Peter.

She told herself it was only natural. At last he knew part of the truth, where William was concerned anyway. Maybe now Peter would understand why she was so disturbed by her unladylike passion for him.

Yet . . . she didn't want Peter to be upset with her. Why did knowing William's identity change things?

At their informal family dinner, her relatives teased

her about Peter's absence, and she took it with a smile. She spent an evening in their company, reading the same page of a book over and over again as she deflected their questions about shopping for a wedding gown and where she and Peter would eventually live.

At last, claiming a headache—but really simply tired of the stress—she retreated to her bedroom after sending word to the servants that she'd like a bath sent up.

If only she were the duchess, she grumbled good-naturedly to herself. Abigail and Christopher shared a newly installed bathtub.

Her bedroom was a refuge of peace for her. Several candles gave the darkness a cheerful glow. Decorated in pale blue and muted white, its simple elegance usually soothed her. She'd picked out the paintings herself, scenes of the countryside to relax her when the city's bustle was overwhelming.

She walked to her dressing table and stared into the mirror, wondering if she recognized herself anymore. Reaching behind her neck, she unfastened her necklace and placed it on the table.

To her surprise, she heard movement within her bathroom. "Teresa?" she called to her maid. "That was quick."

The door opened, and a man peered out at her.

"Peter!" She gasped, even as she caught her bedpost for support.

# Chapter 17

W hat are you doing in my bathroom?" Elizabeth demanded.

"Hiding in case you were one of the servants," Peter said.

She rolled her eyes, even as he casually walked toward her. "*I mean*, what are you doing in my rooms at all?"

"It's been a long time since I've been here," he mused, passing by her so closely that their shoulders brushed. He came to a stop by the four-poster, then leveled her with another intimate look. "New bed?"

She felt her face grow hot. Once again Peter had manipulated them to be alone, and now there was a great big bed between them.

"You were last here when I was ten years old," she said between gritted teeth.

"I believe I saw you from the garden then, as you climbed down the balcony on knotted sheets. Attempting to visit a friend, I think."

With a wince, she said, "That was a long time ago. I have an adult bed now."

He laughed softly. "I like the sound of that."

He seemed so . . . comfortable, so at ease in her bedroom, as if he'd had much practice. He'd admitted his dalliance with women, and for just a moment she wondered if he considered this just another dalliance. It seemed like life and death to her, but perhaps she only amused him.

No, she told herself, that couldn't be. True, Peter had changed for a reason she had yet to discover, but he hadn't become a shallow man.

She felt like stamping her feet in frustration, but restrained herself. "I'll ask one more time—what are you doing here? And how did you get in without anyone seeing you? Please tell me no one saw you," she added with worry.

"I came in through the window just like you once did."

"Peter!"

"No one saw me, of course. I'm wearing dark clothing. Although it is difficult to climb while wearing a fashionable coat. Pulls at the shoulders."

She felt like stalking around the bed and strangling him. "You forgot the most important question—why!"

He took his time, looking at the items on her bed table, from the book she'd been reading to the glass globe Christopher had brought her from Spain, where he and Abigail had spent their honeymoon. And then Peter lifted something from the back of the table. She winced when she saw it.

"I gave you this," he said in surprise.

"It's a birdhouse, Peter. I made it when I was eleven."

"No, now I remember. I helped you make it," he countered. Then he slowly smiled. "You kept it."

She looked guiltily at the little wooden birdhouse, hammered crudely together. She'd put a fake little bird at the front, and attached silk flowers to one side, as if it nestled in a flowering tree. The colors had faded and one of the bird wings had been damaged, but . . . "I thought it was sweet. And I liked that I'd done something little girls didn't normally do."

"I'm touched," he said, hand to his chest, eyes so sincere.

She burst out laughing, then hushed herself. "Stop that! Puppy dog eyes."

He grinned.

"Don't become full of yourself. I was remembering my own accomplishment. I'd totally forgotten it had anything to do with you."

His smile faded until only a twinkle shimmered in his blue eyes as he began to walk toward her.

She backed up. "Stop it! Oh, very well, I remember your part in it now!" She told herself she was furious and exasperated with him, but in truth there was a rising excitement at what he'd risked to be here tonight.

She looked at him differently now, too. Her mouth went dry as he stopped just before her. She had to look up to see his face, and it made her feel strangely small and delicate.

"Your memory is conveniently flawed at times," he said softly.

He reached to tuck a curl behind her ear, and a shiver started there and worked its way down her body.

"What do you mean?" she demanded, trying to sound strict instead of breathless.

"You seem to have forgotten another reason we're connected. Remember the painting?"

The dark night in his carriage flashed back into her mind, where she'd been stretched out almost completely naked across cool leather, while he'd posed her like that painting. Though she'd been overwrought at the time, now she remembered the hunger and admiration in his eyes—and he wore the same look now.

She backed up another step, and found herself against the shelves she used for her books. "What *about* the painting?" She forced exasperation into her voice.

"Tonight is more about the wager," he said, reaching out again.

She tensed, but he reached behind her and picked up a small decorated box from a shelf, shook it, then held it away from her when she tried to take it.

"You don't want me to see this?" he asked.

"Look if you must. The ribbons will surely fascinate you."

He opened the box and poked through it, lifting the ribbons to look beneath.

"What do my ribbons have to do with anything?" she demanded. "And you'd best be quick, for the servants are bringing my bathwater any moment."

He closed the box. "It's what may be hidden beneath your ribbons that concerns me."

"Hidden? I have nothing to hide—" She broke off, realizing that was patently untrue.

"You have so much to hide now. You've made it all so complicated. So I'm going back to the beginning, to what led you to feel you could ask me to lie for you. Because, of course, you had something you knew I wanted."

She bit her lip, and without volition her gaze dropped to his mouth.

"Something else I wanted," he amended, his voice growing husky.

They looked into each other's eyes a long moment, and she held her breath when he set the box on the shelf behind her. His fingers brushed her shoulder and slid to the base of her neck.

"The diamond pendant, Elizabeth," he murmured.

She blinked at him. "What . . . ?"

"The one you wore in the painting. If I find it, it will help me prove you're the model. And then I'll win."

His fingers lingered at her throat, dipping into the hollow, brushing gently over her skin. It made her think too much of his mouth pressed there—his mouth pressed ever farther below.

She pushed against his chest, and although he briefly resisted, letting her know she couldn't overpower him, he stepped aside and allowed her to escape.

Taking a deep breath, she turned back to face him. "My cousins and I share our jewelry, including that piece. You won't find it here. One of them took it on her journey."

"So you say. But if you don't let me search now, I'll simply come back."

He turned back to the shelves and began to look behind each book. She felt invaded, just as he'd invaded every part of her life since that night she'd stolen into his club.

She grabbed his arm, and he caught her against him, holding her immobile while he continued to lift her books. His body was warm and strong, but she had to ignore that. She was about to give him a swift kick when they both froze at a scratching on the door.

"That's Teresa!" she whispered in triumph.

"Should I find a way to explain myself?"

"Get out on that balcony and go away!"

To her surprise, he crossed the room, slipped between the draperies covering the French doors, and seemed to vanish.

That was too easy.

With no other choice, she let Teresa and the parade of menservants in with their pails of hot water. When the men had gone, she could not refuse Teresa's offer to unhook her gown, for the maid would wonder how else she would be able to bathe.

She took her dressing gown into the bathroom and had Teresa unhook her gown there. The girl kept giving her strange looks, for there wasn't as much room, but she asked no questions. When she was wearing only her chemise and undergarments, she pretended she had to make a note of something before bathing and dismissed Teresa for the night. She couldn't very well undress until she was certain Peter had gone.

She wrapped her dressing gown around her and belted it securely. Then she went back into her now deserted bedroom. Though she heard no sound from the balcony, she pulled aside the draperies and found him standing out in the darkness, watching her.

Though she fumbled to close the door, he slipped by her. She tried to put herself between him and her dressing table, knowing he would next search her jewelry box, but instead he went to the bathroom.

"What are you doing *now*?" she cried softly.

He'd already taken off his coat and was standing over the tub.

Her mouth fell open but she couldn't even get words of protest out. He could not possibly think . . . would not dare . . .

He rolled up his sleeves. "I'm testing your bathwater."

Sinking onto a nearby stool, she started to laugh. Peter was standing in her bathroom, sleeves rolled up above his elbows so he wouldn't get wet as he leaned over her tub. It was something she'd never imagined in all of her life.

But then everything lately fell into that category.

"And how does my lady like the temperature of her bath?" he asked, trailing his hand in the water. "Too hot, I think. I'll add more cold."

He reached for the bucket, which was near the candelabrum that lit the room. The light shone down on his arm—and she saw a scar just above his elbow.

"Peter, what's that?" she asked, coming to her feet.

He straightened. "A bucket."

She touched the warm skin of his arm, felt the way he stiffened. Memories of their kisses surfaced to distract her, but she resisted. Instead she lifted his arm and pushed up his folded shirt. There was a scar like a ragged hole in his upper arm.

"It's nothing, Elizabeth," he said, pulling away.

But she'd already felt the far side of the arm, and the

identical mark on the opposite side. "It's a bullet hole," she breathed. "You were shot!"

*A jealous husband, perhaps?*

"Every man has a foolish hunting accident," he said dismissively. He picked up the bucket again. "You were about to tell me how you liked your bath?"

"Peter, why didn't I hear about this? It makes no sense!"

"You don't know everything about me," he said dryly, setting the bucket down again. "And if you don't want my help, I'll simply have to go back to uncovering the diamond. Perhaps Susanna or Rebecca left it behind. I'll go search their rooms."

He tried to go around her, but she blocked him with her body. When he didn't stop, they came flush against each other. He caught her so she wouldn't fall. She knew right away by the way his eyes narrowed that he realized how little clothing she really wore.

"Do you think to distract me?" he asked softly, his face just above hers, the candle behind him shadowing his face in darkness.

"I think I can distract you whenever I want. You've already proven that." The words came out of her without plan or thought—a grown-up challenge, unlike the rash escapades of her youth.

She was so close she saw his eyes darken.

"I don't believe you," he said hoarsely.

She slid her hand to the back of his head and pulled him down to kiss her. It was hot and fierce, open-mouthed with hunger on both their parts. She was breathing heavily when she broke away to stare up at him.

"So who's distracting who?" she asked. He didn't want to talk about his scars, and she didn't want him to search for the diamond.

His smile was slow and taunting. She'd never thought to see such a smile on Peter before. A wicked part of her liked it. She wasn't the only one hiding things about herself.

"Why is it so easy to kiss you?" she asked wistfully.

"Because you like it. And I have a talent."

He kissed her again, sweeping into her mouth with his tongue, pulling her harder against him. Wearing so little clothing, she too easily felt the long ridge of his arousal pressing into her stomach. He wanted her. She should feel worried, but this was far too exhilarating.

She broke the kiss but kept her face lifted to his. Their foreheads brushed as they looked into each other's eyes.

"I don't want to like this," she whispered. It was dangerous and reckless, all things she was trying to disprove about herself.

His hands gently swept up from her shoulders to cup her cheeks. He kissed her again, slowly, gently, too sweetly. It made something ache inside her. And then he set her away from him.

She couldn't give him a reason to come back. It was too dangerous to her peace of mind. "Let me prove to you I don't have the diamond." She brought him her jewelry box and opened it, pushing aside various necklaces and bracelets so he could see everything. "I didn't know you were coming, so I wouldn't have hidden it somewhere else. You made a risky climb for nothing."

"Hardly nothing," he said, brushing a lock of hair from her cheek.

She went still at the touch.

He picked up his coat, went through the draperies and out into the night. She had a sudden urge to run to the balcony and peer over the balustrade, watching to make certain he climbed down safely.

Instead, she stood in the center of the room and hugged herself. Once again he'd been evasive about his past. She'd once foolishly assumed she knew everything about him.

What was he keeping from her?

Peter prowled the club late into the night, drinking too much, playing too many card games—and winning, something he'd proven good at.

William Gibson wouldn't leave him alone, and that made Peter drink even more. Gibson was like a young pup who'd found his new best friend, happily offering drinks and trying to discuss the best way to find a mistress.

Not a wife—not Elizabeth.

Gibson might as well have been wagging a tail.

Peter used the opportunity to study the reaction of other men in the saloon. Gibson was fondly tolerated; he amused most, made some of the older gentlemen shake their heads and mumble that he needed to grow up.

Elizabeth wanted Gibson to grow up, too, but Gibson wasn't ready for it. He was enamored with the excitement of the railroads, asking if Peter had watched them use an electric telegraph, and how many shares he should buy to have a say in the running of the company.

Peter politely answered it all, for Elizabeth's sake.

But he went home that night even more determined to find a way to prove to Elizabeth that Gibson couldn't be what she really wanted.

Falling asleep proved difficult, and it felt like the sky was already beginning to lighten when a restless slumber took him away.

And the dreams started again with the gunshot, the one that made him realize the terrible error he'd really made, that his chance to make things right might be slipping away. He kept running, unable to get to her, the bridge where she was in danger never coming any closer.

He woke even more exhausted than when he'd gone to bed.

If it was just a misjudgment on his part, why couldn't he tell Elizabeth about it? And why did his worry about the danger stalking Elizabeth manifest itself in memories he refused to confide in her?

# Chapter 18

I think you picked out a lovely ring for Peter's engagement gift," the dowager duchess said to Elizabeth two nights later as they waited in the drawing room for the first guest to arrive for the engagement party.

She smiled up at her mother. If the duchess had ever suffered from a language barrier, it was not in reading her children's expressions.

"Elizabeth?" She spoke the name with a tinge of worry.

Elizabeth forced her smile to be light and chiding. "Now, Mama, don't say my name like that. I'm simply nervous. I'm about to be a bride—isn't that natural? My whole life will soon change in a way I've only imagined."

"You know you can talk to me about anything," the duchess said, caressing her cheek.

*No, Mama, I can't. You can't know the truth about me, the lengths I'll go to—*

She stopped her thoughts before they could go further, before tears stung her eyes.

And then the butler announced Peter, and she gave her "fiancé" a relieved smile. He came across the room, dressed in handsome evening clothes that set off his sandy brown hair and light eyes. She'd thought him boyishly handsome when she was younger, but maturity and confidence had only added to his good looks. His smile didn't falter, but she saw him glance at her mother, then back at her. With just a quirk of his eyebrow, Elizabeth understood his question: *What was wrong?* He could read her so well.

Unlike William.

She curtsied to Peter. He took her hand in both of his and brought it to his lips. "I can't wait until this glove is not between my lips and your hand."

She suspected he hadn't meant her mother to overhear, for his eyes widened when the duchess said, "Peter Derby! That is far too romantic for the bride's mother to hear!"

But she was smiling fondly at him, and he gave a boyish shrug.

"Your Grace," he said, "might I steal your daughter away briefly? I have something for her."

"Of course, Peter. You two should walk in the conservatory. Very romantic at night."

"An excellent idea," Peter said, offering his arm to Elizabeth.

Silently they walked into the entrance hall, down the

stairs, and to the far side of the house, where the glass conservatory opened onto the gardens. The doors to the outside were closed, but torches lit the curving pathways in anticipation of their guests' arrival.

The air was cooler, with the faint musty smell of dirt and growing things beneath the scents of exotic flowers brought from all corners of the globe.

Elizabeth inhaled deeply. "I've always loved it here."

"Is the little fort still in the back?"

She blinked at him, the memory surfacing slowly. "I had forgotten all about that."

He caught her hand. "Let's see if it's still there."

She knew she should pull away, should insist they had their guests to worry about, or fret over when they were supposed to show signs of strain before calling off their engagement. Instead, she ran after Peter, her slippers crunching on the gravel. In the far corner of the conservatory, where the glass separated them from the terrace, and the dark gardens spread out below, they had to push past ferns that had multiplied since their childhood, and the shrubbery grouped around a private stone bench. Torchlight flickered just above their heads.

"Peter, we can't get dirty," she reminded him, feeling suddenly elderly compared to her lost, impulsive youth.

"I'm wearing black evening clothes." He ignored her, pushing through fronds, while she watched from the path. He looked over his shoulder and grinned. "It's still here."

He held back some of the ferns, and she saw an edge of the wooden roof that only came up to his chest. The boys had wanted a fort built in a tree, like at Madingley Court in the country, but their parents had refused to allow that, claiming the trees in the conservatory not sturdy enough.

So the boys had to be satisfied with a rough wooden floor they'd built themselves, and green shrubs and ferns overhead for privacy. When the girls wanted a roof, the boys, in their teens by then, had done their bidding, using posts rather than walls to hold up the small roof.

Elizabeth hesitated, for she was wearing violet embroidered silk that could be so easily damaged. Yet Peter's grin made her yearn for simpler times, even as he bent and disappeared underneath. So she pushed aside a few ferns, bent her head, and looked in, surprised to find that some of the torchlight reached inside, faintly lighting the gloom. Weeds or vines hadn't grown up through the floor. The servants had obviously still been taking care of it.

Peter was sitting on the small bench, knees up to his chest, smiling when he saw her. His teeth almost glowed in the near darkness.

"There's room," he said, coming off the bench, hunched over. "Sit here."

Though her corset constricted her as she bent over, she was able to step a few feet sideways and sink onto the child-size bench, her skirts spreading out to cover almost the entire floor, pooling around Peter's legs where he now knelt, looking at her.

She made herself look away, feeling breathless. The glass wall was right outside the fort, but darkness had taken away the view.

With nothing else to distract her, she at last looked back at him, only to find him reaching into the pocket of his coat and pulling out a small box.

"This is a good place to give this to you," he said.

Something twisted inside her chest, but she forced a matter-of-fact smile to her lips. "Of course. The guests will expect to see engagement gifts."

He handed her the box and she opened it, inhaling swiftly at the beauty of the ring set with several pearls. She cleared her throat. "It's lovely, Peter."

"See if it fits."

She took off her gloves and tried it on. It was perfect.

"Your mother lent me another ring of yours so I could match the size."

"Your sister helped me with your gift," she said, pulling another box out of the pocket in her skirt.

He glanced at her in obvious surprise.

"I called for her yesterday and took her shopping with me," Elizabeth said.

"Again? Shopping twice in one week must be a record for Mary Anne. Perhaps you're having an effect on her after all."

She didn't answer that hope, because she wasn't certain what Mary Anne thought of her. She was beginning to feel like a dead butterfly under a magnifying glass, the way Mary Anne studied her when she thought she wasn't observed.

"We did have a nice conversation about the latest Dickens novel," Elizabeth continued. "We both like to read."

"Don't sound so desperate to find something in common," he said dryly.

Shaking her head, she handed her box to Peter and he opened it, smiling up at her as he took out the plain gold ring.

"It seems we had the same idea," he said, sliding the ring on. "I almost purchased a locket instead, but something about the ring caught my eye."

She tried to give him another normal smile, but he was studying her face too intently. Looking back out the window, she wished she could pretend to watch something, but the inky blackness made their privacy far too complete.

He took her hand, and his fingers rubbed over the ring that marked her as his. When he leaned toward her, she quickly stopped him.

"No, Peter, don't kiss me. This isn't real."

His eyes solemn and dark, he murmured, "What if I want it to be?"

For one moment she didn't know what to think. He'd become a man who amused himself with women, with her. He couldn't possibly mean that he wanted to . . . to marry her.

A pang of sorrow and panic tightened her chest—and she bolted. Simply ducked beneath the roof, shoved aside ferns and began to hurry down the curving paths, past the fountain that sparkled with the light glinting off it, and back into the house, where servants hurried down corridors in last minute preparation.

To her intense relief, her mother, far too perceptive, was no longer alone. She was speaking with Mrs. Derby, Mary Anne, and Peter's brother James.

Mrs. Derby turned as she walked in, and her face lit up with joy and gratitude. Elizabeth's tight chest seemed to twist up into her throat.

Mrs. Derby looked at her hand. "I knew the ring would look lovely on you!"

Elizabeth lifted her hand so they could all see Peter's gift. James, a shorter, stockier version of Peter, glanced at it perfunctorily, then looked over her head and grinned.

Elizabeth knew Peter had come into the room, but she didn't turn to face him. She couldn't. Her face would flame scarlet as she thought of his words of longing.

Longing for her? Or longing for the passion they shared, the passion he could have with any other woman?

She'd been such a fool. How had she assumed this false engagement would only hurt their families? And that had been an acceptable outcome, she thought, feeling disgusted with herself.

She hadn't considered Peter's feelings or that it would matter to him at all, except to raise his esteem in the right circles. He had wagered against her, and she'd thought that made him deserve whatever he got.

Yet . . . what if she was wrong? What if she'd been misreading him all this time?

*She* was the one who deserved to feel the pain that squeezed her insides. *She* deserved to be punished for letting all of this happen, and making the wrong choices to solve her problems.

But she was trapped—and Peter had to remain just as trapped in her web.

As Peter approached, James clapped him on the back. "So my little brother has made the engagement official."

Peter smiled. Elizabeth thought that a touch of strain lingered in the curve of his mouth, or perhaps the faint lines at the edge of his eyes.

James looked back at her. "You know you've made him unbearable to live with."

She didn't have to force a blush. "I don't know what you

mean. Surely you aren't warning me about our future."

James shook his head. "For several years it's been Elizabeth this and Elizabeth that, but now it's even more monotonous."

Everyone laughed but Elizabeth, who felt stricken as she watched Peter. Was James telling the truth—or only reporting on Peter's excellent acting skills? Peter laughed even as he met her gaze unflinchingly.

The evening turned into one strained moment after another. Lucy arrived, mortified to admit that her brother couldn't attend. Elizabeth assured her that it was all right, and in fact it was.

Then to make everything worse, Thomas entered the room, even though he hadn't been invited. He mingled with the guests as everyone awaited dinner. Elizabeth was forced to point out his attendance to her mother, who'd handled the seating arrangements.

Her mother only shook her head. "I didn't know why you insisted he not be invited in the first place."

"We don't get along, Mama," Elizabeth softly said, smiling at her guests. "I did turn down his marriage proposal, after all."

"You would never know that from him. He's quite gotten over it."

Elizabeth ground her teeth together. "I hope his arrival does not inconvenience you too much."

"Of course not. But now I wish I'd have invited his mother. I explained to her your worry about hurting his feelings, and of course she understood, but . . ." She shook her head and headed out to the entrance hall, probably to confer with the butler.

Elizabeth had a brief moment alone, and she took it, breathing deeply to calm herself, looking at the dozens of guests who'd come to celebrate her impending nuptials.

Lucy was chatting with Mary Anne and James, and it was good to see Mary Anne laugh at whatever Lucy said.

And then Thomas noticed Elizabeth's solitary stance near the double doors and came toward her with purpose. She stiffened, knowing she couldn't very well flee.

He bowed to her. "Lady Elizabeth, what a wonderful surprise to find myself here."

As if she'd sent him an invitation, she thought angrily. But forcing a smile was getting so habitual, it was easily done. "Lord Thomas, you're a pleasure to entertain, as always."

Amused, he studied her face before saying softly, "You've created the most wonderful charade, my dear."

"Believe what you wish," she said, holding up her hand with its engagement gift outlined beneath her glove. "This ring says otherwise."

"Or it says that poor Mr. Derby doesn't understand what you've done to him."

She didn't think even Thomas could make her feel worse, but it was happening.

"Leave me alone," she whispered raggedly.

"I—"

Something came over his face as he broke off, an expression she didn't recognize. And then to her surprise, he bowed and left her.

Peter stood amidst several old men, all in the House of Lords with the Duke of Madingley. More than one man had said it was strange to celebrate an engagement without His Grace in attendance, and Peter couldn't agree more. If things were normal, they would have waited for him to return to town.

But nothing was normal.

They went on discussing the latest bill that would favor the railways, but Peter couldn't concentrate on business.

He'd made a mistake, he thought, watching Elizabeth and her mother talk. He'd hoped that after her freely given kiss the other night, she might be ready to hear a hint of his true feelings. But she'd panicked and run from him, and everything was worse.

He felt a ripple of unease. How could he prove he

deserved to win her in the end, when she was convinced she loved another man?

He watched her talking to Lord Thomas Wythorne. She was stiff, her smile very forced. Lord Thomas's grin was touched with sarcasm, and Peter had a sudden need to punch that too-handsome face. Was he one of the men who'd tried to force his attentions on her?

"Don't worry," said a soft feminine voice, "she chose you."

Peter knew who it was before glancing her way, and his guilt rose to linger like embers after a fire. "Good evening, Mrs. Leland—Emily," he answered, just as softly.

She smiled. "I'm glad you've finally accepted that we don't need formality between us."

He nodded. "What do you mean by telling me not to worry?"

With her head, she gestured toward Lord Thomas, who was just leaving Elizabeth. "Last year, he asked her to marry him."

"She never told me," he said, stunned.

"There have been several proposals since she came out," Emily said, almost laughing at him. "Surely you know how highly sought after she is."

He nodded. "Of course. I just didn't know he was one of the rejected. How did he take it?"

Emily blinked up at him. "How else could he take it?

In stride, I imagine, since I heard nothing else."

"And he still visits here," he mused, thinking of the glimpse he'd had of Mary Anne playing billiards with him.

"He usually accompanies his mother, a friend to the duchess."

And then as if his thoughts had predicted it, Peter saw Lord Thomas stop beside Mary Anne, who'd been standing near the piano, thumbing through sheet music, something she never did *after* dinner, when someone might ask her to play.

Mary Anne looked a bit defensive, her chin high, considering she'd already enjoyed a game of billiards with the man. Lord Thomas wasn't put off by her behavior, but stood talking to her for several minutes. He picked out a song, and Mary Anne vehemently shook her head. The man only laughed, as if sure he'd get his way.

About what, Peter didn't know, but his gut didn't like it, and he'd learned to trust his instincts. And then he saw Elizabeth watching Lord Thomas and Mary Anne, and for an unguarded moment he'd seen her worry.

He knew then that he needed to look into this man.

# Chapter 19

When Thomas had left Mary Anne, Elizabeth approached Peter's sister, where she still stood at the piano.

"I hope Lord Thomas wasn't bothering you," Elizabeth said. "He can be . . . persistent."

"I think he's very confident. I like that." Mary Anne set down the sheet music, as if she wanted to concentrate on Elizabeth. In a tone that wasn't belligerent, only firm, she said, "I invited him tonight."

Elizabeth's mouth sagged open before she controlled herself. "I don't understand."

"I sent him a handwritten invitation. I saw him watching you and Peter at the opera, and I wanted him to see how happy the two of you were together—because you didn't look all that happy that night."

"I see." If the last sentence were a hint that Mary Anne wanted to know more, she would not get an answer from her. "Mary Anne, couples can't be in perfect agreement all the time. You know how happy Peter and I are."

"So I hear."

"But Lord Thomas—I know you think he might be your friend, since you've played a game together, but . . ." Her words faded away. She could hardly hint at the threats Thomas had made.

"Just say it," Mary Anne said coolly. "I've never known you to be shy."

"You don't know me well, Mary Anne, and I know we can't remedy that in just a couple days. But I'm concerned for you. Lord Thomas can be ruthless when he wants something."

To her surprise, that seemed to ease Mary Anne, who chuckled.

"Elizabeth, you know he could not possibly want anything from me."

"You don't know what he wants."

"Tonight, he wanted me to choose a song he should sing after dinner. Can you imagine? Usually only ladies sing."

"Lord Thomas tends to do whatever he wants at any given moment, little caring of the consequences."

"I guess I'll have to form my own opinion. But I thank you for yours." Mary Anne nodded politely and walked away.

Elizabeth smoothed out her features before her troubled frown could give anything away.

\* \* \*

Mary Anne found herself watching Lord Thomas. And to her surprise, he watched her. After dinner when he came to find her, she didn't scurry away. Her heart trembled in her chest, the feeling of panic she'd lived with so long almost clouding her vision. She'd been less afraid of Lord Thomas alone over a billiards table. But billiards, her obsession, kept her separate from men—from her emotions, she realized.

"Miss Derby," Lord Thomas said with a nod.

"My lord," she answered, her voice steady. "I'm waiting for that song."

He laughed softly. "I thought we could discuss what we were doing at the opera first."

She remembered seeing him there, a scowl on his face, as he watched her brother and Elizabeth argue. Did he want Elizabeth, and she didn't want him? Did the entire city think Elizabeth the perfect paragon of womanhood?

"I think you were spying on my brother and his fiancée," Mary Anne said.

He arched a brow and smiled down at her. "A woman who speaks her mind. I like that. It's one of the reasons I appreciated Lady Elizabeth. I courted her at one time."

"Didn't every man?" Mary Anne asked brightly. Inwardly, she winced. That was too revealing of her own weaknesses. Elizabeth seemed genuinely concerned for her—which only made Mary Anne more intrigued by

Lord Thomas. Why had Elizabeth warned her about him?

"I asked her to marry me," he continued, his smile faint, "but she refused me."

Surprised that he'd reveal something so personal to her, Mary Anne said, "You must have been displeased. Surely you thought you were the perfect candidate for a duke's daughter."

He laughed without amusement. "I must have thought so, because I allowed my pride to become involved."

"And that's why you were spying on them?"

"Apparently I had to see them in a private moment, to decide for myself what I thought about them as a couple. After all, when a woman can have me, and she chooses a commoner . . ." He grinned and spread his hands.

"You're a catch, my lord." She couldn't believe she was speaking so freely to a man. It was frightening, but freeing, too.

His eyes widened, and she thought perhaps there weren't many women who spoke openly to him. Even Elizabeth, she realized.

"I've bared my soul," Lord Thomas said. "Now it's your turn. Why were *you* watching them?"

She hesitated. "They were arguing, though I couldn't hear what they were saying. I want my brother to be happy."

"Because it dawned on you, too, that her choosing to marry someone so much lower in the *ton* is unusual."

He looked around, as if making sure no one was nearby. "*Are* they happy?"

"I can only speak for my brother, but yes, he is."

Thomas nodded thoughtfully.

And then they were approached by a group of young ladies who had seen Lord Thomas at the piano earlier. They demanded a song, and Mary Anne left him to his admirers. When he finally did sing, in a deep baritone that was just as smooth and intriguing as his speaking voice, Mary Anne found herself watching Elizabeth's very impassive expression.

And then she saw Peter watching Elizabeth, too.

To Peter's relief, when he entered his club that night, Lord Thurlow was in attendance.

He sat down opposite the viscount, who folded his newspaper and smiled at him. "Good evening, Derby."

Over the last months Peter had learned to trust Thurlow's opinion on anything, and although that usually involved the railways, tonight he had a different agenda.

"Good evening, Thurlow."

"Surely you're not trying to have some peace from your fiancée already?"

"No, I just left her," Peter said, knowing the viscount spoke lightly, but unable to match his tone. "Would you mind answering a question for me?"

"If I can."

Peter lowered his voice, although there were card games at several tables, and drinks flowing freely. He didn't imagine anyone cared to overhear them. "Do you know Lord Thomas Wythorne?"

"I do, although not well. More by reputation."

"And that's just what I'm looking for. I know that he's arrogant, and he comes from a well-respected, wealthy, and powerful family."

"All of that, yes."

"But is there more?"

Thurlow studied him for a time.

His hesitation made Peter say, "I know he asked Lady Elizabeth to marry him, and she refused."

"I wasn't certain if you knew," Thurlow said. "He did not advertise it."

"I'm not surprised. Rejection hurts even the mighty." He thought about Elizabeth talking to Lord Thomas— the stiff, formal way she held herself. Had she been . . . frightened? He couldn't stop wondering if Lord Thomas had now latched on to Mary Anne. "But what about him as a man?"

"Honest in his dealings, from everything I've heard. But he doesn't do much business. Leaves that to his eldest brother, who'll inherit the dukedom someday. But he enjoys wagering."

"You mean like horses or cards?"

"Besides those, the books are full of the most outlandish reasons to place bets, like who would be the next mistress taken by a newly titled nobleman, or if someone's by-blow would ever be recognized." Thurlow crossed his arms over his broad chest and frowned. "I find such a display vulgar and uncalled for. And scandalous for his family, although they seem to indulge him as if he were naughty child."

Peter grimaced. "How does he act when he loses?"

"He never does. But he's an arrogant son of a bitch. That kind hates to lose the most."

What was such a man still doing at Madingley House? Watching what he set in motion after being rejected?

Peter felt a chill of sudden recognition, of disbelief. He thought about Elizabeth being forced to save herself with something drastic, risking her reputation on a false engagement. What—or who—could have frightened her so badly?

As if the answer to a prayer, Peter spotted Dekker, a nightly regular, staggering into the saloon, catching a waiter on the way to a table for another order. He well remembered Dekker and his friends laughing over Elizabeth. Peter had been so focused on the affront to Elizabeth that he hadn't considered the rest of Dekker's story.

"Thank you, Thurlow," he said, getting to his feet.

"You're looking rather dangerous, Derby," Thurlow said mildly. "Think through whatever you're going to do."

"I've been thinking far too long. It's time for action."

He knew he was on the right track when he approached Dekker and the man's drunken grin faltered.

Dekker recovered, saying, "Derby!" cheerfully.

Peter acknowledged the man, straddling a chair as he sat to face him.

Dekker hesitated. "Seton will bring over another chair."

Peter looked over his shoulder at the approaching man. "When we're done."

Seton pulled up short, looked from one man to the other, pivoted and walked away.

Dekker gave another hardy grin. "Heard you're getting married. To the catch of the Season. The catch of many Seasons," he added glibly. "I never courted her m'self."

"No, you told me you simply thought to get her alone."

Dekker's grin faded. "So I wanted to steal a kiss. You can't blame a man. There were many couples on the terrace."

"If you want me to forget the slight against my fiancée, tell me the name of the man who took her away from you."

Dekker brightened. "That's easy. Wythorne. Seemed proprietary, too. Not that the lady looked happy to see him."

"Thank you." Peter got to his feet, brushed by Seton, and headed for the door.

* * *

The next morning, Peter went to Madingley House as early as was decent. To his surprise, when he asked to see Elizabeth, the butler led him to the billiard room. He found her trying to line up a shot, holding the cue incorrectly, bent over the table, her skirts flaring high over the small bustle. Peter swallowed hard as he thought of what they could do together on that table. She looked up and saw him. The butler discreetly left, and he entered the room, shutting the door behind him.

Elizabeth straightened, wide-eyed. "You shouldn't shut the door."

"Since my ring is on your finger, who will care?"

"Besides me?"

"We need to speak privately." But suddenly, he wasn't in a hurry to confront her with all he suspected. He walked forward slowly. "You're learning to play billiards?"

"I thought it might help me earn Mary Anne's friendship."

"Still paying me back for being your fiancé?"

She stiffened. "Are you implying that I'm simply tolerating her?"

Before he could even respond, her impassive expression became stricken.

"Oh Peter, forgive me. I don't mean to argue. I'm so confused. I never thought this would become so complicated."

"And it all started because of Lord Thomas Wythorne."

Her face whitened and she slowly set the cue on the table. "What do you mean?"

"Watching you with him, I suspected he might be more involved than I'd thought. And then I found out you'd rejected his proposal, and I imagine he's not the sort of man to take that lightly."

She sagged back against the billiard table, looking at the carpeted floor. "He's not," she said softly.

Peter cupped her face, lifting it to meet her eyes. "He threatened you?"

She pulled away from him and walked toward the windows. He followed.

"Peter, leave this alone," she said, parting the draperies and looking outside.

He yanked the fabric from her hand and spun her to face him, keeping his hands on her shoulders. She gaped up at him.

"Leave it alone?" he demanded. "How could you not tell me?"

"And have you challenge him on behalf of my brother? What good would that have done other than to see you hurt?"

"I'd have been challenging him on behalf of *you*!" he said angrily.

"Peter, listen to yourself! I knew you'd try to protect me, but I couldn't have it. I had to solve my own problems."

"What did he threaten you with? Ruination? Disgrace?"

She sighed. "Marriage."

He blinked at her in surprise.

"He still wanted to marry me, to join our families together. It was for prestige alone. He doesn't love me. He simply wants what was denied him."

He gave her a little shake. "You know I wouldn't have done anything you didn't want me to. Yet you didn't trust me."

"I was so embarrassed," she whispered, closing her eyes. "You kept calling me reckless over that painting, and I was so angry about that foolish wager, and— Oh, but that's not the main problem. I didn't want to believe I'd regressed so badly, but now I have no choice, do I?"

"You've made mistakes; we all do." And he was no different than she, was even beginning to realize that he'd been too lenient on himself, writing off his mistakes as simple misjudgments. His dreams were trying to show him what he didn't want to face. "You can't blame yourself for Wythorne's manipulations. What did he threaten you with?"

"Someone told him about the painting. He said he'd make sure no one else heard, that I'd be protected if I married him."

"So someone else knows? Dekker?"

She shrugged. "I don't know. So far, no one has been obvious about it. Thomas said he'd keep the man in line, because he was certain I would soon be his wife. When he wouldn't see reason about the marriage, I panicked and told him I was already engaged. He didn't believe me, but he decided to wait me out, as if we played a game." She winced. "After he left, I wracked my brain for the solution to the mess I'd created for myself that began with that damned painting. And then I thought of you, and knew I had something to offer in exchange for your help. And now I've hurt you with my thoughtlessness—I'm no better than Thomas."

He stared at her. "What are you talking about?"

"Don't you see?" She leaned into him, hands pressed urgently to his chest. "I am just like Thomas. I've always gotten everything I ever wanted—just like him. And when I didn't—I reacted."

He covered her hands where they rested on his chest. "Elizabeth, don't do this to yourself."

"But it's the truth! When Thomas didn't get what he wanted, he resorted to threats and intimidation. My response to my problems was a fake engagement, not caring who was hurt, as long as I could have what *I* wanted—a triumph over Thomas, and the notice of one particular man."

"You were desperate, Elizabeth."

"And I used you! I'm doing it over and over again. How do I make it better, Peter?"

He stared at her, holding back his protests, wishing

he could tell her he wanted a real engagement. But one hint of that the previous night had frightened her, and now all she could think about was how she'd failed herself and him. They needed a fresh start, without all the deceit between them. He prayed that he could win her in the end.

He stepped back, and her hands dropped away from him. "The only thing we can do is begin ending this false engagement, as we'd planned all along."

Relief mingled with pain in her eyes. But was she relieved about all the lies coming to an end—or relieved that she would no longer be linked to him? He didn't want to believe the latter, not after their closeness, not after the intimacies she'd so willingly succumbed to.

"We'll show more strain in public," he continued. "Certainly we already did that at the opera. I won't visit you as often."

"Oh," she said, her brow furrowed.

But she didn't say anything else, didn't beg him to visit her.

She sank down onto a chair by the window. "You know what I realized about myself, Peter?"

He sat beside her.

"That I have been so safe and protected all my life."

"And that is a bad thing?"

"But when confronted with Thomas, I thought I was standing up for myself, solving my own problems. And what did I do?" she asked bitterly. "I fell back on needing to be safe, this time with an engagement, using you to protect me."

"That's because you know I'll always protect you, Elizabeth."

"But I have to do it myself, Peter, don't you understand?" she asked beseechingly. "I think . . . I think I'll have to tell my brother the truth about the painting, so it can no longer be used against me."

"That might be too hasty a decision. Give it thought."

"I will. I have time. But I'm in charge—do you understand?"

He raised both hands. "Completely."

And then he simply looked at her.

"What?" she finally demanded with exasperation.

"You're in charge. So tell me what we should do."

She thought for a moment, fingers tapping on the armrest. "I think you should storm out of here and slam the door."

"And what did we argue about?" he asked mildly. "It's not as if anyone has ever heard us argue before."

"Have we done anything new that might come between us?"

"Kissing."

They shared a momentary stillness, a sensual memory. She shook her head. "We can't argue about that."

"Why not?"

"Too . . . intimate." She didn't meet his eyes.

"Or because you like it too much. Remember, you did say you would use everything I taught you on William."

She shook her head. "No, no, I had already changed my mind. I could not possibly . . . I could never . . ."

Do what they'd shared, with someone else? His hopes that he could win her lifted a bit. If she didn't want to kiss William—

"Perhaps I should let William realize *he* wants to kiss *me*," she said tentatively, watching him closely.

Peter could swear he felt his jaw crack, he clenched it so hard.

"What about . . . money?" she asked. "As an argument, I mean."

"That would be believable between a commoner and a duke's daughter."

"Good. This is the perfect thing to come between us." She sounded more confident.

"But you know it never would," he said sincerely.

"I know." Then she looked away.

Using the armrests, Peter pushed himself to his feet. He crossed the room, opened the door and looked both ways. Although he didn't see anyone, he knew the immense entrance hall would carry sound far through the house.

Standing the near the door, he said loudly, "We'll discuss this when your brother returns."

Elizabeth hurried to join him. "It's not up to you!" she cried, then covered her mouth, eyes wide.

"We'll see about that." With a bow and a secret smile, he marched out the door and slammed it behind him.

It wasn't difficult to stride down through the house and toward the front door while wearing a scowl. Their false engagement was over—could he bring about the real thing? More than one servant passed by him, trying not to stare. To his satisfaction, he saw Abigail, the young duchess, come out of the library, and he didn't bother to talk with her. It wasn't until he was out the front door that he let some of the tension leave his shoulders.

A break from him was what Elizabeth thought she wanted—a way to stop using him.

He needed to prove her wrong.

# Chapter 20

**E**lizabeth thought she should have been able to sleep that night. She was righting a terrible wrong, freeing Peter from her manipulations and lies. Once she told Christopher the truth—even though she'd lose his respect forever—together they would find a way to deal with Thomas.

But ending her engagement had to come first. Their performance in that first "argument" had been so convincing that even Abigail inquired about what was wrong. Stoically claiming a misunderstanding, she had fled to her room.

But her room didn't provide any solace. She could see Peter everywhere, going through her things, testing her bathwater—kissing her. Sweet kisses mixed with the hot.

Had he truly wanted their engagement to be real? Then why did he suggest ending it as they'd planned? Perhaps he'd changed his mind and wanted their relationship finished so he could return to his rakish ways. Perhaps he was bored with her innocence. Though doubts continued to assail her, she couldn't believe that of him. No, it still came back to the secrets he hid from her, perhaps having to do with that bullet hole in his arm.

She'd mentioned getting William to kiss her, just to observe Peter's reaction. She'd thought she saw a spark of anger, but it was gone so quickly she couldn't be certain.

Perhaps she was feeling so confused because *she* didn't want their engagement to end. Could she be . . . falling in love with Peter?

She was a fool. She'd used him in a terrible way. It was amazing he could even forgive her. Yet he'd introduced her to the art of intimacy.

Then again, he was a man—perhaps he would enjoy doing that for any woman. After all, she was not the only woman to benefit from Peter's intimate focus—and that made her jealous and uncertain. She didn't like some of the ways she'd changed. At the full-length mirror, she stared at herself in dismay, face flushed, her eyes too bright with memories. Her nightdress was so sheer she could see the brief hint of her breasts and the shadows between her thighs. Peter had awakened a carnal knowledge within her. She'd never felt that for anyone but him before, not even William. That was a change she recognized and had to accept.

Pacing back and forth, she could not stop thinking of all the surprising revelations she'd had about Peter these past weeks. He'd remade himself, beginning with very little money, and now helped control a vast railway company. The fact that he loved and worried about his sister showed her that his protectiveness for her, too, when she was a child, wasn't an isolated incidence. And there were things he kept hidden about himself, mysteries she wanted solved. He was not simply the jovial man he'd always shown the world.

Love meant telling the truth—and they were *both* hiding things. She still hadn't confided her fear that Mary Anne was falling under Thomas's spell. But if she told Peter her suspicions, and he went to Mary Anne with them, Mary Anne would never trust her again.

She owed Peter so much—the least she could do was help his sister.

It was a struggle to stay away from Elizabeth for the next two days, but Peter had something to focus on: Lord Thomas Wythorne. He spent the first day discovering the man's favorite haunts; one of his pastimes was a daily fencing match. On the second day, Peter showed up at Wythorne's fencing club, and was donning his chest protector when Wythorne came out of the gentlemen's changing room in shirtsleeves and breeches.

Wythorne came to a stop on seeing him. "Derby, what a surprise. Not with your lovely Lady Elizabeth today?"

Peter tossed a chest protector at him. He pulled on his mesh fencing mask and lifted his sword. He kept the leather tip buttoned on, knowing bloodletting would bother Elizabeth.

Slowly, Wythorne donned the chest protector. "Are we fighting today, Derby?"

"Unless you want a different opponent, one who'll let you win. You seem to like to win, especially against defenseless women."

Though Wythorne's smile didn't fade, it seemed to harden at the edges. He slid his mask into place and took his sword from the servant hovering nervously nearby. Several matches were going on in the large, high-ceilinged room, but one by one the sounds of steel clashing faded away.

Fencing had always been a leveler to Peter, a way to prove oneself an equal by skill alone, not by wealth or birth. And although he couldn't pound Wythorne's handsome face, he could defeat him—and he knew the man didn't like to lose.

They saluted with their swords, and Peter attacked first, slashing diagonally. Wythorne stumbled back a pace, parrying the blow at the last moment.

"Well done," Wythorne said as he lifted his sword with his right hand and balanced with his left arm behind.

Peter didn't bother to reply, only attacked again,

ducking to the side to avoid a leather tip in the chest but constantly forcing Wythorne back toward the wall.

With a last hard blow, Peter knocked him to the ground, then knelt over him, the long blade at his throat.

Wythorne's smile wasn't so confident. "The tip is the sharpest part of the sword."

"But the edge is sharp enough to do damage." Peter leaned closer. "Stay away from her."

"Stay away from whom?" Wythorne asked too lightly.

"Don't talk to her; don't threaten her ever again. She's *my* fiancée."

"Not for long, or so I'm beginning to hear."

"She has my protection, and that's all that should matter to you. Don't make her turn you down again, because you know how pathetic you'll look." Peter rose to his feet, flung the sword and protective equipment on the floor beside his opponent, and stalked out.

It was two days before Elizabeth saw Peter again—two days that seemed to drag on forever. She had to endure her mother's questions, reminding herself silently that even though the lies hadn't stopped, she was trying to make everything right. She said she and Peter had a silly argument about her dowry but that it would all be worked out. It sounded false, because it was false. Her mother seemed disappointed in her, which only echoed Elizabeth's disappointment in herself.

She told Lucy that the breakup of the engagement had begun, but Lucy didn't seem to know whether to be happy or sad. Elizabeth felt the same way. Lucy tentatively brought up the subject of her brother. Elizabeth was uninterested, with more important things to worry about.

And then she saw Peter at a dinner party. He only arrived in time to escort a lady in at the end of the line. Chatting with his partner throughout the entire meal, he laughed and gestured, perfectly at ease. Elizabeth didn't have to pretend the jealousy she felt.

When the men joined the ladies in the drawing room after dinner, she and Peter looked at each other from across the room, and it wasn't difficult to show her hesitation, her confusion. He came to her and kissed her gloved hand, then leaned down as if to speak softly.

"Do I look suitably worried I'm losing you?" he asked.

There was a smile in his voice that he couldn't show on his face. She wanted to smile and tease him—she wanted to touch him.

She inhaled his scent, knowing they shouldn't stand so close, yet knowing, too, it helped in their charade.

"I think you look angry," she murmured.

"Even better. I should drag you out of here to talk."

"Do what you must."

To her satisfaction, many pairs of eyes followed them as they left the drawing room.

Peter found the library—of course. It was ill lit, and when he closed the door and leaned against it, he looked mysterious and far too tempting in the gloom.

"I've missed you," he whispered.

His words were a joyous ache inside her. When he swept her into his arms, she didn't protest, couldn't protest. Their mouths met, and a sweet kiss turned hot and demanding. She couldn't stop from touching him, his hair, his strong neck, the shoulders that showed he was so much more than a leisurely gentleman.

His hands on her body felt divine, like she was a cat lying in the sun being stroked. Cupping her hips, he pulled her hard against him, and she reveled in the proof that he desired her, that at least he wasn't ending the engagement because he was bored with their game.

When he set her away from him, she swayed like an autumn leaf.

"Elizabeth, I didn't intend this meeting to become so intimate."

"Neither did I," she breathed, wiping her damp mouth. "It's not your fault, because I didn't stop you."

"I've become used to your kisses," he murmured hoarsely.

Closing her eyes, fighting for control, she reminded herself she'd forced him into this. He deserved to be free of her web—to make his own choices, regardless of the fact that her feelings had changed.

"You leave first this time," he said at last, his voice that husky timbre that made her shiver inside. "Give them the performance they're hungry for."

"I will." With a nod, she swept by him, opened the door, and slammed it behind her.

In the drawing room, she saw several pairs of sympathetic eyes—and several more with the faintest hint of satisfaction, as if they'd known that the relationship between a duke's daughter and a commoner couldn't last.

To Elizabeth's surprise, Mary Anne came to Madingley House in the morning to ask if she would like to ride through the park. Elizabeth suspected she was curious about the rumors, but couldn't avoid her without damaging the beginning of their friendship.

She changed into her riding clothes, had her horse saddled, and rode the animal sedately through the streets of Mayfair at Mary Anne's side, a groom trailing behind them. When they reached Hyde Park, Mary Anne burst into a gallop first, and Elizabeth did her best to catch up. When they reached the far end of the Ladies' Mile, they slowed to a walk.

Mary Anne stared straight ahead, her breathing slowing down, her expression pensive. Elizabeth waited silently, dreading the accusation.

Mary Anne exhaled. "Did you receive the dinner invitation from Lord Thomas's mother?"

Elizabeth frowned in surprise. "I did. I turned it down."

"I'm not surprised. He told me he asked to marry you and you rejected him."

"He doesn't usually reveal his failings to others," Elizabeth said cautiously.

"I've gotten that impression." Mary Anne met her gaze. "I'm going to attend."

Elizabeth didn't know what she was expected to say. "I'm certain your mother would appreciate that."

"It's not about her."

"What is it about then? Testing yourself? I know something about that, and it can get you in trouble."

She felt trapped in her own lies. How could she tell Mary Anne that Thomas had hurt her, when she herself has been hurting Peter? She'd lose every bit of Mary Anne's respect, and perhaps make her unsociable behavior worse.

"I'm not testing anything," Mary Anne said, glancing at Elizabeth even as she effortlessly controlled her horse. "He's not like other men I've met. He's confident and amusing. I like that about him."

"He's definitely confident."

"And I've only ever been confident about billiards."

"Why billiards, Mary Anne?"

But she only shrugged and wouldn't meet Elizabeth's eyes. "I just wanted to make sure you understood that this isn't about you either. You have your hands full with Peter's adoration. I didn't think you'd mind my friendship with Lord Thomas."

"Peter's adoration?" Elizabeth echoed, trying not to blush.

"Oh, don't worry, your new arguments aren't a secret. I'm not even surprised."

"You're not?" Elizabeth was disappointed that Mary Anne still thought so little of her.

"He's not the kind of man who will meekly grovel because he won the hand of a rich heiress, and everyone thinks he's supposed to be grateful."

"Oh."

"Not that you expect that of him—it's what everyone else thinks. But I know how he feels about you. And I know he'll resolve any arguments you have, because he's determined to make this work."

"How—How does he feel about me?" Elizabeth quietly asked, afraid to hope.

Mary Anne frowned at her. "He asked you to marry him, didn't he?"

"Well, yes, but—"

"He acts like an absolute idiot around you, as if you're the only woman in the room. He's wanted you a long time, Elizabeth. You know he'd do anything for you. But don't make him do that."

Elizabeth swallowed the lump in her throat and

nodded, trying to smile. Their brother James had hinted at the same thing, but she hadn't known if Peter had simply convinced his brother of the charade. Now, she desperately wanted to believe Mary Anne's words.

Her passion seemed too overwhelming to her, too out of control. They were supposed to portray to the world a failing engagement—yet she couldn't keep her hands off him. How was she supposed to forget the calm maturity she'd striven so hard for, all the expectations she had for herself, the only Cabot who could be happy without a scandal?

That night, Peter didn't bother to watch the string quartet play at the end of the portrait gallery at Sydney House. He watched Elizabeth, letting his obsession show for all the world to see. And she deliberately didn't look at him.

Part of the charade—but it only aroused him.

It was easy to appear impassive, with a touch of anger seething beneath the surface. She sat across an aisle from him, acting pristine and pure as she pretended to listen to their host's four daughters play. Above her demure yellow gown, so stunning against her coal black hair, her cheeks were tinged with a pink blush. She played with the paper program in her lap, tearing the edge into little pieces.

At last they were all allowed to escape the music as

refreshments were served. Peter stood at her side as the two of them pretended to be the perfect couple—yet not speaking. He wanted to share a joke about the music, he wanted to ask if he was playing the correct part.

Mostly, he wanted to taste her mouth, fill his hands with her breasts, lick his way down her naked body.

Surely she wanted the same thing. But wanting him and accepting the truth of their future were two different things. He had to be patient, let her come to the realization, for like a headstrong colt, she couldn't be easily led.

Guests mingled throughout the gallery, and he walked at her side, pretending to admire the paintings when he truly couldn't stop looking at her.

When they reached the far wall, where the gallery dead-ended, he saw that they were unobserved, and pulled her behind the foliage of a huge potted fern and up against his body

"Peter!" she whispered, hands on his chest, her breathing fast. "What if someone sees? We need them to think—"

He kissed her, and she turned frantic in his embrace, straining against him, wrapping her arms about his neck. He could have sworn she tried to put her foot behind his leg and would have but for her voluminous skirts.

She kissed her way across his face and down his neck until she had to stop at the high collar.

"Miss me?" he whispered against her mouth.

She leaned her head back and closed her eyes, obviously struggling to control her breathing. "Why is this all I think about?"

"Because you're wild, just like me."

She looked at him for a frozen moment, then slowly her mouth turned up with amusement. "No one would ever think to accuse the two of us of that."

"They don't know us."

She sighed. "In case someone is watching, I'm going to pull away from you as if you dragged me here against my will."

"As if I could ever make you do anything against your will."

Her smile died as she searched his eyes, but at last she nodded.

"I'm coming to see you tonight."

"Peter—"

"I'm not finished looking for that diamond necklace. I know you posed for the painting, but I'm going to prove it."

If she knew he was only using any excuse to be with her, she didn't reveal it.

"I might lock you out," she said.

"Go ahead and try."

Their bodies separated but for their hands, and then she stepped to the side, their hands lifted as if they must touch until the last possible moment. Giving a mighty yank, she frowned at him and walked away, head held high.

Peter came in through the balcony doors just after midnight, and Elizabeth was waiting for him. She was wearing her nightdress, with the dressing gown over it. By the faint light of a single candle at her bedside, she could see that his usual grin was absent, his body tense as he watched her from across the bed.

"I looked for the diamond," she said, her voice too breathless. "I can't find it. Susanna or Rebecca must have taken it."

He didn't say anything at first, just started to come around the edge of the bed.

"Peter—" And then she didn't know what to say.

"I can't sleep but for thinking of you, Elizabeth," he murmured, his voice deep and husky.

Her muscles seemed too weak to hold her up in the face of his smoldering gaze.

"I keep having to pretend anger," he continued, "but I can feel you from across a drawing room, and it's not anger that's overpowering me."

Hope rose painfully high within her, brimming in her voice, which almost cracked as she spoke. "James said—he said you have always mentioned me, even before the engagement. Mary Anne said I was the one you wanted. If it's true, why didn't you ever tell me?"

"Because you only thought of me as a friend—until the painting, until that wager. Then everything changed."

And then he was in front of her, pulling her up onto her toes.

"Let me show you what I feel," he murmured.

"I—I've hurt you, Peter," she whispered.

"It's in the past."

She wanted everything to be in the past—her uncertainty and jealousy, her fears that she was just an amusement to him. He was too good a man to lie to her only to advance their intimacy. He wanted her—surely he could love her. She wanted to show him everything she was feeling, every hope and dream that they could share together. In that moment, she took the wildest risk of her life and reached for him.

His arms sheltered and protected her, just as he had before. Feeling dazed and yearning, she moaned as he kissed lightly down the side of her neck, nipping with his teeth, licking afterward as if to soothe.

His breath floated over her now damp skin, and she shivered. When he let her go, she swayed, but he didn't move away, only removed his coat and waistcoat.

"Your shirt, too," she said, remembering that she'd touched his chest in the carriage but hadn't seen it.

She expected a smile of triumph—but his eyes only seemed to darken, so serious, as he watched her. He pulled off his cravat, unbuttoned his collar and the few buttons near his neck, then pulled it off over his head.

She'd thought before that he felt like one of the statues in the Madingley gallery, but now she realized he looked like one, too. She held her breath and just stared, her eyes touching on the curves of his long, lean muscles, the ridges of his abdomen, the way the hair on his chest narrowed as it approached his waistband. And below that, she could see the bulge of his arousal.

They'd shared so many things—she wanted to share this.

And then he embraced her, kissed her deeply, setting fire to the last of her inhibitions.

Her dressing gown fell to the floor, and then he drew the nightgown like cool silk up her body. She thought she would be embarrassed to be so openly naked before him, but with a groan he pulled her against him for more drugging kisses. His flesh was hot, her nipples tight pebbles rubbing against his chest. His hands slid up and down her back, then around her rib cage to cup her breasts.

"Oh, yes," she breathed, eyes closed, lost in the feel of him pleasuring her. He lifted her breasts, kneaded them, gently tugged on her nipples while she clung to his waist to keep from sinking to the floor.

And then he lifted her up and swung her onto the bed. She came up on her elbows, knees tightly pressed together to watch him, but except for briefly sitting to remove his boots and stockings, he didn't finish disrobing, only climbed up beside her.

He leaned over her, and she was falling back into the pillows, taking him down with her. His weight on top of her was a revelation, exciting, masterful.

He spread kisses across her face and down her body, taking her breasts into his hands as he took turns licking them. He drew her nipple into his mouth, savoring, moaning against her, whispering words she didn't understand, didn't need to understand. He was giving everything he had to her, as he always had.

As he played with her breasts, his free hand slid down over her belly and brushed her curls. She convulsed, shocked by the intensity of these new feelings. But though it felt wicked, she didn't stop him, only opened her legs so he could show her everything.

He parted her wet folds, using his fingers to tease and torment. Her body felt uncontrollable, writhing with each startling caress. He circled and rubbed, matching his movements with his tongue on her breasts. Sensations burned hot inside her, swelling, rising, until she didn't think her body could contain such wondrous pleasure.

And then he simply stopped, sliding off the bed. She

cried out, reaching for him, almost ashamed of how much she wanted him to continue. He unbuttoned his trousers and drawers, bending to pull them off before he crawled back on top of her. She had a quick impression of his sex pointing to where it should be as he settled between her thighs. She felt the press of him intimately, the length of his penis a hard ridge rubbing where his fingers had just been.

She shuddered as the quieting sensations roared back to life inside her.

"It will only hurt this once," he said regretfully.

The hard tip of him slid against her uncomfortably, and she tried not to tense. His face was strained above her, even as he held himself up so she wasn't crushed into the mattress. She felt her body's resistance, the beginning of pain, and then with a thrust he broke through and buried himself inside her.

He froze, shuddering, breathing hard, watching her face. "Are you all right?"

"I—I think so. Is it over?"

And then he gave her the most wicked grin, something she'd never seen before these last weeks, something she now cherished.

"This is only the beginning," he said, then covered her mouth with his as he began to move inside her.

Her awkwardness faded away as she assimilated the rhythm of his body, moving against him. Each thrust, each press of his pelvis against hers, made her body tighten again with that rising tension she couldn't even describe in her mind.

"My sweet," he said against her mouth, "it is bliss to be inside you at last."

At last, she thought, thinking of the years she'd wasted not knowing the true Peter. That was her last coherent thought, as her instincts took over, her body undulating with his.

And then everything seemed to crash together inside her, emotions and sensations battling against each other, showering her in the most exquisite sensation of joy and release and satisfaction.

# Chapter 21

Elizabeth opened her eyes to watch as Peter let go of his tremulous control, arched his back, and sank back inside, shuddering, his strokes gradually slowing. She thought she'd given him the same pleasure he'd offered her, and the satisfaction surprised her.

But he didn't leave her body, and she took in the sensations of them joined so intimately, the perspiration that mingled on their skin. Her thighs hugged his hips hard; her breasts pillowed his chest.

At last he lifted his head, propping himself on his elbows, and looked down at her, his smile tender. He brushed a curl from her forehead and kissed it back into place.

He looked so content—she wanted to be, too. But did he love her? They could never go back to what they'd been before. Her willing ruination was the final proof that she would never be the "good girl" again. But sharing that wild side with Peter felt wonderful, felt . . . right.

Her feelings were too deep and complicated to be

called friendship—it *had* to be love. Real love, not the fixation she'd had on William.

She realized she'd never truly been in love with William at all. Was her pursuit of him a foolish whim, a way to have what she wanted, regardless of what William wanted?

Peter watched the play of emotions on Elizabeth's face. He wanted to stop her from thinking, make her live in the moment, to see how they could be with each other.

But he knew her—she wouldn't blindly accept the truth, not when she thought she had her life so perfectly planned. He wanted her love—but it had to be about him, and not because she felt guilty for what they'd done together these past weeks, or guilty because she thought she'd hurt him. If she was to love *him*, all of him, she had to know everything. And if the truth turned her away from him? He hesitated, but he had to take the risk.

He lifted himself off her and rolled to the side, gathering her against him.

"Peter—"

"No, I have something to say. I've never told you this, and now that you've offered one of the most important gifts you have to give, I need you to know the truth. Will you listen?"

Her head resting on his shoulder, she nodded, then

laid her hand upon his chest. Pulling the counterpane up, he covered their lower bodies, then covered her hand with his own.

"My words can never leave this room. I promised your cousin Matthew and his wife my utmost discretion."

Alert now, the languidness of her body dissipating, she watched him solemnly. "I promise."

"My scar isn't from a hunting accident," he said without preamble. "It happened because of a foolish belief that I knew best, that I could help your family—and prove myself to you."

She inhaled swiftly but said nothing.

"I discovered a very incriminating fact right after Matthew returned from India. He was handling it himself, but I didn't know that at the time."

"Handling what?" she whispered.

He saw the fear growing in her eyes. "Hush, my sweet, it's over now and all is well. But last autumn I discovered a note from a blackmailer who was attempting to force Emily to do his bidding."

"Emily? But she's Matthew's wife! What could a blackmailer have to threaten her?"

"Because when she first came to live with you, after Matthew's supposed death, she wasn't his wife."

The pain that shuddered Elizabeth's beautiful dark eyes hurt as much as his own.

"I don't understand." Her voice trembled.

"Do not judge her harshly. Matthew does not—he loves her. She was a desperate woman, alone in the world, with a cruel man trying to force himself on her. She'd met Matthew before he'd gone to India, and he told her if she ever needed help, to come to all of you. And she did, not realizing that her vicar had sent word ahead to expect Matthew's wife. The vicar was trying to protect her, and she was forced to go along with his deception."

"I remember when we first met her—her terrible illness, and how it seemed to take a long time to recover. But you're saying she was . . . lying to us?"

"You don't know what Emily had been through, how much she hated hurting all of you, whom she'd grown to love."

"But . . . when Matthew said his wounds took some of his memory, that he couldn't remember being married—"

"He was lying. He had his memory, and he planned to get the truth from Emily."

"How terrible for him!"

"Considering there was an instant attraction between them, I wouldn't feel so terrible for Matthew," he said dryly. "They fell deeply in love, two people who'd experienced so many terrible things in life." He took a deep breath. "But now you need to know my part in it all."

She touched his arm, her fingers tracing the ragged scar. "Tell me Matthew didn't—"

"Of course not! I found the letter the blackmailer wrote to Emily. I thought she was willfully swindling your family. I followed her and saw her meet with Stanwood, the man who'd once tried to rape her. I didn't know that at the time, but it doesn't excuse me from my culpability. I should have gone to Matthew then, but I thought I could be the hero," he said bitterly. "I wanted to help the family, but maybe I was only helping myself. I met with Stanwood, who convinced me that Emily was making a laughingstock of your family, that she deserved to be exposed, to pay for what she'd done."

"You didn't know what kind of man he was."

"I should have. Maybe I didn't want to see it. He offered me money to leave a note for her inside the house." Peter swallowed and closed his eyes, the words hard to say even with the passage of time and Matthew's and Emily's forgiveness. "I told myself I wouldn't take payment, that helping your family was all that mattered. Maybe I only wanted to be more important than I was, a crowing rooster next door to the dukedom, just like my father always behaved. But . . . I don't know what I would have done about the money in the end." That was the truth he'd buried inside, that he'd never wanted to contemplate.

"Peter, you don't mean that!"

"I do. It was . . . the lowest point in my life. I felt like my future kept getting smaller all the time. I was the younger son, with no prospect of inheritance, for it was all entailed with the estate. Much as I knew I would always have a place with James, what could I offer a wife?"

"Why didn't you ever tell me any of this?" she demanded, coming up on her elbow so she was even with his face. "I thought you trusted me with everything."

"How could I complain about feeling like a failure, Elizabeth? To you of all people—to the woman I loved, but could never have?"

Elizabeth stared into Peter's harsh face, seeing a man who kept his deepest pain from her. He was bound so tightly to her family, yet always on the outside, convinced by his father that as a young son, a commoner, he could never be good enough.

"Let me finish it," he said gruffly, sitting up against the pillows and letting go of her.

She continued to watch him, pulling the counterpane higher because it felt indecent to be naked at such a painful moment.

"Then I discovered Stanwood's true motives when I found Emily's maid dead, after Emily and Matthew had left on their honeymoon."

"I remember her! She died at an inn, and they suspected a violent lover, but never found him. The poor girl."

He nodded. "At last I knew what kind of man Stanwood was, that the Lelands were in real danger. I followed Stanwood, tried to stop him, but he shot me and left me for dead."

She tried to reach for him, but he held her back, the truth continuing to tumble out of him.

"I wasn't unconscious long, and I was able to follow him to the inn where Matthew and Emily stopped on their way north. They were going to Scotland to be married."

"I'll never tell a soul," she whispered. "But your arm—you're lucky you didn't bleed to death."

"How can you have any concern for me? Because of my silence, Stanwood was able to steal Emily away from Matthew. He planned to use her against the family, extort money. She almost died trying to get away from him. I'll never forget the sound of her screaming as she struggled at the edge of a bridge over rushing water. I was too far away. Thank God Matthew reached her in time. Stanwood fell from the bridge and drowned."

Elizabeth let out a shaky breath, not even realizing she'd been holding it. His words created such a terrifying picture in her mind, it was easy to forget that Emily and Matthew were safe and happy now.

"They forgave me," Peter continued in a weary voice. "It was more than I ever deserved. Matthew wanted me to be happy, to find my own life. He offered to help me, teach me what he knew about investing and the coming of the railways, something my conservative brother had always avoided. He introduced me to Lord Thurlow, which is how I became a part of Southern Railway."

Peter looked so guilty—but how could he believe she'd set herself up as judge of another person, after all she'd done? And her motives were nothing but selfish, where at least Peter thought he was protecting her family. And whatever he said about his monetary motives, she didn't believe it. She knew him too well; he wouldn't have taken money in exchange for betraying Emily.

"Peter, you say Matthew and Emily forgave you, but I don't think you've forgiven yourself. You made yourself over this last year, becoming a rake, letting everyone think the worst of you, because you believe the worst of yourself. When are you going to put the past behind you?"

He slid to the edge of the bed and reached for his trousers.

"Are you going?" she asked quietly.

"I have to. You need to think about everything I've said."

She told herself to look away while he dressed, but she didn't. Every movement of his body fascinated her. As he was slipping on his coat, he turned to face her, and it was then he seemed to realize she'd been watching all along.

Oh, what was she supposed to do? Would he forgive

himself enough to be a part of her family? Or perhaps he wouldn't believe she could love him.

Peter walked toward the doors leading to the balcony. "I'll see you tomorrow for our next fight?"

"We're going to fight?" she asked, having forgotten all their plans after his lovemaking.

He arched a brow. "We're showing the world our engagement is crumbling, remember?"

"Oh . . . yes." She'd wanted to end the engagement, free Peter from her clutches, and solve her own problems. But tonight she'd bound him to her even tighter, selfishly perhaps, but she couldn't regret it. Did he? Was that why he'd told her his dark secret?

"Good night, Elizabeth." And he stepped out through the billowing draperies.

Peter didn't sleep that night, as if reciting his sins had churned everything up he thought he'd suppressed. He spent a lot of time pacing his room or trying to read a book, but he couldn't concentrate. He played the evening over and over in his mind, wondering if he'd made the right decisions. He'd gone to her, knowing he meant to take her to bed, knowing he meant to force a decision.

Had he thought she'd reject him, ending their relationship?

Instead, she'd looked too deeply within him, and made him examine what he'd become.

He didn't like any of his motives where Elizabeth was concerned.

He had to make things right, to somehow prove—to *both* of them—that they belonged together, that they could be happy as man and wife. He didn't want her to feel that she'd only married him because she had recklessly allowed him into her bed.

Elizabeth deserved happiness; he needed to give her that. He would have to risk his future, risk everything, by giving her exactly what she thought she wanted— William. If she returned to Peter, he would know at last that she truly loved him.

# Chapter 22

In the morning, Peter rode to the Gibson home, but found the baron already gone. Lucy must have heard his voice as he spoke to the butler in the small entrance hall, for she came through a far door and smiled at him.

"Good morning, Mr. Derby! Did I hear that you were paying a call on my brother?"

"I am. Do you know when he'll return?"

The butler bowed and stepped out of the hall.

Lucy grinned. "It's because of you he's gone, you know."

"Me?"

"It's been 'the railway this' and 'the railway that' ever since he's become acquainted with you. He won't let his secretary investigate for him. He went to Southern Railway to inquire about purchasing shares, and was told there was a meeting for new investors this morning. And that's where he's gone."

Peter bowed over her hand. "Thank you, Miss Gibson."

As he turned to go, she called, "Wait, Mr. Derby. Can you tell me—is this about Elizabeth?"

With his hand on the door he regarded her. He knew that she would want Elizabeth's happiness whether her brother were involved or not. But he was not going to confide in her.

He smiled. "It seems like everything I do these days is about Elizabeth, isn't it?" He bowed and left her looking bemused.

At Southern Railway, located in the warehouse district of London's West End, the small outer office was crowded with a half dozen men, several seated on the few chairs and three others talking in a small group. The clerk sat behind his desk, and when he saw Peter, nodded toward the inner office.

Peter shook his head and looked about for Gibson, who smiled and stood up when Peter noticed him.

"Good morning, Mr. Derby. As you can see, I decided to take your advice."

"And good advice it is, if I say so myself. Lord Gibson, would you step into the corridor and speak with me privately?"

His smile not dimming one bit, Gibson followed Peter back through the door into the narrow, dimly lit corridor.

"My lord," Peter said, "this is of a personal nature, but I felt I had to inform you."

"Yes, Mr. Derby?" he asked, his smile fading but still there, in the faint curve of his lips.

"You know that I am engaged to Lady Elizabeth Cabot. It is . . . more of a struggle than I thought it would be. We are having some issues and I'm not certain we can resolve them."

Gibson cleared his throat. "I'm sorry to hear that. I'm gratified that you felt the need to confide in me, but—"

"It's not that I need a confidant," Peter said. "It's simply that you deserve to know something I just discovered. Lady Elizabeth has looked favorably upon you for a long time. I believe she turned to me because you did not show any interest in her."

Gibson's eyes narrowed as he focused on Peter. "Why are you telling me this?"

"Because I want her to be happy."

"I would not feel right courting her while she was engaged," Gibson said slowly.

"Then you're interested?" Peter asked, as his gut churned with worry about the consequences of his decision.

"Of course. Now that I've decided to follow your lead in investing, such a large dowry would certainly aid my efforts."

It took everything in him not to punch the fool's face. How could Gibson care about money over wonderful, sweet Elizabeth herself?

"You don't have to openly court her, not yet," Peter said. "But call on her, offer your congratulations. You decide if she's happy or not. Spend some time with her at the next Society event."

"And you won't mind?"

"She can make her own decisions. I'd rather live with that than know she's unhappy."

Gibson studied him. "You're a rare man, Mr. Derby. There aren't many who would pass up a place in a duke's household and the wealth therein."

Elizabeth mattered more than anything she brought with her.

Elizabeth awoke alone, and found it seemed strange to be that way after an evening of making love with Peter. Her dreams had been filled with languorous caresses, soft kisses, and endearments of love.

And then memories of Peter's confession, and her realization of the darkness that still ate at his soul.

She wanted to see him, but knew he was determined to go through with her plans as she'd formed them from the beginning—to end their engagement and free her.

She felt unsettled and lost and wished she could speak with someone. But how could she tell Lucy—or God forbid, her mother—what she'd done with Peter? So she'd gone about her day as if it were any other, as if she weren't slightly sore from the vigorous exercise in bed.

During her at-home hours that afternoon, she was surprised to hear William Gibson announced. There was a time she would have been tongue-tied and giddy at the thought of his attention, but now she realized she was only curious. He'd never visited her alone before— he'd always been dragged by his sister or mother.

Her own mother, who'd been spending time with her in obvious worry, now gave her a look of surprise. "Does this have something to do with Lucy, Elizabeth?"

"I don't know, Mama. Lucy can usually speak for herself."

As William walked across the spacious drawing room, a friend of her mother's followed behind him, and the duchess nodded to William's bow before going to greet her friend.

"Lady Elizabeth," William said, bowing over her hand.

"Lord Gibson," she said, smiling, trying to hide her curiosity even as she curtsied.

She invited him to sit across from her. To her surprise, he studied her as if he'd never seen her before.

"Fine summer weather," he said.

She blinked at him. "Has the mist stopped, then?"

"Oh. Must not have bothered me."

"I guess not."

He drummed his fingers on his knee.

"Did you enjoy the opera last week?" she asked, beginning to realize she might have to come up with topics of conversation.

He shrugged. "The Italian words make it difficult."

"Did you study Italian at university?"

He shook his head. Then he took a deep breath. "Besides opera, what do you enjoy?"

This was better. "Riding. I have done quite a bit with Mr. Derby's sister of late."

"I like horses," he said, perking up, "especially betting on them. What else do we have in common?"

"Reading?"

He shook his head. "Can't concentrate. Would rather be outside or doing something."

Reading was doing something, she thought mildly, but she understood his sentiment. She had always appreciated the fact that he was an outdoorsman. "I have several charities I assist."

"Good of you. Women should always help."

She was surprised how difficult it was to find a topic they both enjoyed. He seemed . . . young. Or course, he'd probably always been this way, but she'd never wanted to see it.

Too often, she had to stop herself from comparing him to Peter.

At the prescribed fifteen minutes, he took his leave, bowing over hand, looking quite pleased with himself.

He smiled down at her, his eyes focused on her, showing all the interest she'd ever wanted.

And it didn't matter to her one bit. Her infatuation was long over.

Elizabeth didn't see Peter until the next afternoon, at a picnic in the gardens at the town house of the Marquess of Cheltenham. Spotting him across the lawn, she caught her breath. This was the first time she'd seen him since they made love. She thought she would feel embarrassed, unsure, but all she felt was a deep, physical longing for him to touch her again.

He stood talking to another man in an animated discussion, using his hands as he argued his point. She thought he looked wonderful, so dear.

Even though she could cheerfully kill him for not coming to visit her the previous night.

People gave her pitying stares or shook their heads, as if the disintegration of her engagement had been so fully expected. Elizabeth only cared about Peter and his feelings for her.

Her sister-in-law, Abigail, had come to be by her side, as if she needed sympathetic company.

"I knew something was wrong," Abigail whispered, trying to be inconspicuous as she glanced at Peter. "Oh, Elizabeth, this is just dreadful!"

"Please, don't worry," Elizabeth said. "I promise everything will work out."

But it was William who paid the most attention to her. Peter was polite but reserved. She kept telling herself this was all part of the plan, but it suddenly felt so real to her.

After their picnic lunch, William asked her to be his partner in a game of croquet. Abigail rolled her eyes at Elizabeth when he wasn't looking.

"Go ask Peter to be your partner," Elizabeth urged. "You can play against us."

The four of them soon had mallets and wooden balls, and they followed the path of iron hoops that were set up all around the lawn. William was not very competitive. He was more interested in talking about his new railway investments, and she found it distracting. She and Peter had always been single-minded when playing games, and Peter was no different now. He and Abigail took far less shots to hit their balls through the hoops, and more than once he knocked her ball out of the way. She wanted to take William's mallet and "accidentally" hit him in the ankle with it.

Every time Peter was about to hit, she watched his body, and remembered the way it had moved over her, inside her. Why wasn't he dragging her behind a tree when he had the chance? Abigail could distract William— and there were so many trees!

Had sex changed everything somehow? Or was Peter still just playing his part in the ending of their engagement?

Peter and Abigail defeated them soundly at croquet, and went on to play the next game against challengers. William excused himself when several young men swore they needed his advice. They all laughed together, walking away. Alone, Elizabeth stood and watched Peter play, her bonnet shielding her eyes, her insides twisted into knots.

"Lady Elizabeth?"

With a start, she turned to see Thomas standing beside her, watching the game. "I didn't know you were here," she said.

"I arrived late."

When he said nothing right away, she glanced at him in curiosity. No subtle threats about her engagement?

Meeting her eyes, he said, "I'd like to apologize for my behavior."

She gaped at him. That was the last thing she thought she'd ever hear.

He looked down, his mouth grim. "My fury at being rejected was more than I thought I could manage."

"So you had to punish me," she said in a low voice.

He glanced at her, his expression lacking even a trace of the amusement she was used to.

"I told myself you were wrong, that our marriage was the perfect match."

"And what you want, you get."

He sighed. "I didn't think about how I was hurting you, and that was deplorable. Perhaps the painting clouded my judgment, which might be understandable to other men," he added.

She thought he was trying to be a bit lighthearted at the end, but failing miserably.

"You don't know anything about that painting, or what it means to me," she said quietly.

"True. But no one will ever hear about it from me. You have my word."

"What about the man who told you about it?"

With a wince, he said, "There was no other man. I'm the only one who deduced it."

Stunned, she asked, "But—But why did you say otherwise?"

"Because I wanted you to think you needed my protection. It was base and cruel of me, I know."

She had worried so much about who knew of the painting that she'd begun to see motives where there were none. Lord Dekker had simply overstepped his bounds trying to be alone with her—not because he thought she was without virtue.

"It had always been easy to have what I wanted," Thomas continued in a low voice, "and you taught me a lesson I should have understood from the beginning."

"Very well, Lord Thomas, I can forgive you. God knows, I have my own flaws."

"And you will be happy with Mr. Derby?" he asked.

To her surprise, he sounded concerned. "I will do my best to see it so," she said, her low voice full of determination. Her gaze sharpened. "But have you learned your lesson? What if a particular woman rejects you?"

"I assume you mean Miss Derby," he said dryly. "I understand you have become her confidante."

That brought a flush of happiness. Had Mary Anne told him so? "I only hope that I have that privilege. But you haven't answered my question."

He considered her words a moment. "Miss Derby likes to make sure men know how tough she is on the outside."

Elizabeth stared at him in surprise at his perceptiveness.

"But she's fragile underneath," he continued. "I find that contrast attractive and compelling. But I don't know if that's the basis of a relationship. I promise not to deliberately hurt her, but how can I guarantee she won't be hurt if this does not work out as she wishes?"

"None of us can make such guarantees," Elizabeth said sadly. She hadn't intended to hurt Peter either—but her intentions could not excuse her.

"Then you will not forbid our association?" he asked in surprise.

"It is not up to me to forbid it."

"But your words of caution will be listened to."

"Not so far," she said dryly. "But I cannot speak for Peter and his family."

"Of course not. Mr. Derby has made his views on me quite clear."

She glanced at him swiftly. "I don't understand."

"He did not tell you? We had a rousing fencing match several days ago. I was quite defeated. He made it clear he fought for your honor, and to warn me away from you. Enough chivalry for a textbook on the Middle Ages."

Soft tenderness swelled within her. "How sweet."

"I thought you might think so." His lips twisted with faint sarcasm. "If I continue to court his sister, it will take much to win him over. It is an honorable challenge. Good day, Lady Elizabeth."

And then he bowed and walked away from her. She gaped after him, strangely pleased that she wasn't the only one to learn a lesson from this debacle.

She took a deep, easy breath, as if her lungs were free for the first time in weeks. The cloud of Thomas's threats no longer hung above her, and she trusted that his guilt would keep him silent. The painting could still be a secret shared between Susanna, Rebecca, and herself—and the three men who wagered over it.

She was free of Thomas, free of the need for lies and manipulations. Now she had to make Peter see that she was ready to take the next step—with him. Somehow she had to convince Peter that she trusted him. She wanted to put their foolish decisions behind them, give their relationship a fresh start. She needed to prove her love.

"Elizabeth?" Lucy came hurrying toward her. "Was that Lord Thomas you were just talking to? I've seen you with him much lately."

"We were just passing the time," she said, smiling.

Lucy took her arm and they walked away from the guests, heading for a gravel path and the shelter of rhododendrons lining it. "I cannot believe I'm saying this, but obviously your plan has been a success."

"Which plan?" Elizabeth asked wryly.

"The one to make my brother notice you, of course! He even told me he called on you yesterday."

"He did," Elizabeth admitted cautiously. She felt a pang of worry—how to tell Lucy that her brother was not the man she was at last in love with? "But, Lucy . . ." She trailed off in dismay.

Lucy studied her face, her expression one of calm understanding. "I was concerned about this."

"About what?"

"That you and William would have nothing in

common. I'm right, aren't I? I know you both too well."

"But . . . why did you never tell me?" Elizabeth asked with exasperation.

"Would you have believed me?"

She began to laugh, hugging her friend's arm close. "Not a bit. I guess I had to learn for myself."

"So who's the one person you've been able to share everything with, Elizabeth? Tell me the truth."

"Peter. Oh, Lucy, it's Peter. But I've treated him terribly! And there are things about each other we never knew, and—"

"Is that going to stop you from trying to make things work?"

"No, not at all. Do you think William will be hurt?"

"It's not as if he's actively courted you and you rejected him. Once he sees how happy you are with Peter, he'll understand."

Elizabeth tried to give a confident smile. When next she was alone with Peter, she would make *him* understand.

But that night, he still didn't come to her, leaving her restless and aching, as if her body were no longer her own, but his.

# Chapter 23

The next afternoon Mary Anne was surprised to hear that Elizabeth was in their entrance hall, hoping to find Peter. She hurried down the stairs.

"Peter's not here." She took Elizabeth's hand in hers. "I need to talk to you. Come up to my room."

She saw Elizabeth's stunned expression, but ignored it as she pulled her along. In her bedroom, she offered Elizabeth a seat before the empty hearth and sat across from her. She saw Elizabeth glance about the room, knew it was rather bare of knickknacks and mementoes for a feminine room, but Mary Anne had never been sentimental.

Slowly, Elizabeth removed her bonnet, her gaze watchful. But Mary Anne found herself hesitating, uncertain of the most tactful way to begin.

"You had something you wished to tell me?" Elizabeth asked.

In a rush, Mary Anne suddenly said, "Lord Thomas invited me to attend Vauxhall Gardens with him tonight."

And then she winced, anticipating Elizabeth's shock.

"I've never been there before," she hurried on. "I've heard about the Rotunda, where ballets are held, and the long walks lit with globes hung in the trees, and arches spanning them. Is there really a pond with Neptune and eight white sea horses rising from it?"

"There is, but I must caution you that—"

"I would attend masked, of course, and I'd even take a maid. Lord Thomas suggested that, by the way," she added, needing to prove he had his good points.

"But you would only be attending with him?"

"Oh no! He said several other couples would be attending as a group, to eat in the supper boxes and watch the acrobats. I've never seen professional acrobats, only street entertainers."

"It all sounds very exciting, but you do realize that Lord Thomas is older and far more experienced in such matters than you?"

"I know." Mary Anne's fears had plagued her ever since the invitation, but she was so tired of being afraid. For once she needed to feel like a real woman.

"It is very easy to be led astray," Elizabeth continued. "And Mary Anne, one reckless mistake can haunt your days."

Mary Anne stared at her, noticing Elizabeth's direct gaze—and very flushed cheeks. "A reckless mistake?" she asked curiously.

Elizabeth took a deep breath. "I recklessly agreed to something that I now have great cause to regret. I want to discuss it with you, but you must promise to tell no one else—although Peter knows, of course."

Mary Anne leaned forward in her chair, intrigued, even as she was relieved. She didn't want to keep secrets from her brother—especially about Elizabeth.

But proper, perfect Lady Elizabeth, doing something reckless? She couldn't imagine it!

"You know that my cousin, Susanna, is an artist, don't you?"

Mary Anne nodded.

"A friend of hers was looking for a model, someone he'd never used before. I allowed myself to be talked into participating as a favor."

Mary Anne blinked in confusion. "It is reckless to pose for a portrait?"

"It is reckless—and scandalous—when one poses . . . in the nude." Elizabeth groaned and leaned back, eyes closed.

Mary Anne gaped at her, lips opening and closing silently until she could gather her thoughts. "You can't possibly mean—"

"Oh, I mean it. Nude. But for a scarf, and the scarf covered nothing."

Mary Anne covered her mouth—but her laughter broke through anyway.

Elizabeth opened one eye and glared at her. "No one was ever supposed to know! It was for a private collection in France."

"So—So who knows?" Mary Anne sputtered, wiping tears from her eyes.

"The painting is hung here in London."

Mary Anne gasped. "What happened to the private French collection?"

"The deal came apart. The artist was desperate and had to sell it here—to your brother's club."

"So my brother's seen—"

Elizabeth nodded wearily.

"He knows . . . ?"

Another nod.

"No wonder he's marrying you." She held up both hands when Elizabeth stiffened. "It is not fair of me to tease you. You must feel . . . embarrassed?"

"I thought the risk worth it. I wanted to do something I'd never imagined doing. Didn't you ever just want to take a risk?"

Mary Anne's smile faded and she leaned forward beseechingly. "Lord Thomas is my risk."

Elizabeth felt sympathy and understanding and worry for her. She'd thought the story of the painting would help, but perhaps it had only made Mary Anne think an evening with Thomas and his friends harmless compared to her own scandals.

"Why Lord Thomas?" Elizabeth asked, her voice softening with sympathy.

Mary Anne opened her mouth, but before speaking, a wealth of pain and resignation crossed her face. In a low voice, she finally said, "I've never told anyone this before."

"Would it help if I held your hand?" Elizabeth asked gently.

That seemed to break the spell of sadness, for Mary Anne rolled her eyes. Then she sighed. "When I was fourteen, we visited my aunt and her husband. I had a sore throat one day, so I stayed home instead of going for a ride to see the countryside. I thought Uncle Cecil was working in his study."

There was a strange, squirming feeling in Elizabeth's stomach, and it took all of her willpower to speak impassively. "Go on."

Mary Anne looked out the window, her mouth working for a moment. "Uncle Cecil came into my room. I was dozing, but I awoke, glad of the company," she added bitterly. Her voice became a monotone. "I thought he wanted to read to me. Instead he wanted . . . he wanted . . ."

Elizabeth's eyes stung dreadfully as she held back her tears. "Tell me, Mary Anne. You've never told anyone, and you should."

"He held me down. He touched me . . . under my nightdress. I struggled, but I was small and he was—he was—" Mary Anne took a shuddering breath. "Before you feel too sorry for me, know that he didn't ruin me. I flailed, and though he covered my mouth, a scream escaped. We heard my maid come running. He told me if I breathed a word, he would tell everyone it was my fault, that I wanted him to—to—"

"Just take a breath," Elizabeth urged.

Mary Anne nodded and did so before continuing. "Then he stepped out of my door onto the terrace to escape. So I never told anyone. My father had recently died—how could I risk adding more to my mother's pain? But I never went near that man again. When it was time to visit, I forced myself to be sick—vomiting quite convincingly, I might add. And I made certain he didn't receive an invitation to your engagement party."

Elizabeth didn't care about Mary Anne's reserve toward her. She leaned forward and gathered her into her arms for a hug. She felt the other woman trembling, but gradually it faded away.

"You were so brave, Mary Anne. You saved yourself."

"But I let him take away my life," she said. "I couldn't even look at men for a long time. Instead, I focused on billiards, something I could control."

"Why billiards?"

"Uncle Cecil plays billiards," she said, her voice tinged with bitterness. "And I mastered it."

"I understand."

"Do you?" Mary Anne asked, giving her a hard stare. "Part of me is so afraid every time Lord Thomas looks at me. But he's always been a gentleman, and I won't be alone with him at the Gardens."

Once again Elizabeth hesitated on the verge of telling Mary Anne about the connection between her and Thomas. But Thomas seemed to be genuinely remorseful. She, too, was granted Peter's forgiveness for her sins. How could she not give Thomas the chance to redeem himself?

"I still believe you should not go," Elizabeth advised. "But if you're determined to ignore my advice, don't walk the grounds alone with him. You don't want your reputation to suffer."

"Don't forget about the mask."

"And don't forget those aren't foolproof. You could give yourself away."

"I won't."

"It's so obvious you love your family, Mary Anne. You never told them the truth, so they wouldn't be hurt. They would have wanted to know—they would still want to know."

"I'll think about it. Now is there a message I can give to Peter for you?"

"Ask him to come visit me."

\* \* \*

When Peter appeared through the balcony doors early that evening, just as she was about to change for dinner, Elizabeth stared at him, drinking in the sight as if it were weeks instead of days since she had been alone with him. She didn't care that he might have scaled her balcony—they were engaged, after all, she told herself. Peter had made her feel like the most important woman in the world, the center of everything he did. He could be serious and spontaneous, fun yet intelligent. He worked so hard to better himself, not knowing that he'd always been worthy enough in her eyes.

She didn't know where to begin, what to say. In the end she simply locked the door and ran to him, throwing herself into his arms. Their kiss was full of desperate longing, their hands touching and caressing and pulling at clothing.

He said her name against her mouth. "I know it's early. I couldn't wait to be with you. But it could be dangerous if we're caught together."

"We're engaged. I don't care. Love me, Peter. Please love me."

She only wore a dressing gown, so it was he they had to struggle to disrobe. It was even more enticing since they had to be so quiet. At last they were naked in each other's arms, broad daylight allowing them to hide nothing from each other.

Peter fell back on the bed, pulling her with him, and she gasped at the novelty of being above him. He pulled on her thighs until she sat astride him, across his hips.

"You're already wet for me?" he growled.

"That's good isn't it?"

He gave a stifled laugh, then reached for her breasts. She found herself arching into his hands, her head thrown back, swept up in the sensations she'd only ever experienced with Peter. He played with her nipples, caressing and gently twisting, until she writhed on him, the feel of his erection hot and hard between her thighs. But he wasn't inside her, and she wanted to be a part of him.

When she would have slid to the side, the better to have him rise above her, he shook his head and held her still.

"Help me inside you."

Dazed, she blinked at him. "I can do that?"

He could only nod.

She lifted her hips, and for the first time allowed herself to touch that very male part of him that was so different from her. It was smooth and hot to the touch, hard, yet coated in the moisture from her own body.

"Tell me if I'm hurting you," she said hesitantly.

"You could never . . ." His breathing was hard and fast, and he helped position her hips with his hands until at last she was able to ease down on top of him, taking him deep inside. It felt strange and wonderful all at the same time, especially when she could watch his pleasure, which almost looked like a scowl.

"My God, you feel incredible," he said hoarsely. "Try to lift yourself up and down on top of me."

Her legs were strong from horseback riding, and soon she found the rhythm that most pleased both of them. With her hands braced on either side of his head, she controlled all of their lovemaking, adjusting her body until the passion spiked dramatically higher. With his hands on her breasts, and his penis deep inside her, she reached for the pleasure, the release, shuddering through it, letting it take her away.

Then he let himself go, holding her hips hard against him as he thrust, his expression extreme with concentration.

And then she collapsed on top of him.

"Heavens, that was . . . amazing!" she said between gasps.

She loved the sound of his chuckle reverberating in his chest, and the way he combed through the damp curls at her temple with his fingers.

"I'm so glad you sent for me," he murmured. "This was the best reason."

"But it wasn't the only reason, Peter."

She slid off his body, then gathered the sheet up

over her breasts as she sat facing him. Before she could speak, someone knocked on the door.

Wide-eyed, Elizabeth held a finger to Peter's lips and called, "Teresa, is that you?" When the maid answered in the affirmative, Elizabeth responded, "My head has begun to hurt. I'm going to lie down for an hour. I'll ring when I need you."

They both remained silent as the maid's footsteps died away.

Peter came up on his elbows. "What's wrong? Why else did you send for me?"

Though she had some trepidation about revealing Mary Anne's secrets, Elizabeth could not keep them from him. As she looked into his face, she had a moment of clarity when she realized that her ease in talking to him, which she considered simply friendship when they were younger, showed her how deeply she trusted him, an almost scary connection that went beyond friendship. How had she ever thought she *wouldn't* want such closeness with her husband?

She took his hand, gave him a faint, reassuring smile, and told him about the terrible abuse his sister had suffered. His look of disbelief and pain was like a stab to her own heart, and she understood why he could not simply lie in bed and take such an awful truth. He stood up and yanked on his trousers, pacing the room while she donned her dressing gown. She tried to take him into her arms, but he gently pushed her away.

"I just can't fathom how someone could do this to a young girl!" he whispered harshly. "There is a special place in hell for such a man, and I'll gladly send him there."

"You can't, Peter. It was her choice to keep silent, and her trust in me that she at last allowed it to be expressed. She doesn't want revenge—and there's no certainty she'd have it, for who would believe her? What she wants is to heal."

"It's partly my fault," he said, running his hands through his hair. "If I'd have been there more, instead of running off every day to be tutored at Madingley Court—"

"It happened on a visit to your aunt and uncle's home. I don't even know if you were there. Regardless, you can't possibly be with Mary Anne every moment. She made her choice to be silent then, and at last she's getting up the courage to make a bolder choice."

He came to a stop and stared hard at her. "What are you saying?"

"First, let me preface this by telling you that yesterday Thomas apologized to me."

Peter scowled. "I saw him talking to you at the picnic."

"Perhaps the fencing pushed him over the edge," she said dryly.

He didn't smile. "He deserved it. I wish I could have done more. What does this have to do with my—" His brows furrowed darkly. "I was worried about this. He's sniffing after Mary Anne."

"Sniffing is a very inappropriate word, Peter. They seem to be mutually attracted to each other."

"Mutually attracted?"

"I told you she's trying to get up the courage to be interested in a man. Surely you can now understand why this has been difficult for her."

"But *Wythorne*?"

"He seems to have genuinely learned his lesson, Peter. He told me he wasn't used to rejection, and dealt with it poorly."

"Damn right!"

"He made a terrible mistake—just like I did. But at least no one else knows about the painting."

Peter frowned. "I thought he said someone told him."

"He lied," she said brightly. "He was trying to convince me that only he could protect me." She put a hand on his tense arm. "I lied to everyone I love. In some ways that's worse. And I used *you*, Peter, which I regret most of all. You've given me a second chance. And weren't you given a second chance by my cousin Matthew?"

Peter froze in the center of her floor and stared at her.

She went to him and put her hands softly on his chest. "I used you to try to have another man, the man I thought I wanted. It was reprehensible. Yet you forgave me."

"The man you thought you wanted?"

"Yes."

"Then you've realized that he's not the man for you?"

She gave him a nod, smiling tremulously. But he wasn't returning her smile.

"Then you should know that I hoped you'd have this realization," he said.

She blinked up at him in confusion. "What are you saying?"

"I felt you could never commit to me fully without knowing the truth about your infatuation with Gibson. You might have always looked back, wondering."

"Peter, what did you do?"

"I told Gibson that you'd always favored him."

She inhaled on a gasp. "Without consulting me?"

"I thought you wouldn't have agreed. And you needed to know. This was your chance to have what you wanted, to discover the truth about your feelings."

"And instead, you betrayed my secrets," she cried softly.

Wearing a scowl, he shot back, "And you don't call encouraging my sister to see Wythorne, a man who treated you so abominably, a betrayal?"

His words made her flinch. She was furious at herself when she had to dash away a tear.

"I've tried my best to help Mary Anne, at your request. I've had to walk a fine line between the both of you, for on becoming a woman's friend, I cannot simply betray everything she confides in me. Perhaps I've betrayed too much already. She wants this chance, Peter. It's her choice."

He nodded and turned away to dress. She watched him, a sick feeling swirling in her stomach.

"We'll talk again when our heads are cooler," he said when he paused at the balcony doors.

She opened her mouth but didn't call him back.

# Chapter 24

Vauxhall Gardens was a mad wonder, both enchanting and overwhelming at the same time. Mary Anne, feeling safe behind her mask, walked at Lord Thomas's side through the Grove, a grand park with an orchestra playing in a Gothic temple, trees lit with thousands of globes high in the branches, and walks meandering through supper boxes crowded with laughing patrons.

The night felt like a fairy tale, and she a princess, especially whenever Lord Thomas glanced at her and smiled.

They had left their party to walk alone amidst the crowd. Mary Anne could not believe how easy it was to talk to this man. Billiards had been their first conversation, but soon she discovered he liked some of the same books she did, and they shared the same irreverent humor about the *ton*.

The crowds started thinning the farther they walked from the Grove. When Mary Anne saw the white columns of a temple sheltered within the trees, she hurried up the steps to peer inside. When she turned back, he was coming up the stairs behind her, their faces level. She froze, her smile fading. But instead of that familiar feeling of dread at being so close to a man, she let the excitement rise inside her, drowning out the unpleasantness.

And then he leaned forward and kissed her, his lips gently touching hers. It was sweet and exquisite, just a brush of soft lips once, twice.

And then he pulled away, his expression suddenly remote. "I shouldn't have done that. You're an innocent and you trusted me tonight, and I'm a man who's committed too many sins."

"And I am so very perfect?" she asked lightly. Trembling with her own bravery, she reached to touch his cheek. "Tell me what haunts you."

He took a deep breath, and his shadowed eyes looked remote. "You should know all of the truth. I told you that Elizabeth rejected me, and that I did not take it well."

Mary Anne nodded her encouragement, even as her stomach gave a twinge of dread.

"I lied and told her that someone . . . knew her secrets and would expose them, to try to force her into marriage with me to protect herself."

She gaped at him, not ever imagining the truth.

"I had no right to try to bend her to my will. Women need to make their own decisions, or a marriage is doomed. But in my fury, I didn't care about that. I thought she was wrong, and I was determined to make her see what was best. And instead I hurt her."

Mary Anne knew the secret was the painting, and imagined Elizabeth's fear of discovery, of ruin. It would have affected her whole family, hurt so many people. Nausea roiled her stomach. She'd thought Lord Thomas was different, but instead he only wanted what he could take from a woman, just like her uncle. "Is that why Elizabeth was so suddenly engaged to Peter? Did she *need* to be engaged, to protect herself from you?"

"I don't know the truth of their relationship," he said a low voice. "But yes, she turned to your brother for help."

Did Elizabeth feel any kind of friendship for her, or was she simply desperate? Did she care about Peter at all?

Instead of wallowing in her pain and confusion, Mary Anne at last realized that she didn't have to accept such behavior from any man. She had the power to change her life, to put herself beyond any man's reach for good.

"Miss Derby?" Thomas said her name, his expression one of confusion and worry.

Then she fled past him and began to run down the paths, back the way they'd come, disappearing into the crowd.

"Mary Anne!"

She heard his voice one last time, heard the panic, but she didn't let it sway her. She'd seen the hackneys waiting out by the entrance.

She kept the mask on, half covering her face but for her mouth. The mouth that had just had her first real kiss.

She didn't want those kisses anymore. She didn't trust them. And she had the perfect way to make sure no man would ever think to court her again.

Only after she'd given the driver the address to Peter's club did Mary Anne sit back in the hackney, cold purpose filling her.

After a private dinner with her family, Elizabeth retired to her room, knowing she wasn't fit company. Her mother would only have questions, and she couldn't answer.

She was concerned about her argument with Peter, the way they still kept things from each other—the way he'd tried to show her once and for all that William wasn't for her.

The fact that he'd been right only irritated her. She'd already figured it out for herself—she hadn't needed him to go behind her back and—

But as far as *he* had known, she was still pining for William. Peter didn't want to be the man she simply settled for, and she understood that.

But if only he'd come to talk to her!

*Mary Anne* had talked to her, she thought, feeling a rise in the unease she hadn't been able to let go ever since Mary Anne left. Vauxhall Gardens could be a scary place for an innocent. What if something had happened to her there? Would she have anyone to talk to? Would she retreat from all the progress she'd made?

Elizabeth looked through the window and out into the dark night, telling herself she could do nothing—that she *should* do nothing. Only weeks ago she'd risked herself by going out into the night with her cousins to steal a painting, and so much had changed because of that one act.

She had discovered Peter's love for her, and realized at last that she loved him in return. She might have spent her life miserably unhappy if she hadn't taken that one risk.

Tonight Mary Anne had taken a risk—and had it worked for her?

Elizabeth needed to know. Buried in the back of her wardrobe, she found the boy's breeches as well as the shirt and coat she'd worn that night to Peter's club. It had kept her safe on the city streets once, and she trusted that it could do so again. She slipped out a side entrance of the town house and into the garden, where she ran past the stables and into the alley behind the house. At the corner, she was able to hire a hackney to take her to the Derby town house.

Approaching the front steps, she realized she could

not simply confront the butler—she might even wake him. As she was trying to remember the layout of the house, and estimate which window was Mary Anne's, she saw a thin sliver of light along the front door—it was slightly ajar.

Creeping up the stairs, she gave it a gentle push and peered in. There was no one in the entrance hall, but she could see light spilling out of the door to James's study. On tiptoe, she crept through the hall, debating how to get past the partially open door and on to Mary Anne's room unseen.

It was not James's voice she heard, but Peter's—and he was talking to Thomas! With her back against the wall, she remained frozen, listening.

"It's late," Peter said coldly. "I don't understand why you need to speak to me."

"I'm not here about Elizabeth."

"I know. Now you've turned your sights on my sister. I won't have it."

"She didn't consult you on that decision," Thomas said impatiently. "She went with me and a group of friends to Vauxhall Gardens."

"What?" Peter shouted.

Elizabeth heard some kind of scuffle, and she tensed, wondering if she should interfere.

In a strained voice Thomas said, "You won't hear what I have to say if you strangle me."

"Then say it and leave before I—"

"Mary Anne knows what I did to Elizabeth. I told her the truth, so she would understand everything about me."

Elizabeth sagged against the wall. With Mary Anne's history of fearing men, what might this revelation have done to her?

"That was the best thing you could have done," Peter said coolly.

"I thought so, but she didn't. She fled from me, and I briefly lost her in the crowd."

"Did you find her?" Peter asked just as Elizabeth almost burst through the door with the same question.

"I was able to follow the hackney she hired. Don't bother to look in her room, because she didn't come home. She went to our club."

"Oh God," Peter said in a strangled voice.

"By the time I pulled up, I only saw the edge of her cloak as she disappeared into the servants' entrance. She's still masked, I believe, but I have no idea what she intends to do. I knew she wouldn't listen to me, so I came for you."

Elizabeth didn't wait to hear more, only ran back outside and hailed a hackney. Another man had disappointed Mary Anne—the man she'd risked herself to know. Elizabeth had no idea what her state of mind was, but she had to be desperate to go to a gentlemen's club, where women weren't allowed.

A man couldn't talk her out of whatever she had planned, but perhaps a woman could.

During the hackney ride through London, Peter said nothing, telling himself that now that Mary Anne knew the truth about Wythorne, she would settle down.

But would she? Elizabeth had told him about Mary Anne's suffering. How would she handle learning that a man she'd begun to trust had hurt Elizabeth?

He glanced at Wythorne. His eyes were impassive as the gaslights of the city reflected in them, but there were lines of strain on either side of his mouth. He'd confessed the truth to Mary Anne; perhaps she wasn't just a woman with whom to amuse himself.

At last they arrived at the club, and Wythorne fell back, letting Peter take the lead as they ascended the grand staircase two steps at a time. Peter stopped just outside the wide double doors to the main saloon, Wythorne at his back. They saw Mary Anne standing at the billiard table, the nude painting a scandalous backdrop. She was still cloaked and masked, and she held a cue in her hand like the scepter of a queen surrounded by her courtiers.

"They never allow women," Wythorne said softly behind him. "How did this happen?"

"They think she's someone's mistress, a fallen woman," Peter said. "Of course they'd let her remain to put on a show."

"Are there many men who know her skill at billiards? Her hair is uncovered, after all. Would they guess . . ." Wythorne's voice trailed off.

"I don't think so. She took several family friends in a game once, but I don't see them here."

Mary Anne made several excellent shots, all to cheers and shouts of encouragement.

"What does she think she's doing?" Wythorne asked quietly.

Peter felt both sad and frustrated, watching Mary Anne touch the mask repeatedly. "I believe . . . she's thinking about removing that mask, exposing her identity."

"But why? Surely she would know that she'd make herself a pariah."

"She told me she doesn't want to be married. This scandal would take care of that problem, don't you think? It's what she's wanted all along, until she took a risk on you."

"I don't understand."

Glancing over his shoulder, Peter really looked at Wythorne, who seemed bewildered and just as worried as he was. "I can't tell you everything, but only know that when she was young, she was abused by a man. She's never gotten over it."

"And now she knows I hurt Elizabeth," Wythorne said, his mouth twisting in disgust. "I shouldn't have told her."

"It was the truth. She deserved to know. And you didn't know her background to anticipate how she'd react."

Wythorne stared at him in surprise, and Peter turned away. He wasn't here to make the man feel better.

He'd never felt so frustrated. Mary Anne continued to play, saying little, smiling the cold smile of a woman who knows she's the superior player. She could best all these men, and was proving it. But she kept touching the mask—assuring herself it was in place, or ready to remove it?

If he quietly confronted her, Peter wondered, would she decide to reveal herself in panic? What was he supposed to do?

"There's a message being delivered to her," Wythorne said. "What do you think that's about?"

Peter put aside his fears and focused on his sister. She'd stepped aside to talk to a messenger boy—and then he simply stopped breathing. He would recognize those breeches-clad hips anywhere.

"It's Elizabeth," he whispered. "Oh God."

He heard Wythorne curse softly behind him.

Peter had asked her to guide his sister, to watch over her. Somehow she'd discovered what Mary Anne had done. He'd goaded Elizabeth for weeks about her recklessness, seduced her until perhaps she thought she wasn't a proper lady anymore. And now she'd come to save Mary Anne, and risked ruining herself—all for him.

Had he somehow wanted her lowered socially, so he had a chance to marry her? From the moment he'd discovered the painting, he'd been trying to prove to her how wild she still was. He'd thought he was over feeling unequal socially to her.

"How are we going to save them?" Wythorne asked quietly.

Peter pulled him back into the two-story entrance hall. "We have to come up with a plan."

"Working together?" Wythorne asked, his eyebrows lifted.

Peter nodded curtly.

# Chapter 25

Elizabeth stood near Mary Anne, hands in her pockets, trying to act like a boy who had no interest in anything but doing his job, waiting on Mary Anne's supposed answer.

Elizabeth didn't look at the painting over her shoulder—she'd seen it enough. But she saw other men staring at it, saw the laughter, the appreciation, the skeptical looks as they debated the identity of the model. Hunching her head lower between her shoulders, she looked out from beneath the cap's lowered brim.

Mary Anne was watching another man take his turn at the billiard table, holding the cue beside her like a walking stick. But she wasn't leaning on it. She was taller than many of the men, filled with purpose.

"Just come with me," Elizabeth whispered. "We can talk."

"No."

"Then stop touching your mask!" she hissed. "You might dislodge it."

"Perhaps that's what I want."

"Please—"

"You didn't tell me what Thomas had done to you."

"He apologized to me, and I felt he deserved a chance to prove he was sincere. I didn't feel it was up to me to reveal all his mistakes. I've made enough of them myself."

"Like using my brother?"

Elizabeth sighed. "Yes. And lying to people. Your brother forgave me. Will you?"

As if their conversation had conjured him, Peter walked toward them. Mary Anne stiffened but didn't turn away.

Peter didn't even look at his sister. His face impassive, he said to Elizabeth, "Boy, if you've finished your assignment, I need you to deliver a message for me."

Elizabeth felt torn. How could she leave Mary Anne in such a fragile state?

"I'm done with him," Mary Anne said, turning away.

"Then come with me," Peter said, a note of beseeching in his voice. "I'll pay you well to deliver this swiftly."

Elizabeth knew she could not linger. It was a disaster to have two women in this club. Peter obviously had a plan to help his sister, because he wouldn't abandon her, Mary Anne had to know it as well. But would it make her reveal her identity?

Elizabeth hurried after Peter, her cap pulled low over

her eyes, afraid she'd lingered too long and ruined his plan. She followed him out into the open hall and across to a small unoccupied room with a single card table and chairs taking up most of the space. Old cigar smoke fouled the air.

With the door ajar, they could still see into the saloon. Elizabeth gasped as she saw Thomas going inside.

"Does he know—" she began.

"We came together. He'll get Mary Anne out of there."

Standing close to him, she longed to fling herself against him as if he could protect her from the world. Instead, she said, "And you trust him?"

"Everyone deserves a second chance," he said mildly, looking over her head toward Thomas. Then he stared down at her, his blue eyes solemn, yearning. "We deserve one, too."

"Oh, Peter," she whispered, leaning against his shoulder.

Mary Anne was having difficulty concentrating on her game. She'd been stunned when Peter ignored her, then took Elizabeth away. Had he thought only Elizabeth could be saved from this disastrous situation?

But no, that was her nerves and fear talking. Peter must be at a loss for what to do next. And then she saw Thomas coming toward her, and she realized they'd split their plan between them.

Thomas and Peter, working together.

She stiffened as Thomas approached. He was still so handsome it made her hurt inside. His stride was confident—the very trait she'd been drawn to.

Her own confidence was such a sham.

Yet here she was, about to prove that she didn't need a man. She put her hand on the mask, and Thomas came to a stop.

His voice full of arrogance, he loudly said, "Are you any man's mistress?"

The crowd of men around the table burst into momentary talk and cheers and laughter, then seemed to hush with anticipation.

Mary Anne glared at Thomas through the mask. "I am not. No man is worthy."

She knew that all these men had only allowed her to remain in the club because they thought she was of the demimonde, the class of women she'd heard whispered about, who survived on the pleasure of men. Now they wouldn't know what to think.

Thomas's eyes lit up, and with his hands on his hips, he said, "Then I suggest we play a game, and if I win, you're mine for the night."

She was disgusted—he would have what he wanted by any means necessary.

But was that her fear talking? She thought of the painful confession he'd made, realized belatedly that it must have been difficult for such a proud man to admit his faults. And now she saw a worry in his eyes that he couldn't quite hide. She tried to bolster her anger, but felt it softening inside her.

He was treating her as a loose woman—exactly what she'd been portraying to all these men. Thomas wasn't the only man who would take her for the night if she allowed it.

*If she allowed it.*

She had the control, and it was time she took it back, instead of hurting her family, hurting herself.

"I'll play you, my lord," she said quietly, confidently.

Men gathered around, and she made the final game worth their while, allowing Thomas the lead, taking it back, then deliberately giving him the game.

With the win, he laughed with his friends, then tossed her over his shoulder to the roar of the crowd and carried her away.

Her stomach absorbed the pounding as he took the stairs to the ground floor, and went out into the warm night. She heard a carriage door open, and then he leaned inside, tossed her onto the bench, and climbed up beside her.

Peter helped Elizabeth in then, and climbed in as well.

There was a very tense silence as the hackney jerked into motion.

"All right," Mary Anne said before anyone else could

speak, "this was a foolish thing for me to do. I responded very badly to finding out how imperfect the three of you are—and I know I'm no more perfect than any of you. I'm sorry that I thought to throw away my reputation because of a man." She stared pointedly at Thomas, who sat at her side. "I'm worth more than that."

He nodded solemnly.

She turned back to the other couple. "Elizabeth, did Peter force you into doing something you didn't want to?"

Elizabeth blushed. "No, of course not."

"Peter, did Elizabeth force you into doing something you didn't want to?"

"Never. I've wanted to marry her for several years."

"That's what I thought," Mary Anne said with satisfaction.

"We need to talk," Elizabeth whispered, taking Peter's hand.

Elizabeth and Peter looked into each other's eyes, and Mary Anne felt a warm envy of appreciation for the love they showed each other. A few minutes later, when the hackney pulled up at the Derby town house, Peter helped Elizabeth out.

"Nice painting," Mary Anne called softly, smiling as Elizabeth winced.

Mary Anne sat forward in her seat, then turned to look back at Thomas. "I could have won that game if I'd wanted to. There will be no coercing me into doing anything—that's assuming I allow you to court me at all."

He grinned at her. "I'm quite confident I can influence your decision."

And there was that confidence she'd been attracted to all along.


Elizabeth snuck through the Derby town house behind Peter, then breathed a sigh of relief when they made it to his bedroom without anyone seeing her dressed as a boy. He shut the door and leaned against it, watching her solemnly.

"We did it," she whispered, hugging herself.

"We did. I still can't believe she let Thomas win. Perhaps you risking yourself for her made her realize what she was doing."

"I owed her more than that," she said quietly.

He held out a hand and she went to him, sighing with relief when he enfolded her into his warm embrace.

"Elizabeth, my one love."

It felt so wonderful to hear that word on his lips. Desperate relief and gratitude made hot tears sting her eyes. She lifted her face. "I love you, too, Peter. I am so sorry it took me so long to realize it." Between kisses, she said, "I promise . . . I'll never tell you . . . anything but the truth."

He kissed the tip of her nose. "We've learned that lesson too well. I love you, Elizabeth. I didn't know if you could feel the same way, until that painting. It made me see even more of you."

"Peter!" she cried, feeling a hot blush stain her cheeks.

"No, I mean the you underneath, the woman ready to take risks again, the woman who is more real and wonderful than any idealized version of a lady."

"I was so blind to what real love and romance are," she said, smoothing down his waistcoat, sniffing back her tears of happiness. "To think because you and I began as friends, I thought to limit us that way. We had love all along. I was just so focused on everything being held to my strange idea of perfection. I never saw that life is unpredictable, even a normal, scandal-free life!"

He smiled, then touched her forehead with his. "I realized long ago that marriage to you will provide enough adventure and excitement to last a lifetime."

"Not too much adventure and excitement," she said. "We have to make some quiet time for babies."

"Our babies," he breathed.

"Thank you," she murmured, "for not giving up on me."

Their kiss was sweet with longing, warm with certain passion—and love.

# Epilogue

On the evening of the Kelthorpe Masked Ball, Elizabeth's entire family gathered in the drawing room of Madingley House to attend. She stood with Peter at her side, so happy to see her brother Christopher and her cousins, Matthew and Daniel, reunited with their wives. She sighed. If only Susanna and Rebecca could have attended, but she had not yet heard from them, nor Julian and Leo.

But she couldn't let the absence of her dear cousins stop her. She looked up at Peter. "Are you ready?"

"You don't have to do this," he said softly, putting his arm around her.

"Yes, I do."

"I'm not certain I approve of such a public display," her brother, the duke, said in a cool voice.

He was so tall and handsome, his darker Spanish complexion always setting him apart from other Englishmen. His wife Abigail tried to hush him.

Elizabeth smiled. "And why not? We're engaged. And I love him."

She heard her mother sniffing back relieved tears, saw her other female relatives giving her soft, happy smiles.

"But I didn't know I loved him for a long time," Elizabeth continued. "I'm so glad I forced him into an engagement, because then I learned the truth about our relationship."

Though many gasped, she could hear her mother's cry of "What?" above it all.

Peter held up a hand. "I hardly had to be forced. The details aren't important. We've had our share of misunderstandings."

"But none of them matter," Elizabeth said, smiling up into his eyes. "And yet they do. Because they opened my eyes to the kind of man my childhood friend has become. Thank God," she added fervently.

"Well, that's mysterious," her brother said, "I can only say that secrets don't stay secret long in this family. If you want a marriage contract, Derby, I might need to know more."

"I don't need anything, Your Grace, except Elizabeth," Peter said. "Now before we leave, I do need a private moment with my future bride."

They went across the entrance hall—to the library, Elizabeth thought, trying not to laugh at how often she'd been in one library or another these past weeks.

"Guess what?" she said before he could speak.

He rolled his eyes. "Very well, your secret first."

"Remember how I told you that William had a big announcement he planned for tonight?"

"And you didn't know if it was about you or not."

"It's not," she said, grinning. "Finally, today, Lucy confessed the secret, the reason William wanted me to be near her tonight. Our families are about to be even more intertwined."

"Another marriage?" he said doubtfully.

"It seems that during my preoccupation with you, Lucy found herself falling in love with—you'll never guess."

"Just tell me."

"Your brother!"

She laughed in delight at his shocked expression.

"I know, I know, she didn't breathe a word! She thought I had too much on my mind, was so worried about my problems that she didn't want to 'boast'— her word—about her good fortune. But our families have been inseparable lately. She and James spent time together and have formed an attachment. Isn't that wonderful?"

"My mother will certainly think so." His smile turned devilish. "My news is far more intriguing."

"Tell me!"

"It seems your painting has disappeared from the club. No one knows what happened to it."

"I can't decide whether or not to be relieved, but since there's nothing I can do, I won't worry. I'm simply happy to know that it is no longer on public display."

"Perhaps we should tell Susanna and Rebecca?"

"And interrupt their conquests of your friends? No, I think not. There's still a wager going on, one we intend to win." She paused and fluttered her lashes at him. "I did promise to tell you the truth about the painting when our engagement was broken."

He pulled her close. "I'm waiting."

"But our engagement was never broken, so I don't have another word to say."

His groan dissolved into laughter as he held her against him. "I'm glad the painting is gone, because now I will have the model all to myself."